Daphne Simpkins/Quotidian Books
Updated December 27, 2023
Updated again for Large Print July 12, 2025

Publisher's Note: This is a work of fiction. Names, characters, places, and incidents are a product of the author's imagination. Locales and public names are sometimes used for atmospheric purposes. Any resemblance to actual people, living or dead, or to businesses, companies, events, institutions, or locales is completely coincidental.

Mildred Budge in Embankment/ Daphne Simpkins. – LARGE PRINT Edition
ISBN: 978-1-957435-26-8

MILDRED BUDGE IN EMBANKMENT

LARGE PRINT EDITION

....

THE ADVENTURES OF
MILDRED BUDGE
BOOK TWO

DAPHNE SIMPKINS

Contents

1

JESUS SAVES

As Sam's burgundy Buick broke through the lightweight road guard and crashed downward through heavy brush, church lady Mildred Budge knew she was not going to die.

Her life story did not pass before her eyes. She felt no panic.

Later, Miss Budge would wonder about that--wonder if she had missed some kind of heightened insight into the meaning of her life. And as a thoughtful person does as she ages, the retired public-school teacher would almost regret that she had not been more deeply touched by a near-death experience. What would she have learned that might have informed the rest of her life and made it better?

But in that moment, Mildred Budge thought first only of the inconvenience of being stranded in a kudzu-filled ravine nowhere near the interstate because Sam Deerborn, the chairman of the pulpit committee, had wanted to take this narrow two-lane back road to their destination on a quiet Sunday morning when there weren't other travelers about.

The church lady thought, too, of missing the sermon hour of the young preacher who was the third candidate under consideration to replace their previous pastor and next on the list for the pulpit committee to visit. Finally, she grieved that the elastic in her left knee-high stocking had failed entirely. The stocking was now rolled down around her ankle fully, and it was going to be a nuisance all day long. Oddly, reaching toward that irritation of a collapsed stocking was the impulse Miss Budge fought against---not death.

When Sam's Buick finally smashed into the ground, Miss Budge did not see the big picture of life and how death informs the understanding of it. She saw a rabbit that woke up when the car slammed into the ground, and her eyes were open long enough for her to see it sprint away.

After the rabbit, Miss Budge saw that the three other people in the car were remarkably passive to have sailed over an embankment. They chugged through brush as the Buick's tires tried to find some traction to counteract the powerful pull of gravity.

When the nine-year old Buick crashed against a trio of drought-parched pine trees, bunching up the sun-faded hood and triggering the front seat airbags to expand while dried brown pine needles showered them, Mildred, perfectly peaceful inside of herself, shouted jubilantly, "Jesus saves!"

"We're all right, Budge," Jake Diamond said in response to Mildred's excited testimony.

Budge is what Jake called Mildred. Just Budge. Mildred liked it. It felt like a nickname, a term of real affection, rather than a misuse of her last name, which happened frequently. Mildred looked down at Jake's brown hand holding hers. She marveled that someone was holding her hand at all, and she knew a start of embarrassment at being caught holding hands with anyone in public. As the car gasped, belched, and the panel of lights on the blood-red dashboard blinked out totally, Budge squeezed Jake's hand and asked, "What in the world?"

It was an open-ended question with broader implications that would later require prayer for an answer. Like the use of her last name as a shorthand method of address, Mildred Budge's question, "What in the world?" expressed stupefaction and concern. It was one of her signature prayers to God when he moved in his famous mysterious ways and was a companion plea to her other frequently uttered prayers of "Have mercy," "Help me, Jesus," and the universal cry of unequivocal helplessness, "Lord, Lord, Lord."

"Sam?" Jake said. "Lizzy? You two okay up front?"

Sam's head and torso were covered by the white billowy airbag which had automatically inflated. He was snuffling. That is, Sam was breathing. Mildred thought the slow rise and fall of his shoulders represented more a sigh of relief than the deep inhalations of breath that come after a big surprise when adrenaline surges and then recedes.

In the passenger seat beside him, Liz's airbag had also inflated, and the serial widow was fighting it, punching it with her small, prissy fists.

Jake let go of Mildred's hand and reached out and solidly gripped Liz's left shoulder. "Steady, Elizabeth."

That was Jake Diamond.

When his door opened and Jake stepped out, the car shifted, not dramatically, but enough to indicate that not all four tires were firmly on the ground.

Mildred went very still as she waited for Sam to become himself again, because he was just breathing deeply there in the front seat, held in by his shoulder strap and the airbag. The passenger door creaked clumsily open, and Jake's brown hand navigated the surprisingly resilient airbag and unsnapped Liz's gray seatbelt.

Unlike Liz's hands that were balled up in little fists ready to pummel an enemy, Jake's hand was outstretched and peaceful. His hand seemed to quiet the troubled atmosphere inside the car that was charged with residual fear and surprise. Jake eased the airbag away with his gentling hands and coaxed the pugilistic Liz to a place of stillness.

He has praying hands, Mildred observed. *Hands that speak to God of us.* The odd idea faded away as her senses took hold and brought her more and more to the moment inside the car where they were now altogether in a new way. They were survivors.

Mildred saw Liz's face captured in the mirror on the down-turned visor. The aging beauty queen's expression was one of torment and fear--not at all the perky, starry blue gaze she was famous for at church, and which had successfully induced four different men to marry her, all of whom she had buried.

"Come on out of there, Lizzy," Jake said. He helped Liz to shift her legs out of the car.

While the other woman made her escape from the front seat and as her first foot touched the earth, Mildred could almost feel the ground beneath her own feet, and that feeling of imminent connection drew her more and more out of that heightened place where she was living, breathing, and still saying inside herself now: *Jesus saves. Jesus saves. Jesus saves.*

Mildred released her own seat belt, felt around for her brown leather Grace Kelly handbag on the floorboard, opened her own car door, and let herself out. Jake's eyes met Mildred's as he continued to prop up the pale Elizabeth. Liz had raccoon eyes from where the fresh mascara she had been applying in the car had smeared. The collapsed white airbag, so like a crumpled pillowcase that now needed to be washed, bore traces of Liz's mascara, too.

"Let's get her over there," Jake said quietly to Mildred, who was now listening to that interior voice that had stopped testifying and was now quietly narrating the story of her life to her while she lived it. It was a very comforting still small voice that sometimes she thought was only her inner Miss Budge, and sometimes she believed it was the eternal voice of Truth just keeping an accurate record of history being lived out in her: *You have been in an accident. Sam is hurt and seems to be out of it. Jake is helping Liz and has called her Lizzy and she hates that. You are still standing, although the elastic band in your hosiery has failed entirely, so don't buy that cheap brand again. You need to see about Sam because Jake is busy.*

"Budge, get a move on," Jake commanded. He caught Mildred's eyes, and she felt the word 'steady' though he did not say it to her, and Mildred was gratified, for Elizabeth Luckie was the type of woman who needed to hear that word of reassurance from a strong man, but Mildred Budge was not.

Retired fifth-grade schoolteacher Mildred Budge was a common-sense, faith-created church lady who could rise to any occasion. She looked at Jake wonderingly, her left hand gripping her brown handbag that she used year-round.

She had given up changing out seasonal handbags years ago as a waste of energy. Now, she used one well-made handbag until it wore out; then, she threw it away. *Who cared if the color of her purse matched whatever outfit she was wearing?* Chin up and ready to march to safety, Budge said forthrightly in a voice that was unfamiliar to her own ears, "There was a deer."

"There was," Jake agreed, finally scooping up the wobbly Liz. "Budge, you need to get over there by that tree in case this car is going to blow up or catch on fire."

Mildred looked around while Jake shuttled Liz quickly to a place underneath a red tree. Mildred Budge had often felt the need to learn the names of trees, but she was tired; and when she was fatigued, proper nouns—and that included the names of trees—escaped her. When that happened, Mildred only identified trees by adjectives and colors.

She stopped, a faint smile on her face as she listed the trees, she now identified that way. There were weeping trees, and Christmas trees, and good-smelling trees, and dead trees, and unkempt trees that needed to be pruned, and today, there was this red tree toward which she needed to move. Budge looked down at her root-bound feet and tried to walk. She blinked at her feet hard as if they were separate entities that could be telepathically commanded to move.

Jake reappeared, put a strong arm around Mildred's waist, and said, "Come on, darlin'."

Mildred could not remember when anyone had last put an arm around her waist or held her hand, though many people in Montgomery, her hometown, call everyone darlin' because they couldn't remember proper names either. She wanted to tell Jake that he was not remembering the rules about how people treated an older church lady.

Even church ladies didn't properly hug or kiss each other; they gave those lipstick-saving air kisses to which Miss Budge had not accustomed herself. Mildred thought air kisses—a pantomime of affection that church ladies inflicted on one another—when unavoidable, were one of the great humiliations of being alive. Air kisses told a terrible story of no one quite making a connection with you—just sort of pretending to while passing through your life. When Mildred Budge thought of air kisses, tears occasionally filled her brown eyes.

"You got out of the car, so your legs can work, and they will work. Move that left foot, Budge. Now move the right foot, Budge."

"Left. Right. Left. Right. Left. Right." And then Jake's arm was no longer around her, and Budge was standing beside the woozy Liz.

"Thank you," Mildred tried to tell Jake, but the words came out all rattled because in spite of the fact that she was the inimitable Miss Mildred Budge and truly believed that Jesus saved, her teeth were now chattering from shock.

2

SAM

Just before the airbag inflated, keeping him from breaking his nose on the steering wheel, Sam thought dismally: 'I have killed them. It's my fault. Belle has been telling me that my driving's not so good, and maybe she is right. Maybe I should have given up driving last month when I ran that "Stop" sign.'

And then, even though the airbag did its job, something in the moment that was akin to impact made Sam black out.

The other passengers assumed that Sam's blackout was due to the accident, but that was not true. Losing consciousness was an impulse that Sam had been fighting for some time. Going over the embankment simply gave the retired Air Force colonel an excuse to allow himself to slip finally into a state of not knowing that had been attracting him for months, maybe years.

All the responsibilities that he had chosen to bear and all the work that made up Sam's to-do list reached a breaking point at the embankment, and Sam simply allowed whatever inner force there was that managed a man's consciousness to say, "Lights out, good buddy."

Sam blanked out. But not completely. There was a part of his consciousness that hovered inside of him, taking note of what was going on while his eyes were closed and his face was learning the contours of the airbag. It was taut and flexible at the same time. There were other people in the car, but the chairman of the pulpit committee was all alone up against the airbag, and he surrendered--no fight left in him.

It seemed perfectly natural to surrender to inertia while the car was airborne and turning the steering wheel a fruitless endeavor. Then, the car slammed against the ground, and Sam exulted in that moment of impact. Would liked to have relived it over and over again in the same way that when you're a kid on a roller coaster and a fast dip on the track makes you swallow your heart, you want to do it again. Sam wanted to hit the ground again and again and surrender over and over again to the experience of smashing into the earth. The collision satisfied Sam, and he hid that satisfaction inside the airbag as the car rollicked hard. They came to a harsh stop against the trio of pines.

Sam felt Liz's fingernails claw his right thigh, but her hand departed quickly when the grabbing onto him did not stop the car from lurching or coming to that final neck-jerking slam against the pine trees that were so young that they really shouldn't have withstood the impact of the heavy car, but they did. Dry needles dusted the top of the car, and Sam thought for a second, *I just washed the Old Girl and now she's a mess.*

He saw instantly that she was going to be past ever cleaning up again. Inside the airbag, a smile too big to emerge on his face showed up inside of him, deep inside of Sam where he kept his grit and his will and the determination to keep going. The Old Girl was stopped, and now Sam could take a time-out from cleaning her up, keeping her up, and assorted other chores that were his daily lot.

The smile inside of him yawned as his memory began to do the job of recording the story, but he was not taking note of the story he would tell; he was identifying those parts of the story that he would never tell anyone ever. Not even God. For inside himself in the deep well of his soul, Sam kept a separate book about himself, and it was the story of what he was really like that no one else knew and which he didn't pay much attention to because what's the point? Life was a mystery, and in many ways, Sam Deerborn, who presented himself as an open book to others, was a mystery to himself.

For Sam had experienced a deep satisfaction in crashing into the pine trees— as if a part of him had wanted to do it all his life. And it reminded him of the mailboxes that lined the sides of the streets in his quiet Southern neighborhood, and how often, when driving down a street, his hand had wanted to steer the car over and knock the mailboxes down like bowling pins one after another, only he never had. *Why would a man even think that?* Today, Sam had hurt his Old Girl, a car which had been a faithful vehicle and which was now, most certainly, going to be called *totaled*. The man others knew as Sam Deerborn, Belle's husband, was sobered by the event. Inside of himself, the other Sam was bemused and curious about what he might do next.

He would have to say good-bye to his Old Girl that had been dependable, and they did not make this shade of burgundy for automobiles any longer. It was such a respectable hue of red, and Sam thought it was so much more reliable a color than the cherry reds of cars painted for younger drivers and which seemed to fade faster in the sunlight. No, the burgundy resembled the deep resonating hue of a good leather rather than a painted tin can, and the Old Girl had mostly retained the depth of her color except for the hood, which had faded some. If Sam had believed in naming cars, he would have called her Ginny after a girl he had gone to school with and whom he had thought of marrying before he had met his Belle.

"Sam?"

Face buried against the airbag, Sam heard his name called. Heard the deep assuring tones of Jake Diamond and then Mildred Budge getting out of the car, and Sam had a vague sense of being sorry earlier that morning that he had been rude to Millie for bringing along that blue Igloo cooler that he had reluctantly stowed in the Old Girl's trunk.

He didn't understand why he had been so cross, for Sam loved Mildred Budge. He loved her in the way that people who are growing older together learn to love each other at church, where one's home life expands so that you are not only residing at your residence, you share a larger sense of family. The reminder of the size of this heaven-bound family was the local church on the corner. Sam and Mildred had been members of their church for years.

Sam decided in that first moment after the crash that he needed to apologize to Mildred about the blue Igloo. Make things right. He would just have to find the right moment.

Before Sam could plan what to say in his head and add it to the always present to-do list that was much longer than the stuff he wrote down on a sheet of lined yellow paper on a legal pad each morning, he heard Liz Luckie whimpering. That was good, because Sam had heard her cry like that at her husbands' funerals, and that meant she would be okay. All three other passengers were going to be all right, and he hadn't killed any of them except the Old Girl he had been driving.

Sam inhaled, and listened to his breath come and go, come and go. One day it would go altogether, but until then, breathing was like walking. Take one more breath. Let it out. Put one foot in front of the other. That was life. One more step. One more breath. Over and over again. And now he had lost the Old Girl. Well, it was his personal loss, and Sam would handle it. He was a man, and he could handle whatever he had to face. Sam's hands still gripped the wheel hard. Needing to let go, Sam held on, and it felt to him like his hands were fixed to everything, and he couldn't get loose.

That is how it felt to him at church, too. At Christ Church, Sam Deerborn was the go-to guy. The senior elder. When no one else could get a job done, good old Sam could. When no one else wanted to do a job, good old Sam would. And he hadn't really wanted to chair the pulpit committee, because he had learned from experience that the grief you got from the congregation for whoever you hired simply wasn't worth it. You couldn't please everybody no matter how hard you tried and no matter how many informal polls you took on fellowship night or how carefully worded the questionnaires were that got mailed out to the congregation to find out what they wanted their next preacher to be.

It didn't matter how hard you worked or how smart you were or if there were fifty great guys applying for the job and you chose the very best man for the job, that man would not be good enough for everybody in a church as big as Christ Church. No, Sam Deerborn had not wanted to chair the pulpit committee again. Three times was enough already!

Still, as much as Sam said that he did not want to do it—be the go-to guy this time--he did not want to see the process fouled up and the church end up with a man they would have to keep at least three years (That was the decent time to keep someone if he wasn't working out). So, reluctantly, against his own better judgment, Sam agreed to form the pulpit search committee and chair it.

He placed the job advertisements in the right periodicals and then logged in the resumes by date, read them, identified the top three candidates in order to save everyone some time, and passed out copies of the resumes to the committee members. All he had left to do was take the committee members to hear the three men preach before they—the committee--voted to invite the right one to come and preach to the congregation, which would then collectively vote yea or nay.

However, once a candidate was brought in for the show-and-tell Sunday morning service, it was considered a done deal. The congregation usually just rubber stamped the hiring selection by voting yes. If anyone disagreed or took that other bothersome position of abstaining from voting either way (Sam despised fence-sitters), Sam would call them up and explain that it was so much better if they could tell the chosen candidate who would be offered the job and who would always ask, "How strong was the vote?" that "We're behind you one hundred percent!"

The four-member pulpit committee had recently visited the churches of the other two men and heard them preach. Today they had been on their way to scout the third and final preacher.

So far, the committee was split two and two in favor of candidates one and two. Sam knew reasonably that there should have been a fifth committee member to break any tie, but carting five people around was awkward even in a big Buick. So, Sam had settled on having only four members to comprise the committee, believing that his powers of persuasion would ultimately mitigate not having a tie-breaking fifth person on board. The two girls would vote with him at least.

There was still this last and youngest preacher who had made the cut and who could, if selected, be the right guy for the younger members of the congregation; but looking ahead, Sam couldn't see how the whole congregation would be able to get along with such a young man or keep up with Steev, who spelled his name with the two e's in the middle, and what was his last name? If Steev, with two e's in the middle, was half the guy he was described as being by his references, he could walk on water, and no man was that light on his feet. You had to read between the lines when you read references. Too much praise of a candidate from a current employer could mean that they were trying to run him off and getting him another job was their way to do it.

Sam Deerborn had lived a long time, and preachers were only human, like the people they were called to serve. He had tried to mentor as many of the preachers as he could, even old Joe, who was supposed to have retired years ago but kept coming back to fill in every time a preacher left. Sam believed he could have been more help to old Joe if that old preacher had been the kind of old dog who could learn a new trick, but Joe wasn't teachable. He had no ambition in him either. That was the biggest problem with Joe—no forward motion in him. That is what Sam had tried to explain to him, but Joe had just smiled and excused himself—said he could hear his mother calling--which was a funny thing for that old preacher to say. It was only a while after that when Sam realized that Joe's mother could not possibly have been alive, so the old guy was losing his marbles, too. Sam hoped that this last time was the very last time they would have to call Joe in to pinch-hit while a new preacher was being identified and called to lead Christ Church.

"Sam?"

He heard his name again, and there was no ignoring it this time.

"Sam?"

Jake opened the door and pushed the airbag away from Sam's face. Against his deepest will, Sam's eyes fluttered open, and he was surprised to see some blood on the airbag.

"Sam, snap to. We've got to take care of the ladies," Jake said.

A hand was placed on the back of his neck. The grip of Jake's hand steadied Sam, calling him to attention. Sam felt his seat belt unsnapped, and Jake tugged on his left arm.

"No reason to panic. Everyone's okay. And no gasoline is leaking," Jake reported. "I don't think she'll blow up. The car is sitting fine."

Sam wanted to say something, but there was blood running down his face and into his mouth; and when Sam opened his lips, he found that he didn't like the coppery taste at all.

3

JAKE

Jake saw it all happening from the back seat where he was sitting with Mildred Budge. They had tried to put him in the back with that woman who had killed four husbands; but thank God, Lizzy had announced that she got motion sick in the back seat, so she was up front with Sam and away from him. Boy, Lizzy had beaten the tar out of the inflated airbag with those little hands of hers, and Jake couldn't help wondering what else she had done with them. A woman just didn't become a serial widow without having done something with her hands. Jake Diamond did not have to think twice about it. He had decided to keep his distance from that one.

Yet, there she was—Liz Luckie--sitting in the front passenger seat, and here he was in the same car with the woman he had decided to avoid, and Sam and Budge and he might all be in harm's way just because the Lady of Death was on board. Hadn't they just flown off an embankment?

How in the world did Liz, a professional beneficiary of men's estates, get put on this real live search committee to find a pastor for real live people who believed in a real live God and a real live Jesus?

Already the Black Widow was a problem. Queen Elizabeth had liked that first guy that preached on grace, and Sam had agreed with her because Old Sam didn't want the rich widow to have an opinion by herself. Obviously, the second preacher was the better choice for their congregation, and Mildred Budge saw that right off, too. At present, it was two against two. Jake Diamond and Mildred Budge were new allies.

Jake had been on enough search committees at the local university where he worked to know how to assess the viability of candidates and to read between the lines of what they put on their resumes and what they didn't and what they emphasized about their missions and what they didn't see as part of their job description. But when you cut to the chase, that first guy preached grace, which meant he wasn't willing to preach Jesus front and center, and fifty-six-year-old Jake was too old not to want to hear Jesus preached front and center.

The second guy had mentioned Jesus seven times in his sermon. He had chosen John the Baptist for his focus. But if John the Baptist was the first sermon—could a sermon on Jesus be far behind? And so, automatically, ipso facto, Jake Diamond voted for John the Baptist—the second preacher, hoping for more of Jesus down the road, and Budge had agreed with Jake's choice, though she had not explained why. Jake had meant to ask her why, but he had not been able to talk alone with Mildred yet. Lizzy was always around, and Sam ran a tight meeting. Sam did not allow any time for just sitting and talking, which was a shame because sitting and talking was what people really needed to do.

You would have thought there might have been some time during the ride in the car for just talking about the candidates, but Sam had gotten them off to a bad start this morning by being irritated with Budge for bringing a cooler on a simple day trip. Sam would not allow the cooler in the car or any kind of eating, and Budge was a church lady that way. She couldn't help taking provisions with her. It was what some old-fashioned church ladies did.

But not what a church lady like Liz Luckie did.

When Sam said that about Budge's cooler, Lizzy had let her icy-blue eyes smile as if seeing Budge put down made her happy. Then, after Sam reluctantly stowed the cooler in his trunk and they had been assigned their places in the car, Budge had pretended to go to sleep in the back seat, but she wasn't really. It was just her way of tuning out Lizzy who was talking ninety miles to nothing in the front seat, and Sam was going, uh-huh, uh-huh, and then the deer leapt right in front of the car and, a split second later, they were sailing over the embankment.

It was strange being in the air. It felt like one of those dreams where you think you can fly, and Jake had thrilled to the weightlessness. Budge had, too, for her eyes had popped opened, and rather than fear death, Mildred Budge had worn an expression of a kind of surprised delight—you just never know with women.

Being a sensible man, Jake did wonder if they were going to die as the ground came at them, but he had a funny peace about the whole thing. He remembered the strangest bliss--that he didn't blame the deer or Sam, who had chosen this dumb route instead of taking the interstate. Jake didn't even mind so much that Lizzy was on the pulpit committee and was putting on eye make-up while they were about to crash. She wasn't much of a mystery to Jake. He knew her type. Liz was one of those women you had to pay attention to, and when you did, you would not see a deer before it was too late. She would cause you to lose your focus about so many other things. Only there were too many things that a man had to keep track of. Jake didn't see how any man with a real life would have the kind of time to give Liz what she needed. Her type would drain a real man dry. Steal his thoughts. Feed on his complete attention. Demand his life as proof of his love, if he let her. Knowing that, Jake resolved as they sailed over the embankment: `Don't court death, but you don't have to fear it. Remember this. Remember life. Remember what it feels like to sail out without holding any grudges against anyone. This is what living is supposed to be.'

It felt like flying did in a dream. It felt like heaven.

Over the embankment they all went, while Liz was applying extra mascara using the mirror in the dashboard visor and attempting to make eye contact with Jake in the backseat, as if he, a black man who had made a comfortable life for himself in a white man's world at the university and at the mostly white church near downtown Montgomery, would mess up his life or, more probably, shorten it, by swapping meaningful glances with not only a white woman but also with a white woman who had buried all her loving husbands.

Jake almost laughed out loud when Liz attempted to twinkle at him. Jake Diamond didn't have a death wish. If he had been sitting closer to Budge, he would have elbowed her, and said, 'Look there. Do you see that? Do you see The Liz making eyes at me? I don't want to die.'

But Budge was hugging her door, doing that 'I'm asleep thing' and fighting the urge to scratch some itch on her ankle. Her hand kept stretching almost involuntarily that way. And then the deer leapt, Sam swerved, they smacked the railing, a limb dragged across the car's roof, and as they sailed out over the embankment, Budge opened her eyes and her mouth made an O, and then, just as a rabbit leapt out of harm's way, she started testifying that Jesus saves! As the car arced groundward, it was like there was no sense of danger for her, and that's one of the chief reasons Jake stayed calm. Everyone knew that Mildred Budge had common sense; and when she didn't panic, Jake Diamond didn't either.

4

LIZ

They weren't the same angels that circled overhead at the last funeral when they had buried Hugh Luckie, her fourth husband. They were a different group of angels, much smaller than angels were generally thought to be, and they were circling so fast overhead that at first Liz thought they were spokes in some kind of celestial wheel. As the car went over the embankment and then rocketed downward, the movement of the angels slowed to the point that Liz could make out their shapes, and the same question that had haunted her for the last four funerals arose out of a deep well of grief that no one who had not buried all of her husbands could understand: 'What in the world is happening to me?'

Almost as soon as she asked that question, she heard FussBudget say, "Jesus saves" and then the same question she lived with when she saw the angels: "What in the world?" Liz was relieved by the idea that plain-as-vanilla Mildred Budge might be able to see what Liz had begun to see years ago after her first husband died. For Liz Luckie saw bunches of angels. And when the angels started showing up like that, usually somebody died. Or just had.

Then, people blamed her.

People didn't say those words out loud. They just made faces about her behind her back. Liz saw those faces the same way she saw those crazy angels out of the corner of her eye. She hated those angels that swirled as flashes of light and hovered and haunted and dared her to try and build a life that they would tear down by simply taking away the one she loved every single time. She had been aware of the angels for a long time, but it wasn't until the death of Hugh Luckie that she put two and two together and got the answer that produced her newest question: 'Why are angels of death trailing me around?'

And having finally figured out what the angels were up to—coming to take away someone who loved her--Liz Luckie had decided that when she saw the angels again, she was going to fight them.

Liz pummeled the airbag, trying to get at the angels of death that had stolen her husbands from her, leaving her alone without a soul to help her fasten a simple necklace or tell her when she needed to touch up the roots of her hair. She couldn't see as well as she used to; and when you have been a beauty all your life and age robs you of your beauty in terrible stages, you don't want to look so closely at your face or the roots of your hair or your poor hands that even wearing plastic gloves while dishwashing couldn't stop from looking older.

Liz punched the airbag. Then, she reached over and clawed Sam on the leg for getting them all into this fix. Then, she caught a glimpse of herself in the visor's mirror and screamed because she had gotten so old, though she was still only sixty (she planned to stay only sixty for as long as she could pull it off). Liz missed being beautiful desperately.

She missed all of her husbands desperately.

And she desperately hated to see the flurry of angels, because that meant only one thing: Death.

But who was going to die this time?

One of them? All of them?

Did Mildred Budge know? That woman knew more than she usually told. Liz had tried to get Mildred to be a friend—had almost succeeded—but then there had been that unfortunate accident with Winston, Fran's sort-of boyfriend. Because Fran Applewhite was Mildred's best friend, FussBudget had chosen Fran over Liz, and Winston's falling off the ladder had not been her fault, but Liz was blamed for it anyway, like always. Right when they were about to become friends, Mildred Budge had pulled away from knowing Liz better. Later, when Liz had tried to talk to Mildred about what had happened, Liz didn't get much out of Mildred except that frank brown-eyed stare that would make an honest judge start confessing his trespasses. Mildred Budge was famous for that cow-eyed stare.

Feeling misunderstood and panicked, Liz prayed in the car just before it smashed into the ground and then crashed through bramble until the pine trees stopped them altogether: "God, don't let one of the men die today."

For the famous widow knew her reputation. She knew how other men and women saw her.

But her reputation had not been built solely upon her husbands all dying. Since her last funeral, Liz Luckie had been unlucky in Sunday school classes, too.

No Sunday school class could keep her.

Liz had gone from class to class at church trying to find a place where she could sit and listen to stories about God without causing a commotion, but she no sooner sat down than the man in charge began to talk directly to her in front of everyone. If there was a cross-referenced Bible verse to look up, any man in charge in any Sunday school class asked Liz to look it up. If there was a name to add to the prayer list on the white board, the man in charge handed Liz the marker and asked her to write that name on the white board. If the leader in charge told a joke, he turned to Liz and waited to see if she laughed. Liz was always extremely polite about laughing at men's jokes. When Liz exercised common courtesy, the women scowled, and the other men felt competition for her attention take root and begin to grow.

During the coffee hour, another man would try to tell her a different joke that was better than the one the teacher had told because men were competitive that way. There had been times when Liz Luckie tried to be rude instead—had not even smiled and even let her gaze go a little frosty (and that could actually backfire because sometimes a frosty woman can make a man's love grow hotter), but it was hard to act cold when a man was trying to please you. Before too long in any Sunday school class or during the fellowship coffee time, Liz Luckie was the center of the men's attention and the object of other women's contempt.

Liz Luckie was a man magnet. And she didn't want to be. She just wanted to go to Sunday school, sit down, and not feel lonely for as long as the class period lasted.

For Liz was not one of those women who could get used to being alone. Many women could. Liz saw the women who could live alone. They all sat together on the pews that had become known as the widows' pews, but Liz would not join them there. FussBudget sat there, although she had never been married. There were women like that who appeared to be widows, but really, they were mostly old-maid schoolteachers or retired librarians or government workers. Whatever their marital status, they were women who were content to be each other's company. Not Liz. Never Liz. She would never consent to that. Never.

Just thinking about it made Liz feel anxious and in a hurry. Life was going by pretty fast, and she couldn't take hold of it or catch up to it. She wondered how other people managed. Did they ever have that feeling of either running or being pushed by unknown forces? As the car hit the ground and the airbag slammed against her face and mashed wet mascara around her eyes, Liz Luckie repressed the question that slithered up in her consciousness from time to time: 'Was there a real devil other than one's own fearful nature, and if so, how could one get away from him? Maybe the devil's real name was Time.'

Liz was haunted by bands of misery-producing angels and tormenting questions that seemed to come from the devil. She was scared.

Liz felt pursued by death, and she wanted to feel at peace with life in Jesus. Even last week she had been chased into church by old

Mr. Peavy who had called out to her to slow down as she climbed the steps of the church. Only he didn't say those words, "Slow down." Mr. Peavy said, "Don't you look pretty?"

Liz had always been able to translate men's language, and she had known that Lem Peavy was asking her to slow down and walk into the church with him. And if they had walked into the church together, they would naturally sit together during the service. Then, he would hold the red hymnal for the both of them, and once she was singing the same song with him off of his page, well, she was done for.

That is how a courtship could begin—as simple as that. But this time, the question, "Don't you look pretty?' did not trap her. Because Mr. Peavy walked slowly and with a cane, she had been able to scoot away, moving right to the threshold of the church where the two deacons handed out the order of service. On the threshold that led to the sanctuary Liz had looked to her right where the widows' pews were and knew she would be safe there. It was a no-man zone, and Mr. Peavy wouldn't follow her there and sit down beside her. Still, as safe as it appeared to be in one respect, it felt dangerous in another. Liz simply could not join the other single ladies in the unofficial widows' section who announced their aloneness like that. She never had been able to join women who seemed resigned to being alone or old.

They were the type who wore those red and purple hats as if bright colors made up for living alone. Liz had a great deal to say about the ways that others duped women into wearing uniforms that made them all alike--even that purple and red combo meant to suggest independence and flair and which was just another uniform after all. Liz Luckie was herself. She was herself, alone now, and determined to be herself, alone now.

With that purpose in her heart, Liz had used her charms to inveigle her way onto the pulpit committee so that other people would see her as someone who didn't just get married and bury the poor man who had found her desirable. She was someone who had a job to do at church. She was going to prove it. She was going to help them find the right man for the job and not marry the man or later ask him to perform a marriage ceremony for her!

Liz was working on her reputation all right. She had been making progress, but there were those angels of death circling overhead again like buzzards in white, and she knew what they meant. God help her and the people who were in the car with her whose lives were in danger now. 'My Lord,' she began. Almost as soon as she thought the prayer, Jake's strong arms scooped her up, and like a groom carrying his bride, that man delivered her to safety, leaving FussBudget Budge to fend for herself.

Liz automatically closed her eyes to absorb Jake's strength. It was the same way she had always been carried by each one of her grooms except Hugh, her last husband who had died only four months ago. As a low humming sound began inside of her sounding like an echo of the wedding march, Liz forgot her intentions to be herself alone and allowed the smile of delight to surface that so many men had found irresistible.

But when Jake lowered her to the ground, he did not stop to receive the glow of her feminine approval. As her hero walked back to get FussBudget, she whimpered in a new assault of grief. Tears rolled down Liz's face, for Jake Diamond was immune to her femininity.

"See there?" she called out to the angels of death; and to her surprise, they zipped away.

5

MILDRED

Mildred continued standing unsteadily, her brown leather Grace Kelly handbag gripped tightly in front of her. Her brown slacks still looked pretty good. Brown didn't show dirt. Her aqua double-knit sweater felt oddly damp. *Southern women don't sweat; they perspire.* She plucked at the cloth to loosen it from her skin, where it wanted to stick.

"Did you all see a deer?" Sam asked quietly when he joined her and Liz underneath the red tree. He had removed his suit coat to drive, and so he was standing in his grey slacks and a white dress shirt. A few drops of blood had landed on his shoulder. He kept squinting, as if the sun hurt his eyes, but it wasn't only the sun. A continuous trickle of blood from a wound on his forehead oozed. He brushed at the blood as if it were a mosquito.

"I saw the deer," Jake said, pivoting slowly.

Mildred read his mind: 'Where are we?'

High above them, traffic could be passing by, but there had been no one else on the road that morning. It was a steep incline, a far way up. Mildred shaded her eyes and shook her head. Jake saw and nodded, almost imperceptibly. He turned toward a stand of trees to the west and considered it.

"I saw the deer, too," Mildred replied. The words rattled out of her mouth. She hugged herself, trying to still the shaking that wanted to rise up and claim her. *God, I feel cold, but it's warm out here. Help me.*

Liz had been putting on mascara and had not seen the deer. She quickly nodded, yes, quite vigorously that she had seen the guilty deer that had caused this problem only she was lying, and that small trespass against the nature of her God-given soul layered upon other small nods of the head when she had affirmed or denied something that she did not know to be the truth or not the truth. Unaware of having gained a kind of weight in that moment from lying casually about so many things, Liz kept staring at the sky.

The speed of angels was faster than almost anything else she knew. They could come and go in a cluster in the blink of an eye. Sometimes, she could feel them flying away, even though she had missed their approach—but she could feel their tailwind, the sudden rush of air as they whooshed off, headed to some other place where they had some kind of job to perform. There had been times when Liz had felt that whoosh and wondered, almost hopefully, if there were other women---and maybe men—who were aware of the angels of death. She would have liked to have met at least one other person who could truthfully say just as each one had confirmed to seeing the deer, "Yes. I know the angels you are talking about." But the widows and widowers at Christ Church would never fall into a conversation like that with her. Besides, most people blamed Liz for the appearance of death; and if she claimed to see angels about the time that death happened, they would smile condescendingly, nod knowingly, and whisper. Whisper. Whisper. That's why Liz did not point when she saw them again. The angels—maybe twenty of them or more-- were now hovering at the horizon, a swirl of white that most people assumed was a distant cloud.

Sam took one look at Liz's concerned expression and knew that in spite of his head wound, he needed to take charge. Someone had to get the group organized. There had been an accident, but life can't be allowed to just happen to you. You have to make a plan, stick to the plan, and control the fall-out when something unexpected happens like this derailment from the schedule that had taken them over an embankment. Sam fought a wave of weakness and the strange desire to lie down on the ground and close his eyes. His mouth opened and words came, like the small trickle of blood that still flowed from his eyebrow where he had bashed it on the steering wheel, "Let's get organized. First things first--we need a latrine."

Sam didn't wait for anyone to agree or disagree. Scanning the options, he pointed with his left hand. "How about over there— behind those bushes? And water. I'll look for water, although we don't have a way to transport it." His face grew almost angry, and he clenched his teeth. "Water could be a problem."

Mildred raised her hand, like a student in school. "Sam, you're bleeding."

Sam yanked from his back pocket an old-fashioned white handkerchief that his wife Belle had monogrammed for him and stanched the blood drizzling from his eyebrow. He was glad for the wound, relieved that he was paying a steeper price for the accident than what the others apparently had experienced. No one else was bleeding.

Liz had ruined her make-up.

Sam squinted hard at Mildred, and he couldn't see anything wrong with Mildred except occasionally her teeth chattered.

And Jake—Jake was all right.

"It is too late in the year for berries, I think, but there might be a pecan tree around, though the nuts won't be edible this time of year. If we can find the right kind of water supply, there might be fish. And I think I saw a rabbit when we landed."

Almost immediately Sam realized that mentioning the rabbit was a mistake, for the skittering of the rabbit had happened when the car hit the ground, a split second before the airbag expanded large enough to obscure the view.

Mildred's eyes had been closed. Jake had seen the deer and the rabbit, but he had forgotten about the rabbit until then.

Liz had seen only her left eye in the visor mirror because she was dolling up. She was a pretty woman, and that is what pretty women did. (He didn't know why other women resented her for it.) Sam, who had supposedly been rendered unconscious by the impact, remembered seeing a rabbit, and he shouldn't have, really, because when you black out like that there is a cloud of amnesia that blocks out certain details of that moment of shutting down.

Only Sam remembered the rabbit, and he had stupidly said so out loud. It was a crack in the story of what had happened to them all that morning, and the crack made him want to sit down and hold his head in his hands and cry like a schoolboy. Instead, Sam clapped his hands together vigorously and asked, "Is everyone holding up okay?"

He scanned faces. Jake, Liz, and Mildred nodded solemnly.

"Are you all right, Sam?" Mildred asked quietly.

The older man pressed the handkerchief to his forehead again. The bleeding had eased, and there was now that crusty beginning of coagulation that would lead to healing later.

"No time to worry about me. We have got to get ready to spend some time here. Maybe the night." Though the news was unpleasant, something ignited in Sam's eyes, and both Mildred and Liz thought simultaneously: *This old Boy Scout wants to camp out all night and brave the elements.* Then, almost immediately, the two women's reactions split and went in different directions.

Mildred wondered why Sam wanted to stay outdoors overnight without the comforts of indoor plumbing and homemade food. And his wife Belle was at home, and she was not so well these days and might need him. *Why didn't Sam want to get home to Belle?*

Liz thought, 'Thank God! A real man!' Something inside of her that had been tied in a knot since her last husband's funeral began to unkink, and she felt, inexplicably, almost giddy. Still seated on the ground underneath the red tree, Liz leaned back against the trunk and exhaled. She didn't have to go home right away to an empty house. She could stay right there with two real men: one had carried her in his arms, and the other was now in charge.

Mildred waved her hand at Sam for his attention. He looked momentarily impatient that she had something else to say. "It is going to be all right, Mildred. When we don't show up at the church, the news will get back to the home front that we have gone missing. They will come looking for us."

"It could be six o'clock tonight or later before anyone realizes we're missing," Jake said.

Sam turned on Jake angrily. This was no time to upset the ladies. A man had to look on the bright side when ladies were around. Sam forced himself to speak slowly. "The young man we were going to see today will realize that we are not there."

"But that doesn't mean Steev will call anyone," Jake responded thoughtfully. "It just means he will think we didn't come. Or, that we got the date wrong."

"No," Sam said. "I told him we would take him to lunch afterwards so we could interview him. It's a rare young preacher who doesn't enjoy a free lunch." Sam attempted a short laugh at his own humor. It was a familiar barking sound that attempted to prove to everyone that he was jovial and good tempered.

Mildred flinched. For some time, Sam's false laugh had felt like a stab in her heart. She could only imagine how his wife Belle felt when she heard it.

Liz studied Sam, taking deep breaths of relief that someone was in charge of her life.

"That was definite?" Jake affirmed, oblivious to the implications of that false laugh.

Something passed behind Sam's eyes. Not anger this time. Doubt.

"I think so." He paused and then remembered the ladies needed him to be right. "Yes, of course, it was definite."

Liz smiled faintly, a contentment growing in her. She had seen the angels, and no one had died. In fact, they had flown away. Maybe they were gone for good now. The

Bible said there were seasons of things, and maybe the season of death's angels had finally passed away. Maybe they would never come back. Sam was becoming himself again. They would be rescued. In the meantime, Liz didn't have to stay in her dark, too-quiet house waiting for the phone to ring. It rarely did except when the politicians put their commercials on speed dial and impersonated real callers.

But in that moment, Liz Luckie didn't have to listen to the politicians over and over again for company or try and read her Bible and pray, which was hard for her. She had never had the knack of doing that quiet-time stuff that everyone talked about at church. The quiet scared Liz. There was plenty of time to be quiet in the grave, and Liz was alive.

In that moment, Liz Luckie felt more alive than she had in months. Two men were in charge. FussBudget Budge was about to remind everyone that she had brought her big, fat blue Igloo cooler. It was in the car trunk where she had stowed it this morning. Sam didn't remember it. But FussBudget and Jake did. Only they were letting Sam have his head for a while so he could feel better about running off the side of the road—a simple country road, and not some major thoroughfare which the State Troopers patrolled regularly. They were out here in the boondocks.

Liz smiled inside herself, thinking about how Mildred was standing there thinking she was about to save the day. That's what church ladies believed was their calling in the church and why they carried all that stuff in their church lady purses and had those Kleenexes tucked neatly up their church lady sleeves. Mildred and other church ladies like her were the kind of women who never understood what men actually really liked.

But Liz did. Men liked to be the ones who saved the day.

"Sam?" Mildred said.

Sam was scanning the depth of the incline from where they were up to the top of the hill where the road curved, but there was no sound of other cars. None at all. And even if someone drove by, their car windows would be rolled up with the air conditioning going full blast. No one would hear them calling out.

"Someone could see the broken railing and call it in. Or a State Trooper might drive by and see it," Sam theorized.

"Sam?" Mildred said.

He turned to her reluctantly.

"Didn't anyone bring a cell phone?" Mildred asked.

6

GLORIOUS VICTORY

It was a perfectly glorious moment for Liz.

Perfectly glorious in that she would one-up Mildred and all of her supplies.

Perfectly and wonderfully glorious because Mildred would have her Igloo cooler with generic water from Food City because one of her former students was all grown up and the vice president of that grocery store chain, and periodically he shipped her a big load of bottled water with little notes about still using what Mildred Budge had taught him in 5th grade. *So what?* She, Liz Luckie, would be the one who was smart enough and sophisticated enough to have brought a cell phone on the trip. Only if she brought the phone out too quickly, she would be the one who saved the day, and Liz knew better. A smart woman never saved the day. She waited patiently, planning how she would bring out her good-looking phone in a metallic blue that matched her eyes when she had used her Visine and the right eye shadows to make the eye color pop.

No, Liz Luckie's cell phone wasn't one of those clunky old-fashioned kind that so many older Southern women toted in their grandmotherly handbags in case—and this was their very reason! —they ever got stranded on the side of the road and needed to call for help. Liz had even heard some of them say, "I only carry it for emergencies."

As if they didn't talk on the telephone. Or ever gossip. As if they had not signed up for the prayer chain, which, my dear, happened through the telephone. Most women were such hypocrites. Self-effacing, self-denying, please-let-me-sleep-through-my-life-dressed-in-red-and-purple hypocrites. And then they always added, stabbing Liz directly in her wounded, grieving desperately yearning heart, "Because my husband wants me to carry one in case he ever needs to call me." Then, every last one of them tilted a still-curled-set-and-sprayed-within-an-inch-of- their-lives head toward their still living husbands who probably never thought about their wives' cell phones, because so many men preferred beepers to cell phones.

It was an absolute fact of life. Men liked beepers better than cell phones, because they didn't have to answer beepers. They just read the numbers. Men didn't like to talk unless they wanted to talk. They particularly did not like to talk on cell phones. Real men had fingers that did not fit the buttons on cell phones. Liz understood men. And because she understood them, Liz did not mention her cell phone immediately.

"I am not on call this weekend, so I didn't bring my cell phone," Jake said. "They always call me even when I am not the one they are supposed to call so I did not bring my phone," Jake explained. "I guess I could have brought it—should have brought it—and just turned the thing off if I didn't want to take calls." Jake said the words, but he didn't look as if he meant them.

There was more to it than that. Jake was embroiled in a controversy at the local university where he was in charge of buildings and grounds, and people were presently calling him night and day about one of the most confounding problems he had ever encountered. The problem was critter management.

Wild, untamed cats had overpopulated the university campus and were being quietly and regularly fed by school employees who were also animal rights' activists. There was nothing wrong with feeding the wild cats that roamed the campus and which were also performing the excellent service of keeping the mice population under control. Unfortunately, the cats were also sneaking into the playground of the university's day care center designed for the employees' children and using the sandboxes like big kitty toilets. Unsanitary, of course.

The parents of the children and the leaders of the daycare wanted the cats evacuated or exterminated. The people who were feeding the cats wanted a fence built around the daycare playground and the cats left to live and thrive as they always had. No one really believed a fence could keep the cats out of the playground.

Someone was also sending anonymous reports to the local newspaper about the problem, and if Jake didn't handle it just right, his face was going to end up on the front page of the newspaper with a headline like: Kitty Cat Killer Works at Local

University. A determined reporter with an agenda had been calling him on his cell phone.

The wildly roaming cats were a problem for the university's Building and Grounds superintendent, and that was Jake Diamond, who had left his cell phone at home because he did not want to answer a reporter's questions or hear any more about roaming hard-to-catch cats on Sunday, a day ordained by God himself for a man to rest. There would not be cell phones in heaven. There would be cell phones in hell.

"So, Jake, you don't have your cell phone?" Sam clarified loudly. "And Mildred and I don't believe in them."

Mildred frowned and interrupted Sam. "I don't disbelieve in cell phones, Sam. They are too expensive for me." That is what Mildred regularly told people about why she didn't carry one and it was partially true, but the rock-bottom reason was that she simply didn't want to talk on the phone. It was enough that people could call you at home. Why would you want to carry some phone around so that people could call you anywhere you went?

"I have a new cell phone," Liz said softly, reminding the two men that she was a woman of means. Money could be so attractive, especially as a woman aged. The more money she had, the better looking a woman still seemed.

The sun came out and covered Liz's powdered face in light where streams of perspiration and tears had made small rivulets in the Merle Norman foundation make-up she used.

She was oblivious in that moment to the imperfections of her make-up; instead, she was feeling better, warmed by how the circumstances were coming together for good. Some Bible verse chimed distantly in her memory, and an inner voice chided her:

Why don't you memorize it one day rather than hold onto stray words? Liz ignored that inner prompt as she ignored the clocks at her house that chimed the passing of time. She smiled her younger smile, the girlish, hopeful version of a smile that she had practiced and perfected at age sixteen after she had been pulled over by the policeman for speeding and released with a warning.

The younger innocent smile had earned her that release, and she had stored the knowledge of that smile's power inside herself with the half-recalled Bible verse as part of a hope chest that sustained her in between marriages when there was no man to help her navigate a world that expected so much more of a woman than Liz felt capable of giving.

She felt the trunk of the tree pressing into her back and knew that the bark was plucking at the silk threads, ruining her blouse, but that loss and even the discomfort of the bark was comforting. She pressed herself deeply into the tree, and it hurt some more, and she wondered if the skin had been pierced and if blood would pool there, and it would be okay if it did, because if people saw the back of her blouse where she had been hurt enough to bleed, well, that would be okay. The tree was her friend. The day was her friend. Jake and Sam were her friends. Only Mildred, standing off in her cow-like way wearing brown pants and that frumpy blue sweater top, was not her friend, not really. Liz closed her eyes when she thought of Mildred--closed her eyes to blank out the vision of the other church woman who represented all the women who were not her friends.

Liz settled into the tree and the moment and the sun that was warm, very warm, and she began to take deep breaths of relaxation and peace. The thought of the swirling angels of death was as distant as they were—

off on the horizon, bothering somebody else now. Even after the phone call was made, it would be hours before someone could come get them and take them home. In the meantime, she was out here with real men, and the world felt right again. Mildred could soon bring out her stupid Igloo and have whatever little snack was in there—after they made the important phone call on Liz's sleek, sophisticated cell phone that she could afford because she was a woman of means.

"It's in my purse," she said weakly, leaning against her friend, the tree. "On the front floorboard. But I simply can't go get it. I simply can't." She waved a hand toward the car which Jake had feared would explode. But it had not. It wasn't even smoking.

"Could someone fetch my purse? I don't want to risk trying to stand just yet," Liz added limply.

Sam spun on his heel, attempting to move like the man in charge that he had always been, but something jarred in his hip. His joint locked up for a second. He took note of the pain and kept going, because it was a man's job to keep going. It was the same kind of stopping and starting that was happening inside of him in a number of ways. There were strange surges of old memories and inexplicable losses of daily facts. And there were brief moments when he could not remember where he was going. Sam would stand up, and then almost immediately upon standing, he couldn't remember why he had decided to stand up. There were times when he picked up a telephone and then couldn't remember who he was about to call; and when he finally did remember who he was trying to reach out to, he couldn't always think of their phone number—numbers he knew by heart. There had been a new incident this past week when he was actually walking—walking toward something—and as one leg lifted, he experienced the strangest sensation of not wanting to place his foot on the ground again. *Was he capable of just stopping walking mid-air?*

Sam ignored the confusions and misgivings that were layering inside of him and walked as best he could toward his smashed Old Girl, gulping hard when he saw the front end. He yanked open the door on the passenger side. He saw a tube of mascara on the floorboard, and there was that thing they used—a wand—which had smeared his floorboard mat. Although it didn't matter now, Sam picked up that messy stick and returned it to the mascara tube, tightening it. He picked up Liz's designer purse with pink polka dots on it that was just like some of the purses that the teenage girls at church used and carried it back to Liz.

"Thank you, Sam," she said, feeling the cloth of her blouse growing stickier against her back.

"You have got some black stuff on your face," Sam announced gruffly.

Her head trembled slightly at the news. Liz plucked her cell phone out and pointed it in the direction of Sam.

Jake intercepted the phone and flipped it open. He held it out to the sky as if it were a compass and he was trying to find the North Pole. "There is no signal out here," Jake announced finally.

"I was afraid that might be the case," Mildred said solemnly. "They usually plan those cell phone towers to track with the interstate system."

They all studied the ground in an attempt not to look accusingly at Sam, who had planned the trip and said to justify his own choice when he told them their route, "They are doing work on the interstate. Probably be all kinds of delays. Let's take the county road."

The news of no cell phone signal did not appear to bother the man whose Buick was totaled and whose hip joint was locked up. "I am going to visit the little boys' room," Sam said. "And then I am going to figure out how to get us home."

7

BUDGE

"Budge, have you been trying to remind Sam that you brought a cooler and that it is still in his trunk," Jake asked.

Mildred nodded. She was being carefully quiet. Her teeth had stopped chattering, and she was feeling stronger. A purpose was growing in her, and with it, a fervent prayer: *Jesus, get us out of here.*

"I am parched," Liz interjected pitifully.

Jake went back to the car, stared at the trunk, then walked around to the driver's side, and opened the door. He leaned over, pressed a button, and the trunk lid slowly eased up. He carried the cooler back to the women and set it down before Mildred as if it were a tea service and he was waiting for her to serve. Mildred nodded, and Jake popped open the lid.

"There is water from Food City," Jake said approvingly as he scanned the contents. "And little baby Dr. Peppers."

"The small cans stack better in the cooler than the regular size ones," Mildred explained. She didn't add that the small cans of Dr. Pepper had been on sale. Ordinarily, she preferred Coca-Cola.

"Diet?" Liz asked.

Mildred plucked a seven-ounce drink out of the ice and handed it to her. She had packed the diet ones just for Liz because she had seen that Liz always used the little packets of fake sugar.

Jake purposely let Mildred hand Liz the drink. It was enough that he had carried the woman from the car to the place on the ground where she now sat and had not moved, like she was some kind of queen and the people around her were her royal court. Jake had seen that act in other women like Liz too many times. Jake cast an approving glance at Mildred who was still standing and taking in their surroundings. He knew what she was thinking, because they thought alike: *Home was that way. Were they closer to home than their destination? If they could get back up that hill, which way would they need to start walking?*

"I didn't make sandwiches," Mildred apologized, "because I thought we would be eating lunch out. But there are some Snickers candy bars in there. The bite-size ones." She shook her head ruefully. "I am sorry everything is so small."

"Budge, you brought more than anyone else did," Jake said. "And it looks like we are going to need it."

Mildred took a Snickers bar and ate it for the sugar. The aftereffects of the adrenaline rush quieted. She sipped her Dr. Pepper with purpose. *Jesus, get us out of here, por favor.*

Sam returned, tramping across the ground heavily. "Might as well run off any sleeping snakes while I am moving around," he said, reaching down into the cooler. "You are a jewel, Mildred," Sam said. It was his apology--the only kind he knew how to give. His hand found a Snickers bar and a drink. "You didn't happen to bring an aspirin, did you?" he asked Mildred.

It had been a long time since anyone had asked Mildred for an aspirin.

Mildred stocked a small supply of medicines in the zipper compartment of her purse where she kept her emergency money. She did have some baby aspirin, but what Sam needed was acetaminophen or ibuprofen. "I always over pack," she explained, her standard excuse for carrying the stuff that church ladies toted everywhere. She had tried to cut back through the years on the supplies that she carried around with her and had, through great will and over time, reduced the content of her purse to two Band-Aids, two safety pins, one bottle of assorted pain relievers including Tylenol regular, Tylenol PM (because when you traveled you often forgot to pack one and in a strange hotel room it was just what you needed to help blot out the sounds), a Chapstick, a package of Sweet n' Low because although she didn't use it, often a companion wanted one, a decaffeinated tea bag, one travel pack of Kleenex in addition to the loose ones stashed in pockets and up her sleeve because some public bathrooms ran out of toilet tissue, and there was the small black change purse with a fifty dollar bill and two dollars' worth of silver change, and a small tin of St. Joseph's baby aspirin for potential heart attack victims to chew if they needed a handy blood thinner. There was also a roll of Honees, an Italian hard candy. Each piece had a drop of honey in the center.

As self-conscious as Mildred had been made to feel that morning about packing the blue Igloo for a day trip, she had been just as surprised by the lack of emergency equipment in Sam's car. For in the trunk of her own car was a gallon jug of water, a pair of jumper cables, a small air compressor that quite efficiently could re-inflate a flat tire, a tire gauge, a first-aid kit, and an extra pair of walking shoes in case she had ever gotten stranded on the side of the road while she was wearing shoes not sturdy enough to get her home.

Mildred had used almost everything in her own trunk at one time or another, and even the people who needed her supplies frequently teased her about carrying them. Mildred Budge did not understand that. She did not understand why other people often felt free to ridicule her and women like her for simply trying to be prepared for whatever might happen wherever she might go.

Mildred opened her purse and passed the Tylenol bottle to Sam. "Will this do?" she asked.

He nodded, holding out his hand. It trembled some, and she pretended she didn't see.

"Anybody else?" Mildred asked.

Liz readily accepted, sighing deeply as she took two capsules.

Jake shook his head. Tylenol wouldn't solve the real problem, and his intensity about finding a way home was greater than any small jarring physical pain that wouldn't show up until the next day. He wanted to get home before nightfall because he liked to sleep in his own bed. He didn't want to spend the night out here with the limp Liz who would need to hold onto a man in the dark, and Sam was undeniably married.

Jake surveyed his three naïve companions. They wore the expressions of people who had been in an accident and thought the emergency was over. But in reality, alone in the dark with a black widow spider was far more dangerous. While Sam was busy scouting out a camp, Jake was looking for a way to get them home.

He spotted a small break in the overgrowth on the far side of the car. It could be an opening that might lead somewhere. Jake turned back and scanned the incline. It was steep, but there were some handholds up the way. If he had been alone, he would have tried it—but he wasn't. No way could the ladies or Sam go up that incline without help.

Jake flipped open the cell phone again and punched the buttons hard one more time. Nothing. He tossed the useless phone back to Liz. She didn't catch it. Didn't even try. The gizmo landed with a thud in her lap.

Jake hated that kind of contrived passivity. Some people thought that Liz's brand of helplessness belonged to a generation; but Jake worked on a college campus, and he saw it everywhere in all kinds of women and more and more men these days of every age, too. "Budge, what do you say after we finish our drinks, we take a look over there?" Jake pointed to a woodsy area where he had spotted what could be a space wide enough to hike toward civilization.

Sam turned, assessed the terrain, felt his hip strain, and said, "We shouldn't leave the site of the accident. That is standard operating procedure." The retired Air Force colonel looked up overhead as if a search plane might suddenly appear, and he could wave his arms and direct the rescue plane to land on that six feet of runway that was all the space they had.

"If we are going to get out of here today, we are going to have to help ourselves. What do you say, Budge?" Jake pressed. He didn't really need her, but he wanted her company—wanted an ally that would insulate him from Liz's neediness later. "Or, I can go by myself."

Mildred took a thoughtful sip of her drink and looked down at her Sunday shoes. They were the lowest heels a woman could buy and still call them a dress pump. Both knee-high stockings were now rolled at her ankles, like an old man's socks that needed garters.

Jake grinned. "Come on, Budge."

Jake finished his drink in one long swig, crumpled his can, and as if they were kids on a playground rather than survivors from a car wreck, he tossed the can high and hard as far away from them as he could.

"Litter bug," Mildred commented, and then with a glint of amusement in her large brown eyes, Budge threw her can hard after his.

8

RESCUE

"Do you think anyone will come looking for us?" Mildred asked as they tramped purposefully off into an overgrown terrain. It was slow going at first, and she was surprised that her legs did not immediately want to obey her will. Noting it, she commanded herself to move. *You had to boss your body around. If you didn't, it would try to mutiny against you.* Mildred had been fighting the mutiny of her body's desire to be in charge for years. She always won, but some days were harder than others.

"No one will come looking for us until tomorrow," Jake said. "By the time anyone figures out we are lost, it will be nightfall, and they won't look for us after dark."

"Sam's wife will wonder where he is," Mildred replied.

"Not until tonight," Jake said, as they reached the denser part of the brush. He reached out and pushed aside some honeysuckle vines. "After you?" he inquired.

"I'll follow you," Mildred replied, her purse still looped through her arm.

"You take that everywhere?"

She nodded, and Jake saw that she didn't want to be teased about her handbag.

"If it gets too heavy for you, I'll tote it," Jake offered, stepping forward. "Watch your feet." A second later, he added, "Watch your head."

Mildred ducked lower and hunched her shoulders. The thicket was overgrown but passable; and within minutes, she was feeling stronger and glad to be moving. The chill that had begun after the accident had run its course. Action eased the gnawing anxiety. Mildred Budge didn't like just waiting for help to come. A woman who lived alone learned initiative.

"I don't like sitting around waiting," Jake said, reading her mind.

Jake pressed on.

Mildred followed.

They moved slowly for another few minutes and in silence until they reached a place where there was enough space overhead for the sunlight to fall through.

Jake gripped the collar of his shirt and shook it. "Getting kind of warm," he remarked. "You okay?"

Mildred nodded and inhaled with satisfaction. There is a time when walking when one reaches a stride that feels good. Mildred had been riding in the car, felt the adrenaline rush and then recede, and stood around while Sam tried to get them organized. Now she was in motion, and she didn't want to stop for long. Sweat was beading on her scalp, but it felt like a release of tension rather than something that would ruin her hairstyle. She had grown up in the generation of women who thought exercise unfeminine, and she had discovered motion later in life and now thrived on it—exulted that she had the strength to walk briskly, enjoyed working hard physically, and she loved the satisfaction that she could do what she needed to do.

"You really are okay," Jake said, as the space to walk widened enough for them to move forward side by side.

"I would be more okay if I knew where I was going," Mildred said.

Jake came to an abrupt stop. Squinting, he raised his arm and pointed toward their left. "What do you see over there, Budge?"

"Trees," Mildred replied, sheltering her eyes with a cupped hand. The metal clasps on her brassiere scratched at the middle of her back, and she wondered for the umpteenth time why a genius had not invented a foundation garment that was both serviceable and comfortable. Surely if they could send a rocket to the moon, they could invent more comfortable women's underwear.

"Higher up," Jake directed.

Mildred paused. She squinted, and her jaw dropped slightly in a new move that her chiropractor had taught her to handle TMJ. "Metal," she said. "We can see the metal rail guard from here. That's the bend in the road over there."

"What do you see leading up to it?" Jake asked. At the university, the professors talked like that to their students. They called it the Socratic method—Q & A--but really, it was a technique that many successful black men like Jake used in the company of white people to avoid sounding aggressive. Some white people assessed self-assurance in a black person as aggression.

Mildred knew the same strategy very well. Although she had gently employed the Socratic method as a teacher with 5th graders for 25 years, she had always instinctively used the same technique with white male elders and deacons who were uncomfortable with a church lady speaking authoritatively in their domain which they considered was ordained by Scripture as belonging to men.

How to read and live out Scripture was a lifelong calling on Mildred Budge's life, and while she had few definitive answers about the potentially contentious issues that were often traditionally or culturally driven, she had a healthy respect for the powerful position of simply remaining silent when certain questions arose. There were times when she wanted to ask God why he hadn't added an 11th commandment: *Everyone be quiet as often as possible.* Mildred believed in the principle of silence. Holding that principle together was another: *Keep your own counsel.*

"I see a portion of the hill we came down. But that side of the hill isn't as steep to climb as the one we came down," Jake said. "That is where we are going," Jake added decisively, and Budge didn't mind.

"Without the others?" Mildred asked, heading off toward the hill.

"Let's see what there is to know before we go back," Jake said, moving into the lead position. "We haven't come so far. It just feels like it."

Mildred glanced at her watch. They had only been walking for twenty-five minutes. In the park, that would be a good mile for her; but in this brush, they had probably only progressed a half mile.

Both of them feeling stronger and also energized by their mutual desire to go home, they picked up the pace, pushing aside the long vines that trailed down from trees that grew intertwined. Suddenly Jake reached out his hand to stop her. The move was instinctual. When he saw the ravine, they weren't close enough to fall into it, but his arm immediately went up to protect her.

The troubling ravine wasn't so big as to be insurmountable, but it was wide enough to be a problem. You could almost jump over it, but not quite.

Jake studied it. "We're awfully close to having to give up and go back," Jake surmised. His forest-green eyes narrowed as he considered their options.

"I don't want to give up," Mildred said. "It isn't very wide."

Mildred looked around for a fallen tree that they could use as a bridge. Jake pushed on a tree that was leaning, but it didn't move.

"Maybe there's another way across further that way," Mildred said. It wasn't a suggestion really. She was thinking out loud. Jake understood the difference.

He scanned that direction thoughtfully.

"If we go too far, you're afraid we can't find our way back to them and the red tree," she surmised. "It's easy to lose your bearings."

Mildred reached past Jake and found another vine. Gripping it, she pulled hard, scanning the length of it to see where the vine connected above. The long vine was intertwined around the top branches of a very tall tree. She swung it back and forth.

Jake took it from her and tested it with several hard tugs.

"Do you think it would sustain our weight?" Mildred asked.

"How much do you weigh?" Jake countered.

"I weigh as much as I should for my height," she replied tartly.

"I weigh twenty pounds more than you."

"At least," Mildred sniffed. "Hand me that vine."

"You're not really going to swing across that ravine," Jake said with a short laugh as Mildred took the vine back.

No, she most certainly was not going to swing across the ravine.

But Mildred Budge wanted to consider the idea before she decided against it. She twisted the vine, and then she backed up six steps. She looped the vine around her right wrist three times. "If I start off running, by the time I get there," she said pointing toward the gap, "I could almost jump that space. It is just about three feet past my comfort zone. Or, I could step up here," she said, climbing up on a larger rock that served as a kind of platform. "And using the height, I could push myself off."

"Give me that vine," Jake said. "Women like you do not jump ravines. I could jump the ravine better than you could just by backing up and taking a flying leap over it."

"Then why don't you go take a flying leap?" Mildred asked, daring him. It felt good to say those words out loud. The notion of an 11th commandment receded, overcome by the friendly goodwill between them.

He held her gaze and laughed. "You're a piece of work, Budge."

Jake Diamond was really looking at Mildred Budge, and his frank approval of her was a heady experience. Mildred Budge had never intended to jump the ravine or use the vine. But her mouth opened, and she said something else altogether different than what she had planned.

"Will you hold my purse?" Mildred asked, tossing him the handbag before he could reply.

Jake caught it instinctively, feeling himself about to laugh. She was kidding.

And then she wasn't kidding. For in the movement of tossing him her purse, Mildred's feet slipped on the rock where she was standing, and off she went, sailing over the narrow ravine in pretty much the same way that Sam's Old Girl had gone over the embankment.

It was a graceful sailing movement, Jake thought. *Kind of like flying.* And for a moment he was in awe of Mildred Budge, who had so many kinds of locomotion in her. Curious about her, too. And he had the strangest thought: *What kind of woman is she?*

Mildred was not in the air for very long. Seconds later, she swung back pendulum fashion; and when she did, Jake caught her around the waist as easily as he had snagged her purse, which was now pushed back up on his arm.

The church lady's feet quickly found the ground, and she let go of the vine as Jake released her.

"The vine works," Mildred concluded, brushing at some imaginary sand on her pants.

"Yep. The vine does work," Jake agreed, looking at Budge with approval.

"You were showing off, weren't you?"

"A little bit," Mildred acknowledged. As she stared over the narrow gap appraisingly, she added, "I would just have to remember to let go when I get to the other side next time." She eyed the vine thoughtfully.

Jake laughed and plopped down on the ground.

Budge settled down beside him, trying to keep her breathing steady. The waistband on her brown slacks had rolled down from her waist about two inches below the midriff bulge that had accrued no matter how much she had exercised or not eaten to prevent it. The long tail of her aqua top covered it.

Feigning interest in the blue sky, Mildred wondered how she could pull her pants back up around her waist without doing it in front of Jake. Stalling, she reached inside her purse and withdrew two pieces of peppermint candy that she regularly accepted at the end of any Mexican dinner that she and Fran Applewhite enjoyed on Tuesday evenings when entrees were 2 for 1 at four o'clock. It was the Early Bird dinner. A piece of hard candy could come in handy, and sometimes Mildred got tired of her signature candy, Honees, which had a little drop of honey inside and were wonderful for low blood sugar or a tickly throat. Peppermint candy was good for your mood. The peppermint gave your spirits a lift, and eating the candy had a way of relaxing your jaws where tension was stored.

"How did you let yourself get talked into serving on the pulpit committee?" Jake asked, as he peeled his peppermint.

"I didn't want to be on this committee," Mildred replied honestly, and she wrestled with where to leave her candy wrapper. With a shrug she tossed the balled-up candy wrapper and saw it land near a particularly handsome rock. She coveted the rock instantly. Mildred desired rocks. Liked to collect special rocks and place them in her backyard to remind her of where she had been. She thought about palming the rock and slipping it into her purse.

Jake smiled, unaware of the rock or her attraction to it. "Me, neither. My daddy used to say they will work a good horse to death."

"Are you saying I am a good horse?" Budge asked mildly, as the second wave of covetousness rose up in her. It was truly a very handsome rock. It would store heat and feel warm in her hand. She could place it in her backyard with the other rocks she had brought home from various adventures. Her fingertips danced on the ground, fighting the urge to go and get it.

"A very good horse," Jake replied equitably.

"You know serving on this committee is a no-win situation too?" Mildred asked, popping her candy in her mouth. It was excellent. Most candy was.

Jake nodded. "I can see how you ended up on the committee. And I guess I can see how I am on the committee. You're a settled-down white woman who represents all of the settled-down church ladies. I am a responsible black man who doesn't cause trouble. Sam's, like, the whitest man on the planet. But which group of the church population does Liz Luckie represent? She is certainly not like other widows. You could actually call her a church lady, too, and there's no reason to have two representatives for the same group on the committee." He studied Mildred more closely. "But she's not really a church lady the way you and Sam's wife are church ladies."

Mildred considered the question and answered it thoughtfully. "Maybe Liz represents all of the other people who don't fit in a category. And I imagine there are a lot of them," she said. "She doesn't really seem to fit in, does she?" Mildred added without criticism.

Jake nodded. "I heard something about her and you in the water park during the Missions Conference. She almost drowned. You saved her."

Mildred dismissed the compliment. The story was far more complicated than that. "She wouldn't have drowned. The water wasn't that deep," Mildred said. "I let her hang onto my inner tube after hers developed a leak. We dog-paddled out of there."

"Her inner tubes will always spring a leak, Budge. Yours never will," Jake said. "That doesn't mean your knee-high stockings won't fall down. That's been bugging you all morning. Why don't you just take them off?"

"If I do, my heels will blister," Mildred replied sensibly. "But when I get home, I am going to set fire to them. Watching them burn will feel very good."

Jake smiled pleasantly—he had good teeth--staring off at the horizon where a white cloud grew darker, hinting at rain.

"You're not worried about something and not telling me, are you? Mildred asked, following his gaze.

Jake shook his head. "No, we'll be all right." He hesitated. "Does Sam seem like himself to you?"

"Sam is as good as gold," she replied carefully, avoiding the question.

"You don't talk about other people," Jake stated flatly.

"His wife is a friend of mine. He is, too, for that matter," Mildred said.

"I hear Belle is sick, but her name doesn't show up on prayer lists."

"If your name shows up on the prayer list, your phone will ring off the wall with people proving they are responsible Christians or that they love you. It's hard to even take a nap if your name is on the prayer sheet," Mildred explained. "The doctors don't know exactly what it is. Belle has good days and bad days. I guess Sam is worried about her all the time. Makes him kind of distracted. Worry does that."

"And he is having some trouble himself," Jake pressed. "You must see it."

"We are all getting older. Sam is getting older one way. I am getting older another way."

"You're not old," Jake said, looking at her with puzzled interest. "Budge, you're one of the youngest women I know," Jake said, and then he shifted, preparing to stand. When he was back on his feet, he reached out a hand to help Mildred, who tried to stifle a grunt as she rose. She made a soft oomph anyway, but managed to straighten out the waistband on her pants as she stood up.

"Shall we go forward without them and try to save the day or go back and collect them?" Jake asked.

"Do you think all four of us could get across that ravine?" Mildred replied.

"We could make it. I hate to leave anyone behind. I say we go get them," Jake said decisively. "We couldn't leave without telling them."

Mildred nodded her agreement. "I think we can get back up on the road from over there," she said pointing. "Once we are up there, we can just keep walking on the road. Where do you think we are?"

"About midway, and I don't remember where the last exit was. Let's not forget the map from the car. We will need it."

Jake was sounding positive, and Mildred was feeling good about their prospects of getting home. "Maybe we won't have to walk far," she said. "Someone will surely drive this way and stop when they see four people walking down the highway dressed in their Sunday clothes."

Jake nodded, as he held back a branch so that Mildred could pass through. When she did, Mildred asked the question that she had repressed earlier, "No cell phone on you? Really?"

"Self-defense," Jake explained, as they fell into step in a companionable rhythm. "I'm in charge of buildings and grounds at the university, and we have a problem with too many wild cats on the loose. There are people who want me to get rid of them.

Other, louder people want me to leave the cats alone."

Mildred nodded her head seriously. "I'd laugh if I didn't know just how miserable some people can make you about a problem like that."

The path narrowed, and they shifted into single file again. Jake explained, speaking over his shoulder as he led the way: "The problem is that the cats keep the mouse population down. The campus is big, and we have field mice and loose white mice from the science lab sometimes, but the cats have been getting into the playgrounds and sandboxes of the children who come to the university's daycare center."

"No fence will prevent that," Mildred predicted.

"That's right," Jake agreed.

"What else do the children have to play on?" she asked, as the path widened, and they could walk side by side again.

"The usual. Swing sets. Sliding boards. That board that goes up and down."

"Teeter totter," Mildred said. "So, it's really just the sandbox that is the problem. The sandbox attracts the cats."

Jake nodded, perspiration beginning to drip down the side of his face.

"As a former schoolteacher, I can assure you that sand boxes are a highly over-rated form of recreation for children. People—parents--naively hope that sand is some kind of artistic medium through which children can express themselves, but that view is overly optimistic. It is only sand. Even at the beach where children make sandcastles, it is not art—it is sand. Sandboxes are nasty, and they are unhealthy in the best of circumstances. More than cats are attracted to them. Get rid of the sand boxes."

"And replace them with what?" Jake asked.

"Not a thing. Just get rid of the sandboxes, and don't try to make it up to people by offering anything else. There's too much of that going around anyway."

"Isn't there?" Jake agreed. "As if everyone is entitled to something every moment of his or her life." He shrugged. "They will get mad though."

"Getting mad is the first reaction immature people have to any kind of change. But once the teachers at the daycare—and those are the people you really need to worry about--get over the idea that they have had something else taken from them without their vote, they will decide they like having the sandboxes gone, because I can promise you, they are tired of cleaning up the sand that gets tracked into their classrooms. The teachers will be on your side eventually, and teachers know how to distract irritated parents. Just do what you need to do and apologize later. Don't wait for permission," Mildred advised firmly. "Just do it."

"Is that how church ladies operate?" Jake asked wryly.

"All the time," she replied easily. "It is one of the unwritten rules. You can wait forever in a church on permission to follow through on a good idea that you feel led to do. I have learned—and I am not alone in this—just to go ahead and do what I think is best; and if someone gets mad, I apologize. It's simpler to ask for forgiveness than it is to ask for permission. And in church they have to forgive you. It's in the Bible." Mildred grinned, and Jake smiled back.

"That's easier for women. A man doesn't like to apologize. It makes us look weak," Jake explained. "People expect church ladies to be weak anyway. They have different ideas about men. Black men especially."

"Is that really true?" Mildred asked, stopping. She looked at him honestly.

Jake stopped, too, giving her a moment to catch her breath. "Do you have another piece of that candy?"

She found one in her purse and passed it to him.

"There is a professor on our campus whose teaching specialty is the shared cultural history of black men and white women."

Mildred blinked and blotted her brow with a Kleenex. Insects were beginning to buzz around them. "Really?" she asked, swatting at something that was dive-bombing her hair. She was not surprised, really, that someone was making a living on that sociological pursuit. She had seen similarities herself more than once.

"It has something to do with winning the right to vote, and that after we let white women help us, we didn't help them as we promised we would." Jake smiled, and Mildred really, really admired his teeth.

"I would like to apologize for my ancestors failing yours," Jake said, unwrapping his second piece of candy.

"I would like to apologize for mine causing yours no end of trouble," she replied easily. "Why didn't one of us bring a drink with us?"

"Sorry," Jake said easily. And then he grinned.

"Me, too," she replied sunnily.

"This could go on all the time," Jake said, resuming the walk. "People just apologizing and apologizing for all that human beings are or have ever been to one another."

"Maybe we should," Mildred said quietly, as a swirl of white caught her peripheral vision, shifting her attention immediately to where Liz and Sam were standing together. As she strained to see what that blur was, the swirl of white seemed to evaporate into the air.

9

KISS ME

Liz and Sam were kissing underneath the red tree.

Both Jake and Mildred saw them and immediately stopped walking and stepped back from what they had seen. Jake studied his shoes for a second as if ashamed that another man could act so foolishly. Mildred fought the impulse to go right over there and slap them both on their wrists—don't touch, don't touch! -- and tell them to go sit in their respective chairs and repeat 500 times: "I won't do that again. I won't do that again. Actions produce consequences, and I know this because I am a grown up."

With a quick wordless nod to Mildred, Jake began to stomp the ground, making as much noise as he could. Jake called out, "Hey, anybody home?"

Though the kiss had ended, the two were still standing close. Upon hearing the approach of Mildred and Jake they broke apart and did an astonishingly good job of feigning innocence.

"We found a possible way out of here," Jake called out, waving in a friendly manner. He went over to the cooler and extracted another Dr. Pepper.

"We can only have two a piece," Sam called out automatically. He had inventoried the contents and decided how the drinks were to be disbursed. "Plus, the water."

"Two a piece sounds like more than a fair share to me," Mildred replied tersely.

Sam's face showed concern. He blustered, "Well, show us the way. I, for one, am ready to go home."

Liz turned, surprised by Sam's statement. She looked small inside her clothes, and Mildred wondered irritably if she was losing weight. Liz Luckie was the kind of woman who would lose weight easily. Mildred's waistband was threatening to roll down below her navel again. She inhaled and told it to behave.

"Let me get my keys," Sam said. "My house key is on that ring still in the ignition."

"Grab the map while you're at it. And don't forget your cell phone, Lizzie," Jake said. "When we reach the road, it might pick up a signal." Jake turned, putting a hand on the small of his back, and Mildred wondered if he had sustained some kind of injury or bruise that he had not yet acknowledged to himself.

Mildred took a quick inner inventory; and while she was physically strong enough to keep going, underneath the intention to get home that was helping her to move was a great pull of fatigue. She felt jarred. Seeing Sam make a fool of himself had added to that feeling.

Sam returned with the car keys and the map. "Do we each need to grab a bottle of that water? You were a genius to pack that water, Mildred."

"Yeah. I'm a genius all right," Mildred agreed, her gaze canny with understanding.

Jake reported briskly, "There is a narrow ravine we have to cross. Budge has already done it. All we have to do is use a vine to help us make the two or three extra feet we need to get to the other side. We are each going to have to take a flying leap, but we can," Jake said.

"I don't jump. And I certainly don't jump over ravines. I have short legs," Liz announced. "And I am wearing a skirt."

"If I say jump, you'll jump," Mildred told Liz darkly. "And you will jump, because we are going home. We are going to be home before dark, and you can write that in your diary when you get there," Mildred declared.

The other woman looked worried and hurried to catch up with Sam.

Jake motioned for Mildred to come up beside him. "Sam, fall in behind me. Liz, it doesn't matter how short your legs are, you need to keep up. The day isn't as young as it was."

Authority shifted then. Sam deferred to Jake, who had placed himself in charge, and Mildred was his acknowledged lieutenant. Liz followed the three of them, taking twice as many steps as the rest of them to keep up.

"Wait for me," Liz said more than once. "Mildred!"

Periodically, Mildred did stop to allow Liz to catch up, but she didn't offer her any encouraging words—just stood and waited. And when the other woman got close enough to smile and look at Mildred as if to say,

`Look how well I am doing,' Mildred replied, "Chop-chop. This is no time for dawdling."

The walk to the ravine felt shorter this time. And it felt different, too. Unlike the hike with Jake, with whom Mildred had felt an easy rapport that had caused her to believe that she could do anything, there was now a kind of deadly pall as if the reality of the accident was finally catching up with her.

Her clothes felt damp and dirty, and her muscles jangled. There was no doubt about it. In spite of Jake's declaration that she was the youngest woman he knew, Mildred Budge was not as young as she had once been. She had been in a car accident. She had witnessed her friend making a fool of himself with a woman who had tried to be her friend, and now Mildred was very glad that she had kept her distance from Liz. Very glad indeed.

Mildred joined Sam and Jake by the ravine that she had an hour ago swung over with heroic energy and fearlessness. Standing beside it in that moment, she didn't know who she had been the hour before. How had she ever done what she knew she had done? Jake's eyes met hers, and she understood that he was thinking the same thing. The ravine seemed bigger now, and the shadows cast by shifting sunlight seemed to distort the distance, making it harder to estimate. It wasn't three or four feet—it had to be almost five, maybe six feet wide.

As she stood looking around and at the ravine, Mildred began to think that they had arrived at some other place rather than the earlier spot near the ravine. Surely there was a better place to jump further up. Then, she looked down and saw the handsome rock and the two peppermint candy wrappers.

It was the same spot all right. Mildred stooped down and picked up the rock. It was a handsome thing. She liked the feel of it in her hand. Its contours. Its warmth. Its weight. She held onto it, and the weight of it in her hand comforted her.

Jake said under his breath, "Does that gulley look deeper to you than it did before?"

"And wider," Mildred replied, with concern.

Sam studied the challenge as Liz came up beside him. She was afraid, cowering beside Sam as she anticipated that something was going to be expected of her. Both Jake and Mildred saw Liz struggle not to take hold of Sam's hand. It was in that instant that Mildred understood something about how lonely the woman must be. Though she was deeply angry at both of them, Mildred saw, too, that something terrible must be wrong for each of them to reach out to the other for what could only be very little in return. The cost to them both could be severe.

"Jake says that you went across that gulley hanging from a vine," Sam said disbelievingly. There was something else in his voice—the undercurrent of a suggestion and a criticism of Jake, too-- that if he had been her companion, Mildred would never have been put in harm's way like that. Mildred felt that—felt the implied promise of Sam's superior form of protection.

Like other women of her generation, Mildred had always counted on men like Sam to protect and lead, and she stopped to question whether that reliance upon them had cost her other small surges of joy throughout her life and the invigorating and unexpected feeling of being triumphant, almost by accident, when she had gripped that vine. Looking at the depth of the ravine, she knew only that beside Sam, the elder who protected her from the responsibilities of independence, she felt unable to try.

"I caught hold of that vine and backed up...." Mildred began, and if Fran had been standing there, she would have told the truth: 'I was showing off, and my feet slipped, and I did go across, but it was an accident. Two accidents in one day!'

"She backed up to about here," Jake said, showing the wedge of rock that Mildred had stood upon to gain perspective. "She just flew across the gap." His voice, which had been admiring earlier, now evidenced a tone of doubt and a trace of guilt, for in that moment he saw himself as Sam and others would. Jake Diamond had let a woman go first in a dangerous situation.

"You really did that?" Liz asked incredulously and disapprovingly. "You don't expect me to do that, do you, Sammy?"

The 'Sammy' slipped out. Sam ignored it. He didn't have to explain himself to anyone. Sam took hold of the vine and tested it. Above their heads, leaves crackled. They all looked up as a squirrel raced across the limb; and as if setting them an example, leapt from one limb to the next. The four stranded travelers traded anxious glances. Sam tugged on the vine again, appearing uncertain.

In different circumstances, Mildred would have felt sorry for her friend Sam—would have tried to think of something to say to let him get out of the challenge before him or encourage him to do the best he could. But it had been a long day, and Mildred Budge was more tired than she wanted to admit. She was disappointed, too. Despite a moment's flash of compassion for two lonely people who were making a big mistake, she asked, "Do you want me to show you how I did it before?"

Sam's temper flashed. He was competing with Jake to be in charge; he wouldn't take much from Mildred who had known him long enough to understand that if he had been with Mildred earlier, she never would have touched that vine or swung over that hole in the earth.

"Just stay out of my way. Go stand over there," Sam directed, looking at the gap. His hip hurt bad, but he didn't say so. And a part of him knew that he had been seen as a failure. It was too soon to name the ways he was failing, but the truth was born inside of Sam and was forging its way to the surface of his consciousness where he would have to own it. But not right then. Sam postponed the inevitability of confessing his weaknesses by trying to be a hero first. It was a lifelong habit.

And something in that habit touched a well of compassion in Jake that was still kindling inside of the younger man who had retained the knowledge of flying into peace off of the embankment. Jake said, "Sam, you ought to stay here with the ladies to catch the vine when it swings back. Then, I will be over there on the other side in a position to catch people as they come across."

"I could catch people as easily as you could," Sam argued. "And I should do it. I am the one who drove us into this predicament."

"Oh, Sammy," Liz said, taking hold of Sam's arm. She looked up at him pitifully.

Mildred was still holding the rock that she planned to take home.

Unabashedly now, Liz leaned her cheek against Sam's arm—the arm that belonged to Mildred's friend Belle. Liz's body swayed against Sam possessively; and when it did, Mildred's arm went up automatically. She hurled the rock like a shot put, hitting the other woman in the middle of her back. After striking Liz, the rock fell with a thud to the ground.

Liz yelped and let go of Sam. Instead of looking back at Mildred, she looked up at a small white cloud that was poised overhead.

Unaware of what had happened to Liz, Sam chose that moment to concentrate. He backed up, holding the vine, and took a few hurried steps as if he were approaching a bowling lane rather than a ravine he needed to cross. And then, pretending to be ten years younger than he really was, Sam, too, sailed over the ravine. Before it was time to let go and just as he reached the other side, the vine snapped. Sam landed in a scramble on the dirt, pounding pain into his bad hip, almost falling to his knees but regaining his stance in time to run a couple of steps to find his footing.

Liz clapped excitedly, stopping all of a sudden to put a hand behind her to rub the sore spot on her back that she had in that second of Sam's triumph forgotten. Then, she looked at the ground, then over her shoulder at Jake who held her gaze steadily and at Mildred, who was thinking about what it meant for Sam to be on the other side now—and the vine now useless.

"Made it!" Sam exclaimed, as if they couldn't see for themselves. "But the vine is broken," he added ruefully. He scanned the limbs over their heads to see if any other means of crossing the gap existed.

Jake had already surveyed the possibilities. There were none. Jake understood their position instantly.

There wasn't much to be said. Sam was trapped on one side; they were stuck on the other. Sam looked with regret toward Jake and Mildred and Liz. Though angry with him, Mildred felt pierced that Sam was over there alone and not up to going for help. Not really. But he had to. Had to try at least.

"See up there?" Jake called, pointing behind Sam toward a break in the incline that led up to the road. "You could get to the road from there."

Sam looked up, and his spirit faltered. They all saw it. Sam looked like he was about to cave or crumple to the ground. Mildred's guilty, rock-throwing hand went up. If Sam had been nearby, she would have patted him on the shoulder with that same hand and promised automatically, "It will all be fine. You'll see." For even in the midst of trouble, a seasoned church lady can recognize a problem and understand that the solution will come. Church ladies know the discipline of patience and the power of encouragement to others.

"What about all of you?" Sam asked, and there was an instant when Mildred thought he was just going to sit down and not move again. She felt, too, that a part of him wanted to be over there—away from everything, set free from his responsibilities by simply being physically set apart from them.

"We'll go back to the car and wait for help," Jake said decisively. "You go get us some help, Sam."

"Take my cell phone," Liz called out, as if she wanted to toss a part of herself to go with

Sam. "Maybe it will work when you reach the road." She walked to the edge of the ravine; and as if blowing him a kiss, Liz tossed her cell phone underhanded toward Sam.

The phone never made it across. The metallic blue cell missed its mark, then ricocheted. Liz watched disconsolately as it tumbled into the base of the rocky ravine.

Turning, she raised both hands as if to ask, what's a girl to do who can't throw or jump? But neither Jake nor Mildred had stayed to watch more of the good-bye. Mildred did not want to see more than she already had. She had turned her back on Liz saying good-bye to Sam, and a part of her thought: *Sam Deerborn might not even try to get up the hill to the road. Sam Deerborn might just sit down, stay right there, and never move again.* And a part of her understood the attractiveness of that call of inertia. There came a time when you really felt as if you could not do anymore.

Mildred had felt that way for a long time after she had retired from teaching fifth graders, and then she had changed. She had rediscovered her appetite to see who she would become after she had fully agreed with her Maker to leave the old Mildred behind. Every now and again, the Lord called for Mildred to leave some part of herself behind, and then a new part of her started living. It was a strange way to live: to keep changing when something deep and true to who you are as a human being who craved routine.

Jake plowed ahead, shoving aside the brush and tangled weeds with determination. Liz walked double-quick to follow him, and Mildred stepped back to let Liz catch up with Jake.

"How many candy bars did you pack in that Igloo? Jake asked over his shoulder.

"Not enough to call it breakfast," Mildred replied tersely.

10

RAVINE

The walk back to the Buick was deadly quiet, broken only when Liz called out, "I am going to stop at the little girls' room."

She had drunk her whole bottle of water and tossed the empty container into the ravine where it had landed near her cell phone. 'A remarkable aim,' Mildred had thought as she sipped her water the same way that Jake partook of his periodically, pacing himself and his water supply.

"Don't forget to lock the door," Mildred replied dourly.

"You wouldn't happen to have another tissue?" Liz asked, her saucer-like blue eyes widening.

Mildred reached into her sleeve and withdrew a Kleenex.

"S'like magic, the stuff you keep tucked in there," Liz marveled.

"If you're not back in an hour or two, I'll send Jake to look for you," Mildred promised.

"Oh, I won't be that long," Liz said, missing the irony. Her short legs pumped quickly past Mildred, and she caught up with Jake. Liz's lavender skirt swished when she walked.

Mildred was stupefied. Sam was just barely gone, and already Liz was smiling at Jake. She trilled her fingers in the air like a former cheerleader for the "B" team and told Jake the same thing about going to the little girls' room, where she would powder her nose. Jake stopped and looked back at

Mildred who shrugged. He stood still until Mildred caught up with him.

"Why does she have to tell me that she's going to the bathroom?" Jake asked. "Do I care?"

When Mildred didn't respond, Jake said, "You and I better figure out what to do if we are going to be here all night. I haven't entirely given up hope of getting out of here yet. Sam could get lucky," Jake added, looking around.

But the two of them had seen Sam—had understood that if they were counting on him to round up a rescue party, they were truly hoping for a miracle.

Their prospects were bleak. They looked up. The trek up the embankment was too steep to hike unaided.

"I guess we can sleep in the car if it comes to that," Mildred proposed with resignation. The idea was discouraging. Her body didn't fit the contours of strange environments as it had when her bones were younger. Her bones were different now. Mildred hated to think of how her joints would creak after a night of sleeping cramped in the car.

"You could take the back seat," Jake proposed. "You won't have the steering wheel back there to contend with, and Liz could take the front seat because her legs are so short. The steering wheel won't bother her," he added. "I will sack out in the trunk with the lid open in case you girls need anything."

He looked up at the hillside as if to reconsider whether there was some way they could climb the steep incline. *No. It was too steep—and nothing to hold onto.*

When he turned his attention back to Mildred, he asked, "Did you know anything about the two of them?" And then he let himself sound exasperated. "I mean—really, Budge. Aren't they both too old to be up to these kinds of shenanigans."

Mildred sighed. "I don't understand any of it. I thought Sam had more sense than this," Mildred replied, and she meant what she said. Sam's reaction to Liz did not fit anything that she knew about him. "Belle is a friend of mine," Mildred repeated, and her tone grew mournful. "Sam is, too." She didn't say Liz's name, and Jake didn't ask her why not.

"Liz has got that learned helplessness routine down to a fine art," Jake concluded.

Just as Jake spoke the words, they heard Liz scream. He looked at Mildred and shrugged as if to imply—*see what I mean*?

It was a sharp yelp. Then, Liz yelped again, and suddenly Mildred and Jake heard thrashing. Liz emerged and ran straight toward Jake. Wide eyed and panting, she flung herself against Jake. "There's a man back there!"

As soon as she announced that news, the stranger emerged--a young man in his thirties with longish sandy brown hair and wearing a slap-happy grin. "I have come to seek the lost," he said, good humor in his eyes. "I didn't mean to scare you."

Jake got his bearings first, staring at the young man's face. He had seen his picture on the resumes they had assessed. "You're the boy preacher we were coming to see."

"I am Steev Emory," the younger man acknowledged.

"Tell me you're not here by yourself. Tell me you brought the posse with you," Jake said.

Steev grinned. "No posse," he apologized. "I wasn't sure I needed one. I was following my curiosity more than anything else. When you all didn't show up in church, I got concerned and a little curious. Checked my e-mail right after service to see if Sam had canceled. No message on the answer machine either. You not showing up and no communication didn't strike me as being like the man who has been sending me e-mails every day."

"Only once a day?" Jake asked.

Steev grinned. "Like I said, not hearing from you all didn't fit with what I knew about Sam. I figured something was up. I didn't know what it was. Could have been a flat tire or a radiator. After I spied the break in the guard rail I stopped. I stood up there and looked down and saw that big old car and called out. Nothing. I got worried and started looking for a place to come down. Finally, I tied a rope to my van and rappelled down. What happened to you folks?" Steev asked, looking around.

"We fell off a mountain--that's what happened," Liz said, and she began to whimper. She balled up both hands and pressed them to her cheeks as if to stop the tears from hitting the ground.

"A deer ran in front of us, and Sam swerved to avoid it," Jake explained.

Steev turned toward Mildred. "You must be the famous Mildred Budge."

She gazed intently at him, unaware of how the gaze of her large brown eyes affected others. Children who had cheated on tests immediately confessed when she looked at them that way. Strangers in waiting rooms or lines in stores told her all their troubles. In the grocery store, men holding a shopping list given to them by their wives occasionally held it out to her helplessly when that gaze fell upon them, asking pitifully and hopefully: "Do you know where the pimientos are?"

"I heard about that Missions Conference incident," Steev explained. He took hold of her hand fully, not wagging the ends of her fingertips limply. His hand was strong, the skin rough. "Are you all right? Anything broken?" Steev looked around again. "Where is Sam? Is he all right?" Steev walked over to the car and peered inside.

"He has gone for help," Mildred explained. She looked toward the steep incline Steev had rappelled down. She saw the rope he had used then, partially hidden by vines and kudzu. She looked at him questioningly.

Steev read her mind. "It is not as hard to do as it looks."

"Maybe coming down isn't, but going up will be," Mildred predicted, tilting her head back and covering her eyes with one hand to block the sun while she examined the path of her future. She understood instantly what was in store for them all. Jake, too.

Steev tilted his head in Liz's direction and said, "She will have a harder time than you will."

"How do you know that?" Mildred asked, wishing she could go lie down in the car for a while by herself and not have to talk to anyone. She lived alone, and there were times when she was involved in social activities that she reached a point of social saturation, and her inner-most private self cried: 'Too much talking!' Then, she needed to be alone the way thirsty people crave ice water.

"I hope you don't think I am going to climb up the way you came down, because really, I do not climb," Liz said, overhearing their conversation. "Why didn't you send for a helicopter with one of those hanging baskets?"

Steev ignored the question. "I bet you folks are hungry," he said, still looking around.

It wasn't a pretty place. The ravine was sandy bare in some places and overgrown with kudzu and what could be poison oak in others.

Then, Steev looked over at Liz and said, "You all should be in worse shape than you are. Other than her two black eyes," Steev said, jabbing one thumb in Liz's direction, "you all look fine. Are you really all right?"

Steev asked, looking to Mildred for an answer.

"Are my eyes black?" Liz asked, pressing her fingertips to both eyes.

Everyone nodded.

"Rocky Raccoon," Jake said.

"I tried to clean off the mascara, but it's hard with just an ice cube," Liz explained with a whimper.

Jake and Steev laughed.

"I don't like to be teased," Liz complained irritably, rubbing at her eyes. Her lavender skirt was also hitched up in the back from where she had gotten it caught in the waistband of her underwear after a mad exit from the powder room.

Mildred was just trying to figure out how to sneak up behind Liz and pull it out when Steev said very simply, "Your skirt is hiked up in the back. You might want to fix that. There are mosquitoes out here."

Liz yelped again and began to pull frantically at the back of her fulsome skirt. The sound of surprise or fear was quickly becoming her signature yelp. Mildred had heard it when they went over the embankment, when the rock she had thrown had hit Liz in the back, and now with her underwear on display. One type of yelp seemed to fit all kinds of occasions.

Mildred wondered what it would feel like to give voice to every upset in your life. To yelp and yelp and yelp again. Maybe she should practice doing it. Liz relied upon it heavily to communicate all kinds of information, the way babies cry for any of the reasons that require others' attention.

"Have you got a plan?" Jake asked, while Liz began to fidget with the rest of her clothing.

'She was like a cat that keeps grooming herself,' Mildred thought.

"Nope—don't have a plan to speak of," Steev admitted easily. "But I did bring that rope, and it is tied to my van so it will hold us one at a time. I have a cell phone, but it didn't work out here."

Steev smiled at Liz. "I don't know how to call for a helicopter, but I would have called the police after spotting the car if I had been able. It seemed a better idea to jump down here and see if anyone needed any immediate help." He scanned their faces again to confirm that all were fine.

Beads of sweat had caused his skin to glisten, and Mildred marveled that he could be smiling so broadly when he was so hot. Her own clothes were sticking to her uncomfortably. When the prospect of being able to get home took firmer hold with her, Mildred began to catalogue physical discomforts that she had paid little attention to until then.

"Thank you," Liz said in a small voice. She was disappointed about the helicopter.

Steev pointed over his shoulder to a heavy knotted rope hanging from above the embankment, which he had used to come down. "I can and will go back up there and drive until I can pick up a satellite signal and call for help if that's what you would rather I do.

"However, the day is getting away from us and by the time any real help gets here, it will be dark and a good deal harder to negotiate the terrain. If no helicopter is immediately available, I imagine that they will simply send a fireman down here with a rope and try to bring you up individually that way. Or, we could try to help ourselves. If we don't do something, we will end up spending part of the night out here and..."

Steev surveyed the incline. "It would be hard for anyone to come down here and help us in the dark no matter how many floodlights you turned on."

Jake said the words first. "We could try to climb back up. It isn't a mountain, Elizabeth. It is only a hill. People climb hills all the time. It is a matter of putting one foot in front of the other while holding onto that rope. We could all try."

"I have very short legs," Liz argued. "Besides, I am wearing a skirt." She patted the fabric again.

It did not wrinkle, Mildred saw. How did Liz have a skirt that looked as if it were made of cotton and didn't wrinkle? There was even a satin sheen to it. Mildred eyed the skirt with heightened curiosity. It was an old-fashioned skirt, but it didn't look old or well worn. *Where did one find a skirt like that nowadays?*

"We've already seen your underwear, Rocky" Jake said, cutting off her excuses. "No biggie. We are not going to let the indignity of a strenuous climb keep us down here all night."

Liz did not like the nickname. The appellation attacked her femininity at a core level that made her uncomfortable. Liz looked around for a protector and remembered that Sam had left her. Her lower lip trembled. Her mauve lipstick had been chewed off. Tears came into her bright blue eyes. "Don't call me Rocky," she said.

Steev's gaze swept the Old Girl. It was mangled on the front end but otherwise looked unscathed. "It may not be a total loss. However, an impact like that most likely shook some of its innards loose. If she would crank, we could back her up and try climbing up on to the trunk, but I don't see that saving us many steps."

"I think Sam took the car keys with him," Jake said. He cast an appraising look at the sky; and in the distance, they heard a faint rumbling.   Almost immediately the sun disappeared behind a cloud.

Steev craned his head back and covered his eyes. "Rain is coming, too. Look at those clouds over there."

Liz peered intently in the direction of his gaze. Another tear fell.   A shiver went through her body.   "We need to get out of here," she said with conviction.   "Before those clouds reach us."

Jake assessed quietly, "A fast heavy rain could wash down that hillside."

Neither man said anything more as Liz went to the Igloo, opened a bottle of valuable water, poured some into her open palm, and began to try and cleanse the mascara more thoroughly from her eyes.

Mildred wondered what it would be like to battle a flash flood; and if they had to, would they climb back in the car—or try to swim? She looked about for a tree she might climb and hold onto, but there wasn't one with enough sturdy branches that looked like it could hold all of them. Liz poured some more precious drinking water into her hands and patted her face.

Mildred reached the same conclusion the men did. "I don't think staying here is a viable option. Let's go home," she said.

"We're spending precious daylight. Let's not waste it here talking," Steev agreed. "We can do that while I'm driving you folks home."

Jake agreed. "Lead on."

Liz fell into step beside the preacher when he spoke with authority. "I have very short legs," she reminded him.

Mildred came up beside her. "If I can do it, Liz, you can do it."

"You don't know if you can do it yet," Liz replied tartly as they grouped around the end of the hanging rope that Steev had used to come down the embankment.

"I can do anything I need to do," Mildred said with resolve. She had never felt more tired in her life.

"That's right," Steev agreed, and he flashed her an approving grin.

Mildred was about to allow herself to feel just a bit superior to Liz, but that flicker of rivalry and ego was stamped out very quickly by the young preacher's next two remarks: "Miss Budge, you are a trooper. My mother is, too."

11

UPHILL

Jake stood beside Mildred while she gathered her nerve and her thoughts. When confronted with the hill to climb, she doubted very seriously her ability to best gravity by hoisting herself to the top.

Jake scanned the area that Steev had rappelled down. "If I went first, I could pull from up there. I don't want to leave you, Budge, but I think I need to be up there first. If I were up there pulling on the rope from the top, all you would have to do is hold onto the rope and get your feet to help you," Jake said. He squinted up at the sky and at the unforgiving slant of the hillside. "You could do it, Budge, and if you do it, Rocky will have to do it, too," Jake said; and when his eyes met hers, Mildred believed him. "Let's go home, Budge," he said.

Mildred met his gaze solidly. There was no telling how tired he was. Jake had been carrying the load for everyone and was keeping the cost of it to himself.

Mildred understood that she would have to try, and that she would have to try in faith that she could climb up that embankment holding onto that rope. 'I am going to have to believe I can do it, or I won't do it,' she told herself. But she said something different to Jake Diamond.

"Yes. Failure is not an option," she agreed.

Jake fastened the looped rope about himself and tried a couple of practice tugs to gauge the tension.

"She'll hold," Steev promised. "I tied it to the van's hitch."

"I don't think I can pull a van down on top of me," Jake said, backing up. Using his hands, Jake levered himself up as far as he could until his feet began to dangle, but not for long.

Mildred watched carefully, taking note of Jake's every move. She had seen this sort of thing on TV but not in real life. She watched, trying to memorize the steps she needed to take in order to succeed. Inside, that interior voice that maintained unceasing prayer began to whisper, *Help him, Jesus. Help me. Help Sam wherever he is.*

As soon as Jake's feet were airborne, he used one to kick himself back and then planted his feet against the side of the hill— against vines and dirt and rock and sand-- and began to take small steps, at first sideways until he found his footing, and then he began to go up the hill using the same motions with his hands that Mildred had used long ago to pull taffy, one hand after another. Taffy pulling was harder than most people knew. Climbing the embankment would be harder than pulling taffy.

There were a couple of occasions when Jake's feet lost traction, but he recovered quickly. He caught hold again and began the climb, his hands working in concert with his feet.

Mildred paid close attention to Jake's feet, tracked the placement of them, and prayed for every foothold. When Jake reached the top, she grinned and called out, "Well done, sir!" And then she wished she wouldn't say things like that. No one said, well done, sir!

Once Jake was securely

on top, he looked down at her and connected with her eyes. He held her gaze, and his eyes blazed with truth. "I was wrong, Budge. It's harder than it looks, but I still think you can do it.

"Your hands will burn. The rope cuts into your skin. Don't focus on the pain. Keep your eyes on me. I will help you, Budge. Just keep coming, and don't look down."

Jake released the heavy rope, and Mildred tried to catch it, which was a mistake. The thick hairy rope slapped her hard in the face and brought stinging tears to her brown eyes. She was ready to quit in that instant, wanted to go find Sam and sit down with him in the dirt and wait for Jesus to send Liz's helicopter.

Jake saw what happened and winced. Mildred saw him shaking his head in an apology. She ducked her head so that he couldn't see that she felt like crying, and she hadn't even started the climb yet.

Steev came alongside Mildred and whispered conspiratorially the way Mildred had seen Little League coaches encourage baseball players who were about to go out on the field. "I don't want you falling down the hill and breaking your neck. I will be right under you to catch you, and I will catch you. I will not fail you, Miss Budge."

"I don't want to break my neck either," Mildred said, denying the pain of the rope burn on her face and the itch of the first burnings of the hemp in the palms of her hands. Growing older taught you how to put pain in its place. Mildred tossed the rope back and forth between her palms-- searching for the feeling that Jake had found before he climbed.

"Let me try," she said, despite her misgivings, "before we give up."

Steev waited beside her, letting her think and feel and assess the climb ahead of her. When Liz started to say something, Steev held up one hand, and the other woman shushed.

Mildred took hold of the rope, whispered her "Help me, Jesus" prayer again, and did not look to see if Steev heard her. Instead, she looked up at the embankment and said,

"I am going to do this because we need to go home."

"You just go right ahead," Steev encouraged. And when she stole a quick glance at him, the young man's eyes beamed with confidence and a kind of irrepressible belief that she would do what she said. Her eyes lingered inside his gaze, and the smile he wore invaded her, enlivened her, and as she had thought earlier about Jake's hands being a kind of prayer, she thought: *The boy preacher prays with his smile and his eyes the way Jake prays with his hands.*

It was an incongruous moment of encouragement.

Then, Mildred tuned out the presence of the young preacher, forgot about Liz's reluctance to follow her, and began to concentrate on the job at hand.

She would have to hold tight to the rope.

She would have to manage a different way of walking—a different balance.

She would have to remember step by step that she believed she could do it.

That was key.

Church ladies had understood faith like that long before it became a popular expression of athletic coaches mentoring athletes to victory through visual imaging.

"I step back like this and lace my hands like this," she said, imitating Jake's approach. "And then when my feet are loose." Almost immediately her feet were suspended, and she flailed for a split second before instinctively bringing her knees up toward her chest. With the same ease that Steev had told Liz her underwear was showing, the strong young man now stepped forward, crouched, and put his right shoulder under Mildred's hips and hoisted her up while she put her feet out to find traction on the hillside.

"I do beg your pardon, Miss Budge," Steev muttered, balancing her indelicately on his shoulder. Then, reaching behind his head, Steev placed both hands on her bottom and pushed her higher by three more feet.

The rope tightened in her hands. Mildred ignored the ungainliness of the position she was in, closed her eyes against the sharp intake and hiss of air that was one more yelp from Liz, and held tightly onto the rope, willing her hands to make the next move.

Determined, Mildred felt the rope bite into the flesh of her wrists, knew they would be bleeding soon, dismissed bleeding as insignificant, and concentrated on taking the first step up and then the next in order to stand the way Jake had—perpendicular with the hillside.

"Miss Mildred. Maybe we are wrong to expect this of you," Steev gasped. He stepped back to lower Mildred to the ground, but her grasp of the rope was secure, and Jake, sensing the tightening and the timing as he watched from above, gripped from his end and hoisted mightily. Mildred moved rapidly up three feet out of Steev's reach with her feet planted as Jake's had been against the side of the incline.

Steev stayed put, ready to catch Mildred should she lose her hold, but it became obvious that Mildred was determined and that Jake was strong enough to act as a human pulley.

"You with me, Budge?" Jake called down.

She couldn't answer. She could only concentrate on the rope and will her feet to move. Every bit of her breath was reserved for the work of climbing and helping the others by making it to the top.

Jake called again. "Budge?"

Her eyes connected with Jake's, and she nodded wordlessly. Jake pulled again, lifting her forcefully while she used her hands and feet to keep traction with the hillside. They found a rhythm then, and determined, each sensing the other's timing and respectful of the other's will, worked in partnership.

For the third time that day Mildred Budge felt herself take flight, her legs moving faster than she had imagined possible. It felt at once alarming—and then liberating. She told herself to breathe and to trust the hands that were helping her.

Jake grabbed her forearms as soon as he could reach her and lifted her the rest of the way. Slamming into the dirt as she ascended, Mildred ignored the grit and her pain as she clambered up over the edge of the embankment, slicing a gash in the calf of her left leg on the broken metal guard. Her brown pants legs crawled up her calves as she scrambled over the top, revealing the pitiful knee-highs around her ankles and the faint trickle of blood coming from the wound caused by the broken shard on the metal guard. Jake saw only the stockings and grinned.

"You've got to stop shopping at the Dollar Store," Jake advised.

Budge nodded tersely, breathlessly, in response, brushing off her aqua top and the front of her dirty brown slacks. Back on her feet, she looked around. They were closer to the highway than she had remembered. There was no traffic, only an old blue Chevrolet van with a bumper sticker that read "Honk If You Love Jesus!" and a magnetic white sign stuck on the side of the van's body that identified itself plainly as "Church Van."

No denomination.

No name of a preacher.

No listed hours of service.

Jake tossed the rope back down to Steev, who was now encouraging Liz about her climb up.

Mildred could hear Liz laughing in a high-pitched voice because she was close to hysteria. Even from where she was standing,

Mildred could hear Liz saying over and over, "But you don't understand. I am not like her. I have on this skirt. My legs are too short."

Suddenly, Mildred Budge wanted to be home more than anything else. She was thirsty. And there was nothing to drink. There wouldn't be anything in the van to drink, because men didn't think about bringing refreshments.

"Budge, go sit in the van. I will handle that one," Jake urged, while he turned his attention to raising Liz the same way he had brought Mildred up.

The rush of pleasure caused by her moment of triumph faded quickly. Her leg hurt, and she could feel warmth oozing there. Her hands were skinned. Her wrists were scored by the rope and gravel. Little dots of blood were rising to the surface. She needed a Kleenex, but had forgotten her purse, she realized with a start. *How had she forgotten her purse*? And she couldn't go back down for it.

And just that quickly Mildred Budge, who had been focused and determined seconds ago, was now just as suddenly disoriented. She would have to ask the police to get her purse. And then she would have to wait for someone to bring it to her. And her wallet was down there—and her checkbook and her house keys. She felt her eyes water. And all the Kleenex she had left. She blotted her moist eyes on the sleeve of her shirt.

She saw no reason to witness Liz's coming up the hill because Liz would come up the hill no matter her protestations. There was one sure thing to say about a widow of four dead husbands: Liz Luckie was a survivor.

Smiling wanly out of habit alone, Mildred left Jake to wrestle with Liz and walked over to the church van and eased into the back seat where it was dark and she could be alone with her thoughts.

She was safe, at last, and now rescued, instantly ready to be back in the quiet of her house. Alone. Her feet hurt. Her wavy brown hair was messy and itchy from sweat and outdoor grit. As she sat there cataloguing her range of discomforts, she stopped suddenly. That interior voice that sometimes narrated her life also chastened her: 'Don't grumble. You've had an adventure in the midst of routine. All the wounds you know about will be healed—and some you don't understand. Be grateful.'

Gratitude was often, initially, an act of will. A discipline. A conscious choice that was a response to Scripture that urged you to be grateful in all circumstances. It took a long time to learn the power of gratitude. Mildred knew that expressing gratitude to God had a mysterious power to reestablish a balance that she needed. Praise or expressed gratitude would not stop wrists or legs from bleeding or erase a well-earned fatigue, but

the truthful expression of gratitude to God
for his providential care would put her soul
back in a place where she needed to be in
order to live. Gratitude was the pilgrim's
position of recognizing the Sovereign will of
God that allowed for His own to sail off an
embankment while they were doing a job for
him and then to provide the means to climb
back up. Or not. Any kind of ending was
possible with God, and Mildred had learned
that it was wise to be thankful for anything
that happened.

"Thank you, Jesus, for saving me. Us," she
whispered into the shadows. There was real
power in real gratitude as there was real
health in praising the Lord, which was why
she liked to weave singing songs of praise
throughout her day; and because she was,
when she stopped to think about it, truly
grateful and disciplined in expressing it, she
continued telling the One who had come to

fix what Adam broke that she recognized his hand in the day.

Mildred stopped in her prayer of gratitude to consider the implications of someone with leadership abilities like Steev's, and then the retired fifth-grade schoolteacher mused softly: "He spells his name with two e's in the middle, Lord. I don't see how we could ever add his name to the church sign on the front lawn of our church, or post it with that spelling on the website, or print it week after week in the church bulletin. Because Jesus, You and I know that is not how you spell the name Steve." Mildred sighed then.

She had expressed her gratitude, and having finished the good work of recognizing the Sovereignty of God in all things, she gave herself permission to be truthful about her physical condition. She was tired. Deeply tired. Tired in ways she had not named before.

Tired of being under Sam's leadership, which surprised her because she had submitted to his leadership for years without complaining. She had a complaint now.

She was tired of the limp stockings rolled around her ankles.

Tired of the dirty clothes she was wearing. She coughed.

Tired of being thirsty and hungry, too.

She could feel the trickle of warm blood on her leg, and because she had no other choice, she reached down and pressed the fabric of her pants against the wound and held it, applying direct pressure. That was all she could do.

Pressing her hand against her leg, she leaned her head back against the seat, felt grit falling from her hair and down the neck of her top, and some onto the seat, and closed her eyes. When she did, the sounds of Liz's climb up became easier to hear. Gone was Jake's earlier disdain and distrust of the

Black Widow. Now, Jake was speaking soft and low to Liz as the other woman climbed with her short legs, and Mildred knew without even thinking hard about it, that it was easier to lift Liz to the top than it had been to help her.

Liz was a petite size eight, and Mildred was a sturdy women's size fourteen. She had stopped regretting her size years ago, when she realized that there were advantages to being strong and having two good feet planted on two strong legs to carry you around.

Still, she remembered what it was like to feel girlish and lighter. The one thing she missed most were skirts that swished—even good dark-colored slacks, as practical as they were, did not compensate for a swishing skirt.

As she sat up again when it was clear that Liz was almost at the crest of the embankment, Mildred couldn't help but peer out through the open doorway of the van and watch as Jake easily helped Liz to her feet, and without thinking brushed off her skirt, which had become twisted. And just as he did, Mildred saw something dive-bomb the other woman's head, circle, swirl, and Liz beat about her head as if shooing a monster horse fly away.

Jake pointed to the van, but Liz didn't move. Instead, she maintained her position to watch for Steev.

The rope was situated again, and Liz stepped back to watch as Steev made his ascent. Mildred leaned back again and closed her eyes and listened to the sounds of Steev coming up the hill. Sometime in the midst of listening, her mind wandered, and so she was surprised out of her reverie to hear Steev say suddenly, "Miss Mildred, are you okay in here?"

She opened her eyes and saw the young man mopping the perspiration from his forehead. Mildred felt him let go of some urgency that he had been carrying with him, and she realized then that attending to all of them must have felt like a big responsibility. And they weren't home safe yet. But they were much closer to it than they had been in the ravine.

And then the dear boy—genius young man with the slap-happy smile-- handed Mildred her purse with all the life-saving essentials that she took with her everywhere. She looked past him. He had brought Liz her purse, too. And then, Miss Budge budged. She thought, 'Maybe he could be one of us— no matter how he spells his name.'

In the distance, the thunder sounded again, and Liz turned toward it, and then looked back at Jake, her face swapping the expression of relief for one of a fresh anxiety. She was a fretful woman.

"Thank you, yes," Miss Budge said, though her mouth was dry, and she relaxed back into the shadows of the van, wondering where Sam was. She reached into her purse for a Honee that had a little drop of moisture in it. She popped a piece of the hard candy in her mouth, counting how many pieces she had left—enough to share.

They would be home before it was very dark. She would soon be in her own house and have some quiet time alone before she talked with Fran.

When she did talk to Fran, Mildred would tell her best friend about flying over the embankment and how it had felt to be weightless, and then, holding the vine and swinging like that, and how she had climbed that hill and felt her legs hold her up.

She would try to remember that feeling for a long time because when you grew older you doubted that your body would do what you wanted and needed for it to do. And it felt important to remember that sometimes you could do more than you believed possible.

But she wouldn't tell Fran about Liz and Sam because maybe that would blow over before it got any worse. One or both of them could come to their senses.

"You came up that hill like a champ," Steev said approvingly. He smiled at her. The smile began first in his eyes, and like a fire that catches hold of whatever it touches, it arced through space and electrified her with warmth and a welcome.

A part of her that had been braced and ready for trouble since the car had taken flight relaxed then. That part of her that was always braced and ready for trouble and prepared to meet it head on, and then bear up under the consequences, eased.

Inside the boy preacher's smile, Mildred Budge felt inexplicably safe—and welcome.

This young man would deliver her to her house safely, and she wouldn't have to do a thing to help. She eyed him with fresh curiosity. "How did you know to come to the highway and not the interstate to find us?"

"God didn't tell me," Steev assured her, leaning on the van.

She stopped herself from asking if God ever spoke directly to him, but asked instead, "So Sam told you our route?"

Steev grinned and nodded. "Not exactly. But he does have the kind of mind you can read if you pay attention," Steev answered mysteriously, looking back toward Liz and Jake, who was gathering the rope.

And then Steev turned suddenly and broke the rule of decorum by making a personal statement about her to her, "You don't have that kind of mind. I can't tell what you're thinking at all."

"Oh, I am just an ordinary church lady," Mildred replied politely.

Steev laughed out loud then. "Ma'am, I have known women like you all my life, and nothing about any of you is ordinary."

He was about to say more when a patrol car suddenly swerved over on the side of the road and parked with a screech in the gravel next to them.

The policeman emerged from his cruiser, leaving the blue light flashing as he looked around, trying to deduce what had happened and called out, "What's going on here?"

Liz twinkled at him briefly, and then suddenly, it was as if someone had pulled the plug on her. She slumped, and the hysteria she had been fighting finally arrived. She began to sob from exhaustion and nerves and because her legs were so short and the men had seen her underwear.

Just as he had after the crash, Jake put an arm around Liz and steered her over to the van and into the back seat next to Mildred, who automatically checked her sleeve for a tissue, but they had all been dispensed. Her hand moved inside her purse, where the small packet of back-up tissues was stored. She handed the packet of Kleenex to Liz.

"You always have everything you need," Liz said.

But her comment didn't feel like a compliment.

"I can't help thinking about what might happen and trying to prepare for it," Mildred explained unnecessarily.

"I stopped trying to do that years ago," Liz replied honestly, as the crying began to ease. Her shoulders shook. "Nerves," she explained. "Sometimes, I just have to let myself cry. Later tonight, I may let myself have a whole nervous breakdown." Her voice dropped. "And a big glass of wine."

"I've never had a nervous breakdown in my whole life," Mildred stated.

"You've missed out. It can be very cleansing for a girl's system."

"When I feel like I need a cleansing, I get out my can of Comet cleanser and scrub the bathrooms."

"I am not built for housework," Liz replied, as the policeman conferred with Jake and Steev. Then, he spoke seriously into his car radio.

"They're probably calling in about the car," Liz explained to herself.

"They are reporting that Sam is missing, and I guess he is missing," Mildred said.

"Bad luck," Liz said. "That's what I have. If I didn't have bad luck, I wouldn't have any luck at all. And when people are with me, they have bad luck, too."

"Any preacher worth his salt will quote some theology about the sovereignty of God to you if you use that expression about bad luck around him."

"Bad luck?" Liz asked. "A lot of people have bad luck. Christians, too. Look at me."

"Are you referring to your loss of four husbands?" Mildred asked pointedly.

"What else could I be referring to?" Liz sniffed. "If being widowed four times isn't bad luck, I don't know what is." At that moment, a small white cloud puffed on the horizon, and Liz thought: *Good, they're going to bed for the night.* And suddenly she wanted to be home and go to bed, too, but not alone. Getting into bed at night by herself was the worst part of her day. The second hardest part was waking up the next morning, still alone, and remembering that the bad luck called her life was not a bad dream after all.

Jake went around the van and slipped in on Mildred's other side.

"Budge, I will sit back here with you." He didn't wait for her to agree. Just sat down and shoved with his body until Mildred moved over. He offered her a conspiratorial grin, and Liz shot Mildred a curious glance.

Men didn't pay attention to plain women like Mildred Budge when Liz Luckie was around.

"Let's hit the road, folks," Steev said. He waved his thanks to the two men in the cruiser. "The police are going to look for Sam, and I am taking you folks home."

Just as Steev said the words, an old man, drooping from age and the heat, appeared on foot coming from the other direction. Mildred didn't recognize Sam at first. He looked so beaten down and small. The determined spring in his step was gone, and something else was, too. He didn't know that anyone was watching him, and his gait was different; his posture, defeated. He was trudging, putting one foot in front of the other. His shoulders rose and fell with breathing that looked like it was a hard job for him to do.

Liz waved excitedly with both hands, then got out of the van and hurried toward Sam.

Steev followed her, but Jake and Mildred stayed where they were.

Sam stopped to speak to the patrolman. Pulled out his wallet. Showed him his driver's license. Nodded *yes* a couple of times and then handed over his car keys. Sam's hands trembled slightly when he gave them over, and Mildred sighed deeply inside herself. Belle would grieve at first that Sam's giving up the car keys had finally happened, and then she would be relieved.

The officer shook Sam's hand and said something that made Sam stand up straighter. Sam looked past the policeman toward the coming storm and nodded in agreement with something else the policeman said, and then finally turned toward the van and the occupants who were waiting for him.

The way Sam walked changed as he came toward them. His military bearing returned, the one where he expected people to salute him. There was no band playing in the background, however. There was just Sam's sense of who he should be in front of other people that caused this extra effort in him. He waved, and Mildred raised a hand automatically, but her old friend—Belle's husband-- couldn't see her.

Because it was the only place left, Sam climbed in the front seat beside Steev. Staring straight ahead, he said without enthusiasm, "Well, we're all alive. Praise the Lord."

"We're all alive," Liz repeated, and there was wonder in her voice.

Jake sat behind the driver's seat. Mildred was stuck in the middle. Liz was seated directly behind Sam.

"Anybody need to phone anyone?" Steev asked, clicking on his phone. "No signal yet. But we'll keep an eye on it. When it's alive, you folks can call anybody you like. I have got lots of roll-over minutes." Steev steered gingerly out onto the road, and the police cruiser fell in behind, temporarily. When he did, the policeman read the bumper sticker and gave two short blasts on his horn.

Steev blasted his horn back and grinned broadly. "He knows Jesus."

Then taking a quick assessment of Sam and with a curious appraisal in his rearview mirror of the other members of the pulpit committee, Steev asked, still smiling, but his eyes were watchful, searching for the truth, "How about you folks? Do you all know Jesus?"

12

CHEATIN' HEART

Mildred should have slept well, but she didn't. She swung her legs over the bed and tested the floor to see if the hardwood floor was still solid. It held her; and at a quarter to five in the morning, she made herself get out of the bed, padded barefoot to the kitchen and started the coffee.

Then she went to her living room where she twirled the clear prismatic bar cautiously opening her blinds in case someone was outside staring back in at her. That had happened one time, and the shock of facing someone on her front lawn peering into her house had changed the way Mildred Budge opened her blinds each morning.

Her peeping Tom was a strange man from down the street who had been standing in front of her window and pantomiming some ritual of his. Fran had theorized that it was some kind of mating dance. But Belle Deerborn had explained, *"No. It is Tai-chi. He drifts around the neighborhood looking for some kind of vibe and when he finds it, he goes through his exercise routine. But I don't know what vibe he felt that caused him to choose your house, Mildred."*

Mildred didn't care what vibe had brought the man to her house. It felt strange to have some man acting like a mime between her house and the Garvin house that was now, sadly, empty. Front blinds open, Mildred was relieved that the strange man was not present and performing any kind of ritual or dance. There was only the vacant house across the street and its kind of plaintive moan that no one else seemed to hear, but Mildred heard it. Her father, who had also been able to hear those kinds of empty house sounds, had explained to her a long time ago: "*When one house remains vacant too long in a neighborhood, the other houses are affected. Property values go down. An empty house often attracts intruders. Intruders survey an empty house and become aware of who the neighbors are. They start casing the joints.*"

Mildred still agreed with what her father had told her. No, it would be so much better for the house to sell or rent. People needed to live there. The once bright yellow 'For Sale' sign was growing less distinct, showing signs of aging fast in the weather. It was depressing. Empty houses always were. "Lord, will you kindly send someone to buy that house?" Mildred prayed automatically, and then she prayed for the family that had left in the dark of night. She had befriended them.

A young boy she had helped learn to read had lived there with his parents. But the family of organic cereal makers had disappeared recently, moving out as quickly as they had arrived, with no word of explanation, no forwarding address, and owing three months' rent. Their organic cereal business had not been as successful as they had liked to pretend.

The coffeepot gurgled loudly in the kitchen, signaling that there was enough brew in the pot to pour some into the stoneware cup Mildred had been using for as long as she could remember because it kept coffee hot but didn't burn her hands.

She poured out the first welcome steaming cup and placed the carafe back in to finish the cycle. She carried her coffee back to the living room, where her Bible lay open on the sofa. She was up to the famous thirteenth chapter of First Corinthians in her morning quiet time. Old Thirteen painted broad parameters for what love should be, but it didn't answer the question of what one was to do if the expression of love was not a part of one's daily life.

Do you get married a fifth time after burying four husbands?

Cheat on your wife of forty-three years?

Mildred read the chapter, asked God to let it take root in good soil, took a sip of coffee as if she were indeed watering freshly planted seeds, and then asked God to help Sam and Liz and Jake and Belle, and then the other names came.

Ruth and her wounded face because her brother had died.

And Dottie who had come back from brain surgery with her head shaved. There was something besides the hairstyle that was different about Dottie. It was in her eyes that seemed colorless now—translucent with eternity and distance and new knowledge. It wasn't that expression of stored pain, like Ruth was wearing; it was that 'I live somewhere else now, and I am going through the motions of living here' expression. Dottie made small talk that didn't sound like small talk. There was a farewell inside all of Dottie's small talk and a kind of forgiveness of everyone around her.

`What is she forgiving us all for?' Mildred wondered, as she cast her eyes upon Old Thirteen again: "Though I speak with the tongues of men and of angels but have not love I am as clanging brass or sounding cymbals." The words roamed inside of Mildred Budge, touching places, lighting up darkness, calling forth memories that became a confession, repentance, and inexplicably--hope. "What is love?" she asked God again, for you could spend your whole life trying to solve that mystery, and she had asked the question many times before. So much of what people ostensibly did out of love for others was driven by personal ambition. It was rare to see a true act of love for love's sake. "Help me to love," she prayed. "And to see the ways that I don't love."

Prayer inside Scripture reading had become part of Mildred's daily habit, for she had accepted that the impressions that came to mind and the questions that bubbled up during prayer time were meaningful. There were various expressions in the Bible that would validate the meditation as God's Spirit searching her spirit or even that provocative idea espoused by Paul that there were gifts of discernment.

Mildred didn't need to attach Bible verses to the moments of her meditation to approve of her time spent in abiding with God in the morning, of being in the vine. She had reached that place of rest years ago and come to increasing intimacy as God happened to her over and over again. In answer to Steev's question, "Do you know Jesus?" she could unhesitatingly reply, yes. Knowing Jesus was unlike other types of relationships. You learned the features of living inside Jesus Saves over time, acquiring a language and a context for being able to say 'yes' to his unceasing call to live in love and the light that did not fit the language and contexts for other relationships, which were not as authentic, meaningful, or loving as the one with Jesus.

The relationship one had with Jesus was so different, so personal, that to hear it validated by the honking of a car horn seemed absurd and also loudly true. A sharp blast on a horn was, in its way, very appealing and uncharacteristic of a well-behaved church lady schooled in discretion and silences.

Mildred moved her Bible to the side and left it open. She would start there again tomorrow—or sooner. Sometimes Mildred finished her day with the same Scripture, but because, like so many women her age who had trouble sleeping, Mildred found that the Bible was so riveting it did not lead her to sleep but rather to a kind of riotous excitement at night. Mildred resisted reading the Bible too close to bedtime. She wondered if a young preacher who spelled his name with two e's in the middle could understand that.

That concept was something a young preacher most likely wouldn't understand yet. He was keen on checking people for their salvation, but did he know that God saved you from yourself and then began to redeem the days with an intimacy so exquisite that there was no single word that could explain the phenomenon? Prayer released the reality of it into the stream of daily life and created Eden. *Yes, Eden,* Mildred Budge concluded once more that she now lived in Eden with Jesus although her address was in Cloverdale, the garden district of Montgomery, Alabama.

A forceful knock on Mildred's kitchen door stopped her meditation, which had become an energized rumination—a kind of rhythmic mental waltz that would create a bridge from prayer to her daily chores.

Clutching her snapped yellow robe, Mildred went to the door and asked brusquely, "Who in the world is it?"

"Who do you think it is?" Sam asked, matching her brusque tone.

They weren't angry with one another; it was simply a tone of voice that old friends used when they didn't have the energy to sound more cordial.

"It shouldn't be anybody knocking on my door this early in the morning," Mildred replied, twisting open the lock. "And it especially shouldn't be you. Why aren't you still in bed? I am surprised that Belle let you out of the house."

Sam pushed past Mildred as if he had a standing invitation. He did, but he didn't usually exercise that privilege so early in the morning.

Closing the door, Mildred thought about getting testy herself—then remembered the expression in Dottie's eyes, and the word 'love' pulsed inside of her. Sam's friend realized anew that they could spend their whole lives forgiving one another their trespasses. She decided not to be upset but to listen to what Sam had come over too early on a Monday morning in such a hurry to say. He must have come to apologize. After his quiet time when he must have thought about his wrongdoings, Sam had surely come to his senses and was up early and in her house to apologize to Mildred for the several ways he had trespassed against her the day before.

Mildred thought an extended apology from Sam was both unnecessary and very important. As far as she was concerned, he was already forgiven, but Sam needed to say the words, because people needed the discipline of humility to keep them well balanced. She stifled a yawn and a sigh and motioned toward the coffeepot. "There's coffee. You know where the cups are."

Sam turned toward Mildred as if she hadn't spoken. His eyes burned with a mission, and she wanted to pat him on the head and say, "Go back to bed. All is forgiven. It was an accident. And you were rude about my Igloo, but I don't care. Didn't then. Don't now."

But before she could make an apology easier for Sam, he declared, his eyes blazing, "You hit Liz with a rock."

Mildred brown eyes widened. That had happened a long time ago. Way back when she was someone else. Was it only yesterday? She had confessed that sin—had been forgiven. Had she done that? Repented? She had meant to. Had she told God she was sorry? The act of throwing the stone resurfaced, and Mildred relived it. Yes, she had picked up the palm-sized rock, held the weight of it, felt the warmth of the rock, was planning on taking the rock home as a treasure—wished she had it after all even though it had become in a moment of something beyond words, a murder weapon--now that she thought about it-- and she had thrown it at the woman who was hurting Sam and Belle.

"And don't deny what happened because I saw you. I didn't know exactly what I was seeing, and it took me a while to remember it. But I saw your arm move, and I heard Liz holler, and she says there is a big bruise in the middle of her back. She told me on the telephone when I called to set up our next pulpit committee meeting, which is tomorrow night. I wanted to go ahead and get things wrapped up tonight, but Liz says no one feels like meeting tonight. She is considerate of others that way." Sam stopped speaking, but his feet began to move, and he reminded Mildred of a fighter who has just entered the boxing ring and was dancing back and forth on his feet, waiting for his opponent to show up. He needed a fight. And a shave. His beard was gray. A hard stubble.

"You threw a rock at that poor girl—and she a recent widow. How could you do that, Mildred Budge? I don't know what's wrong with you women."

Mildred felt herself grow smaller as she stared at her old friend, who was wearing a grayish-white T-shirt that had been washed too many times and was thin enough to have long ago been relegated to the rag basket. Sam was so used to it that he couldn't see that for himself. Neither could Belle.

Mildred suspected that the grey stretch pants Sam was wearing were his pajamas. They were a pair of those exercise britches that Fran had forbidden every member of the Berean Sunday school class to ever wear. *No woman should ever get caught dead in a pair of pants that does that to her belvedere.* They weren't doing much for Sam either.

"It isn't even eight o'clock in the morning yet," Mildred replied weakly.

"You women at the church are mean to Liz Luckie. She can feel it. I see it. A lot of the men do. It is like you are all a bunch of high school girls jealous of the prom queen or something. Just because the girl is pretty and can dress good because of the money she's inherited...."

"From her four husbands, and she is hardly a girl...." Mildred injected. She led the way back to the living room where her cup was.

Sam followed her. "I thought you were better than that, Budge." Sam was mimicking Jake's nickname. It didn't sound right when Sam used it. If he used her last name like that one more time, Mildred would tell him to stop.

"Better than what?" Mildred asked, sitting down beside her open Bible. The words about love were still there, but they were distant now and hard to read. Her eyes grazed over them, and she could barely remember what she had been thinking—praying—receiving, asking God to plant deep, deep inside of her and water so that love would grow.

"You stoned her," Sam said, and just that quick Sam ran out of steam and sat down. "She is one of us," Sam reminded her. "It doesn't matter that you women don't like her. Liz Luckie is one of us. We are not all feet or hands. Liz has a different role to play in the church body, and you women want her to be just like you all. She's not like you women."

"A foot or a hand?" Mildred asked. "Is that what we are?" Mildred reached absentmindedly for her pink stoneware coffee cup. She watched her hand, saw her mother's likeness in it, felt glad and sad in the same instant, and then picked up the cup. There wasn't much coffee left, and what remained was cold.

Seeing her holding the cup, Sam decided he wanted some coffee after all. He stood up, and Mildred saw that he was sockless, too. The grey pants with elastic where a cuff would have been rose up past his bony ankles, exposing that vulnerable part of anyone's anatomy. Sam's ankles looked bluish and brittle, birdlike, weak.

In her kitchen, Sam helped himself, and Mildred could feel his thoughts gathering. By the time Sam returned, he wasn't as angry anymore—just confused, with a puzzle to solve, and determined to solve it. He came back and sat down on the sofa where he always sat when he and Belle came over for a visit.

"What exactly do you women have against Liz? I have been wanting to ask you that for a long time. Liz didn't kill her husbands, you know. And they didn't commit suicide, so there's nothing wrong with her, but you women all act as if there is something wrong with her. The four men died. It's as simple as that. You could feel some sympathy for her. Think of how many times her heart has been broken," Sam said.

Mildred puzzled over that. Being broken-hearted was such a part of one's life that it barely seemed worth mentioning any more than one would complain about gray hair or hot flashes. Having a broken heart was part of being alive. Was Liz's heart more broken than anyone else's—and if so, had she and the other women in the church been unfair to her?

"You women are jealous. That's what it is. Liz has gotten four men to propose to her, and that's just the four men we know about. Four men to marry her. And now she has all that money and the liberty to do what she likes --and she looks good for her age--and you women are jealous." A flash of anger surfaced again. Sam looked at Mildred in disbelief. "And you hit her with a rock, and that's not the first time you've been up to no-good around her," Sam asserted. His eyes glinted, for he had his suspicions of other nefarious actions by the women in the church but no proof of what he was thinking.

"You women take the cake," Sam said finally.

"Stop calling us 'you women'," Mildred objected finally. The memory of trying to prevent Liz from developing an intimate relationship with Sam at the Missions

Conference resurfaced. Mildred had tried to stop it—had obviously failed. In that moment she saw also that her resistance to Liz wasn't just about Sam—it was about Hugh. Mildred had turned down Hugh, but that did not mean that she wanted Liz to have him. But Liz had married him. It didn't make any sense to be jealous of someone who had accepted the man she had refused, but there it was: another motivation for why she had thrown that rock. Maybe it was the real reason.

"Stop throwing stones at her. You women..."

"You men..." Mildred said finally.

Sam met her gaze squarely. "Go ahead," he said. "I've been dishing it out."

In spite of her own growing guilt in the matter, she was still sure that Sam was wrong. "You men are stupid about a certain kind of woman."

Sam's chin went up. Unable to hold her gaze, Sam took a big slurp of coffee. The light caught his face, and his day's growth of beard was greyer than it had ever been before. If Mildred were meeting him for the first time, she would think he had a drinking problem. His eyes were ringed in circles and red from lack of sleep and from worry. He had to be worried. That was why he was so angry. She saw then that Sam was angry with himself and taking it out on her, his friend, because he could.

"Why do you think I threw that stone?" Mildred asked and waited. Inside, her inner Mildred Budge confessed, *because I didn't like what happened to Hugh, and I don't want it happening to Belle's husband.*

Sam leaned back on the sofa and took a deep breath. "It is hell growing old," Sam said finally.

"You are making it worse by getting involved with that woman." Mildred heard the contempt in her own voice and wished she could change it—not judge Sam or Liz— but there it was: puritanical disapproval that had, at its core, disappointment and fear of how her old friend could hurt his wife, himself, and the reputation of the church of which he was an elder.

"Good grief. I am not involved with Liz," Sam said tiredly. "I don't have the energy to get involved with another woman."

"I saw you," Mildred said frankly. "Jake, too."

Something passed behind Sam's eyes. Confirmation. Surprise. Resolve. The emotions came quickly.

He sat up straighter, angrier. "Although it's none of your business, I have not kissed another woman in forty-three years. I don't even know how that happened. It was a strange day. Liz felt weak. I felt.... stupid. I had gotten us all into that mess. And she started talking, and I tried to comfort her....

And it was what it was. And it was only, only a kiss that had started as......" Sam held up his hands in supplication. "Comfort. We had just survived a possibly fatal car crash. She was afraid. The accident was my fault. I hugged her. The hug turned into a kiss. That is all it was, and you and I are old enough to put only a kiss in its place. Aren't we old enough to do that, Mildred Budge?"

A dull pang of embarrassment hit Mildred Budge. Was she so unworldly, so unfamiliar with the way kisses happened between men and women that she had not understood that from the beginning? Was she such a faithless friend that she had believed the worst about Sam right away?

"When I talked to Liz this morning—I waited a day to figure it out for myself--I explained that, and I apologized for my part in it. Although I think she already knew. She has been around the block. She knows what a kiss like that is. She knew before I did."

"You talked to Liz this morning," Mildred said, sitting up straighter. "Before coming over here?"

Anger resurfaced in Sam. "I told you that already. That is when Liz told me about that bruise on her back. And then I remembered what I saw, and you didn't need to hit Liz, Millie. Liz Luckie is liable to leave the church; and if she goes, she'll take her tithe with her."

Mildred didn't respond to that. Tithing was a private matter.

"Did you tell Belle about the kiss?" Mildred asked.

"Why would I do that?" Sam replied, looking exasperated. "Belle is not herself these days. You know that. She wasn't there. She can't know how it all felt. Belle doesn't like Liz any more than you do. Belle wouldn't understand, and I wasn't about to give her something to worry about when there is nothing to worry about in that respect. We've got a real problem to worry about. Belle and I are without a car. What did you do without your car while it was gone?"

Mildred's car had been stolen for four days a few months before, but was found abandoned in a mall parking lot in Tennessee. Mitch Harper's brother worked in Tennessee and had driven it down. Mitch had brought it over to Mildred. Not a scratch on it. But Mildred had never felt the same about her little black and red mini-Cooper, which she had previously relished. It had never again felt as if it were hers. "I walked until I got my car back, or Fran drove me where I needed to go," she recalled. Not having her car had not been a great inconvenience.

By the time she said the words, Sam had forgotten his question. Almost immediately, he asked another one: "Are you going to apologize to Liz?" he demanded, moving toward the front doorway.

Sam never left her house through the front door. He always used the back door that led to the field connecting Mildred's house to his and Belle's—the one he had used to come inside. The front door was for real visitors who were parked in the driveway or on the street.

Mildred followed Sam to the front door.

"Liz is home, and you could call her right now and get it over with. Or you can tell her you are sorry tomorrow night. We're having a pulpit committee meeting at her house to figure out what to do next. Be there at 7 o'clock." Sam recited Liz's phone number then, and said, "Call her."

"She could use a friend," Sam added meaningfully.

"I will think about it," Mildred said woodenly.

Mildred thought Sam was gone then. Really. Sam had never been one of those people who didn't know how to say goodbye and exit her house. But, unlike himself, Sam kept turning, turning back, and this time when he spoke, Mildred felt as if her old friend was finally saying what he had really needed to say.

"Millie, when the car went over the embankment, did you feel something?"

Her head bobbed yes, gently.

The look in Sam's eyes changed, and she could see that he was remembering, reciting the feelings his memory had recorded.

"I saw the deer. Wasn't he the beautifullest thing you've ever seen? When I saw him, I had the funniest feeling, like I was the deer, and I could move like that in great bounds. Did you see him leap—that deer? I was Superman there for a minute while the deer was leaping, and when he sailed away, I turned the steering wheel, and we flew over the embankment. I know it was an accident, but when that happened, I was the deer." His voice filled with wonder and longing.

"And even when we crashed, it wasn't so bad, was it?" Her old friend looked to Mildred for forgiveness, and she gave it as instantly as she would have the moment he had walked in through her back door, stomping and getting himself mad at her and the world. She saw that Sam was mad at himself more than anyone else for not being like the deer any longer, but he was taking it out on his friend Mildred and probably his wife Belle. She remembered her conversation with Jake: *Yes, we could spend our whole lives apologizing to one another for all the trespasses we commit all day long.*

Suddenly, Sam kicked at a lizard that was threatening to cross the pathway to her front door. Kicked at it harder than was necessary to make it go in the other direction. And

Mildred thought, *we people—even Christian people—have plenty of violence in us. Look at Sam with the lizard. Look at me with that rock.* "We're all right now, Sam. Everything will be all right. Maybe even better than before."

Hope hung in the air between them as Sam considered the prophecy, and then as easily as he kicked at the lizard, he said brusquely, "You call Liz. You owe her and me that much."

And then Sam turned and walked away from her house and to the sidewalk that was the longest route possible back to his home and to Belle.

13

TELL ME WHAT HAPPENED

Ordinarily, a member of the Berean Sunday school class did not take Sister Schubert's cinnamon rolls to her best friend when she was sick or had been in an accident. Instead, a best friend generally helped eat the Sister Schubert's rolls that other people who weren't your best friend brought over to prove that they cared about you and that they were well-behaved Christians who exercised themselves in the kinds of acts of mercy that were not only biblically approved of but socially approved of, too. In the South, sharing Sister Schubert's rolls with someone who had received them was one of the perks of being a best friend.

There are exceptions to that common rule, however, and when your best friend was involved in a car accident that happened while you were on church business, it is appropriate to bring her the Sister Schubert's rolls yourself to prove that you are her best friend and that you know what she really, really likes. Fran placed the sweet cinnamon yeast rolls in Mildred's preheated oven. After closing the door, Fran asked bluntly, "What did Liz do that caused Sam to drive the car off an embankment and almost kill the whole pulpit committee in one fell swoop?"

"Liz is innocent," Mildred replied, uncomfortable. "A deer crossed the road, and Sam swerved to avoid killing it. Liz wasn't doing anything but putting on mascara. She can do that while a car is in motion."

Fran nodded. The oven made the clicking sound that indicated it was now officially baking the rolls at the desired temperature that would produce optimum results. The centers would be done, and the tops would lightly brown but not enough to harden the lovely white icing that was very, very good. "Liz was in the passenger seat?"

Mildred nodded. "She gets motion sick in the backseat."

"Of course, she does. Otherwise, Liz would have been sitting in the backseat where putting on mascara would not have distracted the driver," Fran said, with a canny smile. She scratched the side of her neck below the ear, a habit of hers when she was thinking hard. It had been Gritz's habit first. She had acquired it from her husband—still had it all these years since he'd been gone.

Mildred tilted her head to one side the way her mother used to do when she was thinking. "It would distract me if someone were putting on make-up while I was trying to drive."

Fran nodded knowingly. "She has to be admired. Remember that."

"I had my eyes mostly closed."

"In the backseat," Fran confirmed.

Mildred nodded. "You will never know what a strain it was being in the car. It was two against two the whole way."

"You and Jake and Sam and Liz."

Mildred inhaled and patted her sore leg absentmindedly.

"What happened to your leg?" Fran asked, pointing to the bulge under the red jersey pants.

Mildred looked down at the leg that she had bandaged. The wound had been a surprisingly angry one. About three inches long, the jagged cut reminded Mildred of an insignia some superhero comic book star wore on his chest signifying a lightning bolt. She felt as if she had been struck by lightning on her leg, and the bulk of the bandage made a mound against the cloth of her red jersey pants, which she had not planned to wear when Fran could see her in them. This type of stretch pants was the kind Sam had been wearing, and it was expressly forbidden by Fran that any thinking church lady ever wear them.

Next to blue jeans, stretch pants, a.k.a. athletic pants, were the worst fashion choice any lady could make because they did absolutely nothing for the appearance of her behind other than to bunch back there in a most unflattering way. If the pants did not bunch, they hung too loosely. And if a lady needed to wear any type of additional undergarment that was thicker than ordinary undergarments, the reality of it was often showcased incontrovertibly in a way that no lady would want known. Fran's rule was: "Never be caught dead in a pair of stretch pants, and you never know what the day will bring!"

Mildred had bought a pair on impulse one day at Wal-Mart. Three bucks. Bright red. Who could turn down a bargain like that in your favorite color even if they were inclined to bunch up in an unbecoming way in the back? What did that matter if you planned to never leave the house in them?

After Sam had left, Mildred had tried to get dressed, and the stretch pants were the only pants that didn't press the bandage hard against the wound on her leg.

Fran was studiously ignoring Mildred's contraband pants. But she didn't have to speak. Mildred knew what Fran would say, because Fran, a former New York model, had explained the dangers of not only stretch pants but all kinds of pants that women mistakenly wore. "Look around you,

Mildred," she had said on more than one occasion when they were standing behind many women in church who were wearing the right pants and many who were wearing the wrong ones. The wrong pants always clung, revealing panty lines, derriere dimples, dents in the thighs, and unfortunately, at times, Depends undergarments.

Knowing everything Fran thought about stretch pants (the elastic in the waist is an inducement to overeat; maintain the discipline of a real waistband, and you will be less likely to gain weight), Mildred had previously only worn her three-dollar pants from Wal-Mart late at night when it was cold and her legs got chilly and when Fran could not see her in them. *Besides, if she died in her sleep, Fran would be the one who found her body, and by then she would never have to hear: "Didn't I tell you this could happen?"*

"I cut my leg on the metal guard when I climbed up the embankment," Mildred explained, her voice indicating that she didn't want to say more about it. *It was just a cut, just pain, would probably scar—what difference did it make? It was just a leg.* If she could distract Fran from the wound, maybe she wouldn't nag her about the pants.

"I am having a hard time imagining you climbing up an embankment," Fran said, ignoring the red elephant in the room. She eyed her friend thoughtfully.

"Jake was above, and he was pulling on the rope that I was holding," Mildred said. "Rope burns your hands, by the way."

"Hoisting you?" Fran said, brow furrowing. "That could not have been pleasant for either of you."

Mildred swallowed hard and hurriedly added, "That is not the worst of it."

Fran held Mildred's gaze. It was best to get it all out while she could still say the words

"The boy preacher helped me get started up the hill."

"How exactly did he do that?" Fran asked. The wrinkles in her furrowed brow grew deeper. She did not rush her friend's story. There were Sister Schubert's rolls baking in the oven, and Mildred was notorious for rushing the baking time of the rolls. The conversation now was not only a fact-finding mission but a roll-saving gambit. Fran was skilled at it, but Mildred was not oblivious to the different motivations for the discussions. As long as she didn't have to defend the red pants, Mildred was happy to keep talking about her adventure.

"Jake pulled on the rope and lifted me, and then Steev came over and put his shoulder under my hips."

Fran's expression immediately glazed over. Realizing that the oven was now past comfortably warm and was now uncomfortably hot, Fran shifted her own belvedere away from it. "You sat on a strange preacher's shoulder," Fran confirmed, trying to see it in her mind. She shook her head to dispel the image.

"In a way," Mildred said, uncomfortable. "Steev used both hands to lift me up, too. It wasn't all Jake who was above me holding the rope."

"The boy preacher pushed your belvedere upwards?" Fran verified. "The boy preacher that you just met?"

"Palms out, dead center, the whole of my weight in his hands," Mildred declared. She closed her eyes to try and obliterate the memory. She couldn't.

For the first time since she had arrived, Fran's eyes registered the pain that she had worn alone when she first heard the news of the accident—before the details had come out, before the rescue was explained, while she was still in that state of, oh, no, is Mildred all right? Sam? Jake? That woman? What has happened to our people? Fran's eyes had worn the news of deep personal sorrow, and only tamped it down as she digested the details that came forth. *There had been an accident. Everyone is fine. They are all headed home.* Mildred had called Fran late Sunday evening and confirmed that report, adding, "It's been a tiring day. See you tomorrow."

"See you tomorrow," Fran had promised, going right to her freezer to confirm that she had her pan of emergency Sister Schubert's cinnamon rolls. The sorrow for what her friends had experienced stayed in her eyes until she was on her way to see Mildred, and only fully dissipated when she reached her friend and Mildred's face registered unabashed delight at seeing the cinnamon rolls.

But the shock of the misadventure returned with the description of her Mildred's ungainly ascent up a steep incline and her dependence upon a young man who could become their next preacher and who had held her up with arms and hands uplifted in a way that no church woman who had lived long enough to remember what white gloves and real hose felt like could bear to consider, imagine, and now remember. For the rest of her life. Until she died. It was the kind of event that might even be one of the last thoughts you had before you left this world forever. Only the arrival of eternity could blank out a memory like that.

"I am terribly sorry that happened to you," Fran said sorrowfully, and she stifled a sympathetic wince. She tried not to look at Mildred's leg ensconced in the red jersey fabric. Mildred's ordeal ranked up there as one of the worst events that can happen to any church lady, and Fran knew her best friend well enough to know that Mildred Budge had lived through the moment by concentrating on the task of climbing the hill that needed to be traversed.

After a considered pause, Fran offered a verdict. "We cannot, under any circumstances, hire Steev Emory to be the next preacher. You could never really listen to him preach, could you?" Fran was halfway joking and deeply serious. "Did he do the same for Liz?"

"I don't know. I was in the van by then. Jake pulled her up, too. It didn't take them very long."

"That's bad. I hope Liz doesn't target him as her next victim. Jake's too nice a guy to die so young."

Mildred looked toward the oven. She could smell the yeast, the cinnamon.

The clock on the wall ticked. Mildred was counting down the minutes. The rolls were almost ready.

"There is more," Mildred confessed softly.

Fran heard the tone of her friend's voice. Her gaze careful, Fran nodded silently for Mildred to go ahead and confess what needed to be said.

"I threw a rock at Liz." Fran waited for more details, but that was all Mildred could say out loud in that moment.

"Why did you throw a rock at Liz?" Fran asked sharply. Her friend was not known for gossiping or throwing rocks, one being very much like the other.

Mildred didn't answer her. She stared at the oven. She had not meant to go there; but telling the story had begun to help her, and she had lost track of the boundaries that she had intended to maintain. Mildred often forgot the boundaries of good sense with Fran, because Fran was so deeply inside the boundaries that defined private and public. Mildred trusted Fran. However, in that moment, Mildred had only wanted to confess her sin out loud. She didn't want to talk about Sam and Liz, not really; and if she could take out the rolls, she could put one in her mouth and chew and chew and not talk, not talk.

Fran concentrated hard, Sister Schubert's rolls ignored. "Why would Mildred Budge throw a rock at Liz Luckie?" she asked out loud. The question echoed in the kitchen.

Mildred looked past her, out through the sun porch that led to the back field that connected her yard to the Deerborns'.

Fran turned and followed her best friend's gaze to Belle's house, where the driveway was empty, and might stay that way. To the soft lights glowing in the back of the house. Toward Belle and her Sam.

Fran pivoted back to Mildred. "Don't tell me.... don't tell me that our Liz twinkled at Sam again. I thought that was over way back when."

"Okay, I won't," Mildred said quietly.

"Are you kidding me?" Fran demanded. She crossed her arms in what most people considered to be a self-protective stance; but when Fran did it, she was getting fierce. Fran had a fierce side.

Mildred shook her head.

"I know that Liz twinkles at men randomly the way most of us just blink our eyes to keep them moist. She did that a while back and Winston took her twinkling personally."

Mildred nodded almost imperceptibly.

"But she twinkled at Sam specifically?" Fran clarified. "A married elder in our church?"

Mildred met her friend's gaze and did not shake her head.

"She arranged to sit in the front seat beside him," Fran theorized.

Mildred's face became a picture of immobility.

"But you saw something? Something that bothered you...." Fran continued thinking out loud, as Mildred neither agreed nor disagreed. Instead, Mildred stared hard at the oven door.

"And when you realized what was going on, you had found one of your rocks," Fran deduced. "And you were holding it?"

Mildred nodded.

"And she did something."

Mildred nodded. The smell of cinnamon grew rich in the room, the aroma of yeast, strong. In the Bible, yeast is almost always a symbol for sin. When the Israelites made their famous exodus from Egyptian capture, there was no time for the bread to rise; consequently, they ate unleavened bread on the run from captivity toward their promised land. A yeastless bread became a symbol for remembering then—for God's providential supply of an escape. But there was none for Mildred Budge. She had yeast rolls in her oven, and her best friend was beside her with a series of questions. No escape from the truth for her.

"And your hand threw the rock, like a reflex?" Fran asked, eyes narrowing. She looked at the Deerborn house.

Mildred nodded slowly.

"For Belle?"

"For Sam, too," Mildred said. "And for Hugh. I think I am mad at her about Hugh."

Fran ignored the confession about Hugh and turned back toward the Deerborns' house and eyed it thoughtfully. The oven beeped three times, signaling that the rolls were ready to eat. She did not turn toward the oven. Neither did Mildred right away.

Fran said with a heavy sigh, "I knew something was wrong over there. I just didn't know what it was."

"You're not shocked," Mildred observed, as she placed the rolls on the table before them. They were perfect. She twisted one out--the one with the creamiest white icing.

Fran held up one hand that meant: *I will wait until they cool.*

Fran had a dozen ways of not over eating. Waiting for food to cool was one of them. Mildred had seen her friend exercise a number of strategies to keep her calorie consumption at a minimum. Sometimes, at a fellowship supper or at the Country Club, Fran walked around the dessert table as if she were going to make a selection, and then she didn't exactly decline. Rather she just walked quietly away. She gave the appearance of participating but didn't and without causing others to think she was a party-pooper.

She was discreet in other ways. Sometimes at a Lunch Bunch meal at a friend's house, Fran got up to stack the dishes in order to avoid second helpings. Sometimes, she claimed wide-eyed, as if she found the news unfathomable as well, "I'm simply not hungry."

Mildred blew on her roll and nibbled. Perfect. Sister Schubert's rolls almost made it all right to be listed formally on the prayer chain, and there was nothing she could do about it. Being on the prayer chain could be very inconvenient, and typically Mildred nixed it when someone asked her if she needed to be placed on the list for some malady.

But this time, no one had asked. The news of their car crash had put every member of the committee on the prayer chain. As a result, the phone would ring too much. There would be cards that came in the mail that she would have to answer or at least recall when she saw the well-wisher the next time at church.

However, and she had not thought of this before, Mildred wondered if someone else might bring her another pan of Sister Schubert's rolls. Maybe, two pans. They would be very welcome indeed. Mildred imagined for a moment what it would feel like to have a freezer full of Sister Schubert's cinnamon rolls. The comfort that would bring! The fantasy did not last long.

"Nooooooo. Something like this does not shock me. Sam will come to his senses fast enough. Sam Deerborn is many things, but he is not a complete fool."

"What do you mean—he is many things?" Mildred asked.

Just as Fran often used questions to direct people to do the tasks that she had mentally assigned them, Mildred asked questions to cause someone else to talk, especially if she wanted to eat another roll without having to contribute much to the conversation.

Mildred ate with appetite. She was feeling much better. A burden shared is half as heavy. A sin confessed loses its power to condemn you. Besides, Sam had explained that the kiss was nothing. Nothing. Mildred had thrown the rock at nothing. She would have to think about that some more in order to repent fully of her own folly in seeing what was not there. And she must find the right time to apologize to Liz. So far, the words felt tamped way down, and she could not imagine a time when she could say with authenticity, "I am sorry I threw a rock at you while you were trying to steal my friend's husband after you had already married Hugh and he's only been gone a few months."

"Sam is arrogant, controlling, a hypocrite, and probably a terrible husband, but Sam Deerborn is not a fool," Fran said. "And I'm not judging him. I am just telling you the truth."

Mildred's hand stopped with the thickly iced roll halfway to her mouth. The experience of time changed for an instant. The delectable warm sugar dripped slowly onto the napkin on the table in front of her. Mildred registered the loss of that large drop of sugar, considered the roll, hesitated. *Was she supposed to say something?* She had never heard Fran Applewhite speak so frankly about their mutual friend that way

"Well, you see it, don't you?" Fran demanded.

"I thought he was well-organized and zealous for good works and uncomfortable retired, so he liked to keep busy, and there's always plenty to do at a church," Mildred mused.

"You do not live in the same universe as the rest of us, Millie. I have warned you repeatedly that seeing the good in others doesn't do them any favors, ultimately. It just postpones reaching the inevitable conclusion that no one is a hero really, not even Christians."

Mildred considered the roll she was holding. How quickly life can change. A turn of the steering wheel and a car flies over an embankment. A sentence spoken suddenly and a lifetime love affair with yeast rolls mutated. The dainty roll didn't look quite as appetizing as it had seconds before. The icing, seconds ago so desirable, felt uncomfortably sticky on Mildred's fingertips.

"Sam Deerborn tries to run the church, and it is my considered opinion that he has run off more than one preacher," Fran said, finally sitting in what was her chair by the dinette in the kitchen where they always sat together. Most visitors joined Mildred in the living room, but the kitchen belonged to Fran.

"They left for greener pastures," Mildred theorized softly. It was what she had told herself when anyone left the church. *Sheep and shepherds often leave for greener pastures.*

"Honey, preachers don't just quit churches. They get run off by people like Sam who can't be pleased no matter what you do. And any preacher worth his salt wants to lead the flock himself. Sam presents himself as a helper, but he's really a self-appointed chief disguised as a helper. When people won't follow his vision or do what he tells them, he makes their lives uncomfortable until they leave."

Mildred laid down her half-eaten roll. She eyed the others wistfully, nostalgically. Reaching for a napkin, Mildred wiped her fingertips. It was now beyond the pale to keep eating—akin to eating heartily at the gathering of mourners after a funeral. Only polite eating is supposed to happen there: the kind of eating that says, *we are only eating because we must keep going*. But not the other kind of eating that Mildred often suppressed the urge to exclaim about: *Wow! These are the best rolls I have ever tasted in my life! The best cake! The best green beans! The best squash! The best tomatoes!* Not that kind of eating. Mildred took a deep breath, consoling herself with the idea that she could wrap up the rolls and bring them out for her supper later. *A little cup of cocoa....* She composed the expression on her face because Fran was getting into one of her moods, and the fastest way to help Fran get past a blast of irritation was to be attentive, show that you were really listening, and after Fran was really, really heard, she usually would change the subject herself.

I know other people in the church feel that way. I just didn't know you did," Mildred said.

"Sure, Millie. Sam is a bully dressed up like a nice guy."

"Do you think Belle knows?" Mildred asked.

"Wives always know, even if they don't know they know," Fran replied cryptically. Sometimes the long-time widow did slip into the secret world of married women, and while Mildred was occasionally adept at faking knowledge about what husbands and wives felt and kept from one another, Mildred did not try to fake it with Fran.

Instead, Mildred revealed, "Sam keeps saying that something is wrong with Belle."

"Belle knows," Fran said with quiet authority.

"Lord have mercy."

"Amen," Fran said, finally reaching for a roll. She took the smallest one with the least icing, as she changed the subject. "How long has it been since you got a tetanus shot?"

Mildred shrugged.

"Millie, you were cut on a piece of metal yesterday. It was probably rusty. You need a tetanus shot. I think you're supposed to do it within 24 hours or else."

"Don't want one," Millie said. She didn't ask what *or else* meant. She knew. You foamed at the mouth and then died a horrible death if you didn't get a tetanus shot. That's what they said anyway.

Fran went to the drawer where the roll of tin foil was stored, unfurled a piece, and zipped it off. She laid it gently over the rolls, covering them loosely.

"Well, wash that icing off your hands and grab your purse. I will drive you over to the doctor's office so you can get a tetanus shot."

"I don't need a tetanus shot," Mildred objected, unreasonably.

"I have known you longer than ten years, and I know for a fact you haven't had a tetanus shot in ten years. You don't want a tetanus shot. That is not the same thing as not needing one."

"I don't want to go anywhere if I have to get in another car." It was a rare kind of objection for Mildred to make: the kind that expected sympathy for the ordeal she had endured.

"It is not far, and we don't have any deer crossing the roads. I think we can make it there and back. I'll drive. You can sit in the front seat."

Mildred shook her head emphatically. "I'm not leaving the house. I promised myself in the van that if I ever made it home, I'd never leave the house again."

Fran's expression did not change.

"I don't want to go," Mildred said, crossly. She looked down at the pan of Sister Schubert's rolls that were all covered up now.

"There are some givens in this life: utility bills, taxes, tithing, and tetanus shots when you get cut on rusty metal."

"You don't know if it was rusty," Mildred argued weakly, turning toward her bedroom. She hated going to the doctor for any number of reasons. It was just asking for trouble. In an ongoing effort to not be sued for oversights or malpractice, doctors were very likely to schedule you for painful and unpleasant tests just to make sure they didn't end up in some kind of legal trouble.

"Do something about your face while you're back there," Fran called out.

Mildred heard the tin foil rattling as she walked down the narrow hallway to her bedroom. *Was Fran a secret nibbler? Was she getting into the rolls now that no one was looking? If Sam was a bully hiding out as a helper, what kinds of secrets could Fran have? What kind do I have?* Mildred wondered.

As she stared into the mirror over her dresser, wondering what she could do about her face, she stared into her own large brown eyes. *Steady as she goes.* That's how her father had christened her when she graduated from college. Mildred had heard the words spoken to her mother as she marched by on her graduation day in cap and gown. *Steady as she goes.* Mildred had made it through some pretty hard times by remembering her daddy's assessment of her resolve, her perseverance, her temperament, which she was born with and did not consider a virtue.

Ironically after changing and adding a quick touch of blush and lipstick, hoping that those brief ministrations to her face and the changing of the red jersey pants would be enough to silence Fran, the proclamation of her father's that she was a steady individual was undermined by the sudden trembling of her wounded leg.

The pain showed up on her face as she joined Fran by the front door.

"What's wrong?" Fran demanded. She was not angry. She cared deeply about her friend, and when something was wrong with Mildred, she got scared. Fear could sound like anger in Fran.

Mildred inhaled and reached for her purse. "My leg hurts," she said simply.

It was enough. Fran motioned toward the door with the hand that was holding her keys.

"Anyway, I should tell you that really there was nothing to it between Sam and Liz. He came over here this morning and explained that when I saw them kissing it was only a kiss—nothing more. And so, I threw the rock for no good reason, really. Maybe I was temporarily insane from adrenaline overload or the heat."

Fran laughed out loud. "You poor thing. You see them kissing with your own eyes. He comes over here before you have a chance to talk with his wife and tells you it was nothing, and you believed him?"

"Yes. Sam came over here this morning, and he told me that there was nothing to it."

"Honey, get in the car, and I will explain the facts of life to you on the way to the doctor's office."

14

CLOVERDALE

Traffic was light. It usually was in Cloverdale, Montgomery's most famous neighborhood. You could still drive through the garden district of Montgomery, Alabama at the proper speed of a life: slowly.

Mildred loved her neighborhood. Loved the pace of it. The fragrances. The easy access to anything she needed. Neighborhood shops created a village-like quality. Some had been around forever. Others were new, like Ex Voto Vintage, a jewelry store that specialized in creating one-of-a-kind pieces of jewelry out of beautiful artifacts from around the world. Elizabeth's shop was situated near

Richardson's Pharmacy, which had always been there. You could find just about anything you needed at Richardson's, from cheese straws to gift items. It was a local gathering place. When you were feeling social and didn't want to go home, you could go to Richardson's and visit with the girls there, whether you bought anything or not.

Around the corner was The Capri movie theatre. As Fran drove past it, Mildred remembered the dates of her youth and her first kiss, and they were distant but warm memories—the kind she vowed not to mention so that others wouldn't accuse her of going down memory lane.

You reached a time in your life when you had to monitor the stories you were inclined to tell, for it was a great temptation to relive the best memories over and over again—only others didn't want to relive them with you. So, Mildred kept the stories of The Capri and the kisses that had happened there to herself, and surveyed the crowd at Sinclair's next door, which was not a restaurant of her youth, but she liked it.

If you lunched at Sinclair's and had the time, you could leave your car parked and just walk up the street to the neighborhood bookstore, Capitol Book & News and hide out from the world.

If Mildred's leg hadn't been hurting, she would have suggested that Fran park the car and take a stroll with her. But the familiar and present potential delights of the neighborhood shops were left behind as Fran drove purposefully toward the doctor's office where they did not have an appointment.

Mildred and Fran had been going to the same doctor for as long as they had been friends. They knew the nurse and had seniority as patients in good standing. They were well-behaved patients. They finished antibiotics when they were prescribed. They did not wake up a doctor in the middle of the night for non-emergencies. If they needed medical guidance, they had the good sense to call the office before 5:00 PM and speak with the nurse or place a call early in the morning. They paid any bill that insurance did not cover. A tetanus shot that medical protocol and common sense demanded be administered within 24 hours of a cut on a piece of rusty metal was not asking too much of a long-time doctor—no matter who he was or how busy. They did not waste time calling for permission to come over. *What was a doctor going to say? No? I won't give you a tetanus shot that could save your life.*

They drove peacefully past the people and businesses they knew, while Fran explained the facts of life to Mildred Budge.

"When a man shows up at your house before 8:00 AM to deny that he is involved with a woman who isn't his wife it is as good as a confession that something is going on," Fran explained.

Mildred stared straight ahead. She felt the same disorienting confusion with Fran that she had with Sam when he had explained that a kiss could be nothing.

"We have our follow-up meeting tomorrow night at Liz's house," Mildred added in a monotone.

"That is fast. Very fast, considering you have all been in an accident. He told you about that meeting this morning before I got there?"

"Uh-huh. I was still in my bathrobe."

"That means he talked to Liz before he came to your house."

"That's right."

"And you still believe that there's nothing to it."

Mildred shrugged. Sometimes she liked to get her chores done early, too. She could understand how Sam might have just wanted to cross her off his to-do list.

"Why would a man make a phone call from his home very, very early in the morning before his wife wakes up, Mildred?"

"He has a long to-do list?" Mildred asked.

"What time does Belle usually get up?"

"Not as early as Sam does," Mildred replied with a frown.

"Exactly. Belle was still asleep. Sam could call Liz without her knowing. You should have used two rocks and knocked some sense into both of them."

Fran made the left turn toward the doctor's office over in the next-door neighborhood of Mulberry. The doctor's office wasn't far from Cates Optical, and if Mildred could have had her way, she would have stopped to say hello to Mr. Cates and his sweet wife.

She smiled as Fran drove past the old Southern home that had been converted into an optometry business and where cars were already lined up because Mr. Cates had the good sense to open before 10:00 AM. People like Mildred and Sam preferred to get their chores done early, and when your glasses needed adjusting, that was usually first on the list. She patted her brown plastic frames and concluded that she was overdue.

Her body leaned toward Cates Optical where she could have a good visit with Mr. Cates and his sweet wife. *What was her name?* Sometimes Mildred knew Mrs. Cates's first name right away; other times, she had to think about it. When she couldn't recall it, she called her Honey. Mrs. Cates called Mildred, Honey, too. Mildred smiled when she remembered that.

"We're not stopping to see the Cates," Fran said, as she made the next turn that took them to the parking lot of their doctor's office.

"I didn't say we should," Mildred said, as they parked.

Each woman got out, and Mildred heard the Honda's horn beep twice as Fran used the remote control to lock it down.

Inside, Fran went over to the receptionist's desk, whispered, signed the sheet for Mildred, and motioned for her to grab the chair nearest the water cooler and away from the TV that was suspended in the other corner of the room. Fran hated the sound of televisions in public places. She boycotted them by placing herself as far away from them as she could.

"How big a rock was it?" Fran asked suddenly, taking the seat next to Mildred, where she could watch the door through which the nurse would come and call Mildred to the back.

"It fit in my palm," Mildred said. "It was a very nice rock. I had planned to add it to my collection."

Fran ignored Mildred's confessed desire for more free rocks. "Good. Sometimes behavior modification is the right approach, like those electrical impulses they give to rodents who go the wrong direction in a maze and can't find the food," Fran said.

"Don't blame yourself. Liz made you do it the same way she makes men show off and almost kill themselves. She's a dangerous woman. Death follows her around. Some people die in her company. Four husbands have. Other people are tempted to commit murder and throw away a perfectly good rock. I have explained that before. Let's stop talking about her. Liz Luckie is not that interesting. Let's talk about us and our business."

As Fran briskly changed the subject, she inhaled deeply before announcing the news that she had been keeping to herself concerning their antique booth at The

Emporium. "The booth space beside ours has become available. We could expand."

"Which one closed? The Scarlett O'Hara booth or the Zelda Fitzgerald booth?"

"Scarlett is gone with the wind," Fran said, with no expression.

"Imagine that," Mildred said. "It's the end of an era."

Fran dismissed Mildred's overture to discuss the exodus of the memorabilia of a movie that was only faintly popular now. "Since that booth is now available, what would you think about doubling our floor space at The Emporium?" Fran said the words casually, but she had been planning them for quite a while. Fran didn't do very much casually.

Mildred came to full attention. "Twice the floor space means twice the inventory which means twice the work. That's a lot of carrying and dusting."

"Don't give me that. You don't dust. It's twice the profits is what it is. We could go to Greece in twice the time!" Fran beamed. She was asking Mildred's opinion, but she had already made up her own mind about it. Fran was a full-steam-ahead-kind of woman, and Mildred was a driver who preferred slow routes where there were only right-hand turns.

Mildred considered the idea. "We would have to start going to more estate sales very seriously because we don't have enough inventory in our own attics to justify the rent."

"I'm ready to go. It will be fun. What else have we got to do? There is nothing for us to see at the movies anymore, because James Garner is not making any new movies."

"He made that Christmas movie a few years ago with Julie Andrews. Before that he was in that movie with Mel Gibson."

"Mel Gibson needs prayer," Fran replied automatically. "We've got a few months before Christmas, and then they'll run that movie several times on TV. You can watch James Garner then, if you like."

Mildred frowned. "I'm not thinking about James Garner. I'm thinking about serving on the pulpit committee, and you're on half a dozen committees yourself."

Fran waved aside the objection. "You were on the same kinds of committees while you held down your full-time teaching job, and you managed just fine. This enterprise is much simpler. Once the furniture is in place, the business simply runs itself."

Fran shrugged as if the idea didn't really matter. "It's just an opportunity. I just thought we could do it; but, if you're not interested in going for pretty drives to small Southern towns and scooping up bargains at estate sales and auctions and then selling the merchandise for four times what we paid for it, that is entirely your affair."

Mildred remained silent. Her leg hurt. Her Sister Schubert's rolls were getting colder by the minute. She wondered if Fran had tucked the tin foil in securely. They would dry out and get hard if they weren't tucked in properly.

"You won't be on the pulpit committee forever, Millie. Sam will tell us who the new preacher will be, and then you will be off the Deerborn clock. How was the boy preacher, anyway?"

"He has got a good head on his shoulders. He came looking for us on a lonely road and found us. That proves that he has initiative."

"Is he too young for us?" Fran asked directly. The earlier objections she had made about his hands on Mildred's caboose were dismissed as irrelevant now. Now, she wanted the facts.

"Yes," Mildred said. "But there's more. After we were all in the van, he asked us if we knew Jesus."

Fran laughed out loud. "He asked Sam Deerborn and Mildred Budge if you two knew Jesus."

"Liz was in the van, too."

"Hire the boy. I don't care how young he is or what kind of post-traumatic stress syndrome you may suffer from your close encounter with him. The field is white, and some of the crop that needs to be harvested is sitting right in the church building."

"I imagine we will discuss trying to go and hear him at the meeting tomorrow night," Mildred said.

"Like I said, it will be over soon. You all will settle on the right guy, and then you will be glad you have extra floor space at The Emporium and the adventure of finding inventory with me."

"Have you already signed the paper?" Mildred asked, holding Fran's gaze.

"Now you know that I wouldn't sign anything without your agreement. But I think we better get over there. It's primo real estate."

"No, it isn't," Mildred replied.

"Well, maybe not to others, but it is to us."

"Mildred Budge," the nurse called from the doorway.

"Coming," Mildred said forthrightly. She stood up, and the room felt swimmy. The unsteadiness surprised her, and Mr. Budge's daughter experienced an unsettling question: *What if for the rest of my life I am no longer steady as I go?*

15

A SHOT FOR WHAT AILS YOU

After the nurse weighed Mildred Budge loudly and asked her twenty loud questions as if she thought Mildred had a hearing problem, the patient who was being "worked into the doctor's busy schedule because you don't have an appointment" was delivered to the examination room, where every instinct in Mildred Budge went on high alert. At that moment, it became her primary job to escape.

The doctor was not her regular doctor.

The doctor filling in for her doctor was younger than Steev.

The doctor was short, and short men often had too much to prove and did that in dangerous ways. Mildred Budge was cautious around very short men. She considered them potentially very dangerous indeed.

The doctor's white coat hung almost to his ankles, and his stethoscope looked like it banged against his navel.

The doctor could have been one of her former fifth-grade students all grown up now and expecting her to remember him. She did not.

Mildred Budge composed her face, tried not to scream, 'No. Not a chance. Not gonna happen. No kid's gonna take care of me. I know kids, and they don't know people like me. They don't know how to weigh and measure symptoms and be patient while your body adjusts itself to change. What they call a symptom, I call the dust settling.'

Instead, she shook his proffered cold, uncalloused hand and before he could ask her to do anything unpleasant, like undress, she announced in a tone of voice that would brook no argument: "I just came in here for a tetanus shot."

He had a childlike glint in his uncreased eyes, and his unlined face was pink with youth. No aberrant hairs grew out of his ears or overtook his eyes. He had a fresh-scrubbed look, as if he had used a pumice stone with alcohol to wash his face.

She exhaled slowly, attempting to master her self-control, which was threatening to slip. *But really! She had not wanted to leave the house!*

It was the business of older people to be patient with the young, and the retired schoolteacher steadfastly accepted that responsibility, except when medical care was involved, and then she did not want a child to attend her. It wasn't personal. It was her survival instinct operating in high gear. It was life and death.

"We haven't seen you in two years, Miss Budge," Doctor Jon chided her, perusing a folder that had her name on the tab: Miss Mildred Budge.

"I haven't been sick," she said a little louder than was necessary. Her voice echoed off the walls of the small room that was efficiently appointed. The narrow examination table with the metal devices on it was positioned in the corner. A small sink promised hand washing. Two green trash bins had signs that indicated the safe disposal of medical devices and trash, like needles and swabs.

"You missed your flu shot this year," he said, studying her chart. The tone of his voice condemned her.

She felt accused, and replied sourly, "I forgot."

"You have gained six pounds."

"Living does that to you," she said woodenly.

Doctor Jon smiled, and she saw the contours on the top of his head as he studied her file.

"Where is my doctor?" she demanded sharply. "Why aren't I seeing him?"

"He is out west on vacation. I'm filling in," Doctor Jon replied easily, as if she had no choice in what happened next.

The explanation came too quickly. Mildred Budge had the sudden notion that her doctor was retiring and was in the process of handing his practice over to this child with a bumpy head. She wanted to test the bumps of Jon's head with her hands and see what they could tell her. A ripe head held clues about the mind inside.

"We've got your blood work going, and the nurse said you were in an accident yesterday. I didn't want to let you go without following through on a few questions that you might not have thought about. Did you hurt your head?"

Her right hand involuntarily went to her head. She shook it. "Sam hit his head on the steering wheel, but I only hurt my leg."

Doctor Jon leaned over—he didn't have to go far—and eased Mildred's pant leg up. His hands were gentle, his touch cool. He peeled back one of the Band-Aids, his face showing concern. "Too late to stitch it. You will have to keep it very clean."

"I just need the tetanus shot," she said, wishing he would put the Band-Aid back. The air didn't feel very good against her skin. A burning sensation threatened. Besides, a doctor's office was the worst place in the world to pick up germs.

She was just about to tell him to put that Band-Aid back immediately when he asked, "How did you get the marks on your hands and wrists?"

She looked down at her wrists. They still bore the marks of the rope burn. "I was in a car accident yesterday. We went off the road and into a valley of sorts. We had to use a rope to climb up an embankment. Those are rope burns."

"How far up did you climb?" he asked automatically, and Miss Budge noted that he was like many students she had taught who avoided giving information by asking rat-a-tat and often random questions. It was not the same activity as the Socratic method, but it could sound like it.

She answered him anyway. "About 30 yards? Maybe more." In her mind she tried to retrace her steps. How many times did she plant her feet against the side of the hill? 'Did each step count as a yard? Was it shorter? Was it only two feet instead of the usual three that you count when you are marking off flat ground?

"You should put some ointment on those scratches." Doctor Jon advised, and then he came to life in front of her. Until that moment he had been playing the part of the doctor, *pretending to be one,* is how Mildred thought of him, but in that instant when Dr. Jon looked at the scratches and saw that they hurt, compassion came to life.

She wondered if compassion for others was his motivation for becoming a doctor or was it only ambition: to make money. To be significant. To play God.

When Mildred looked into his eyes—more innocent than they had appeared when the mask of doctor was in place—she dismissed the latter. Mildred was suddenly sorry that she had been aloof and cold. Dr. Jon couldn't help his age or his height, and maybe her doctor was only out west and not about to abandon her. She smiled faintly.

"I will add some ointment before I go to bed tonight," she promised.

Dr. Jon grew serious then, talking to her as if she were too young not to know that you need to cleanse wounds and dress them well. "Wash them first with soap and water."

Mildred nodded. He was such a kid.

Reaching for her, he found a place on her wrist that wasn't bruised, and tenderly, with those refreshing cool fingertips, he took her pulse. The touch was surprising. It always surprised Mildred to be touched by anyone.

A few seconds of silence later, he said, "Your resting heart rate is optimum. And your blood pressure is 116 over 68 after the day you had yesterday." There was a note of wonder in his voice, and he eyed her curiously.

"Always," she said.

"You're a healthy woman," he declared "And very lucky to have fared as well as you did."

"I know," she said

The door opened, and the nurse reappeared with a tray. An injection was on the tray underneath a white paper cloth. Mildred averted her gaze. She did not like needles. They seemed so violent. The little guns that fired inoculations directly into the skin weren't any better.

Mildred wondered if more women had been doctors through history would there be fewer tools for administering medicine that didn't have the connotations and shape of weapons.

She let her mind drift while he prepared the injection, watching him out of the corner of her eye while she wondered if the language of medicine--shots, guns, attack the germs--were the right words to use to regain a healthy status quo.

In her world of faith, where words merged with breath to become an instrument of creation, Mildred had developed a healthy regard for choosing and using a mindful vocabulary that respected the creative job it had to do and sensitively sought resolution to problems, like ill health.

"Hip or arm?" he asked.

"Arm," she replied. She pushed up the sleeve on her shirt.

"Where did these bruises come from?" Dr. Jon asked immediately.

"The fellow who helped me up over the incline yesterday grabbed me by the arms. I think those are his fingerprints."

"Are you sure that is how you got them?" he asked, swabbing a place on her arm with an alcohol-enriched cotton ball. "Elder abuse is against the law."

He jabbed the needle in the way that someone does who sees an arm as an object rather than as a destination. It hurt. He held it in a long time, releasing the medicine slowly.

Mildred sent her attention to Jesus. *You do still remember that being human is very painful, don't you*? The prayer brought an instant balm to her spirit.

"There. All done," Dr. Jon said with satisfaction. He stepped back and surveyed his patient. "No broken bones? No head injuries?"

"No elder abuse," she confirmed. "My friend was truly helping me up over an embankment."

"If that's your story," he said, neutrally, "you're good to go."

16

NOW AND LATER

Fran had more self-restraint than to ask Mildred if she wanted to go over to The Emporium to look at the floor space now available next to their booth and sign the lease for it right away. She took one look at Mildred's face after she emerged from the doctor's office, understood immediately that her friend felt old and violated, and said, "I'm buying you lunch at Derk's, and I won't take no for an answer."

"My answer is not no," Mildred said, but the smile she offered was wan, and for the space of the walk to the car, the two women felt their age together, their aloneness that friendship could not altogether bridge, and one more thing: in spite of her objection to going to the doctor, Mildred now did not want to go home right away, and Fran didn't either.

Derk's Filet & Vine on Cloverdale Road was the perfect place for lunch. It was a neighborhood restaurant and close to downtown. Often the people who worked in downtown offices joined their family members at Derk's. Consequently, you often saw very casually dressed people sitting at tables with very dressed up people, and you knew instantly that the dressed-up people were stealing some time away from the roles of their professional lives downtown to be with the people from home who loved them.

Seeing people being together at Derk's in the middle of the day made up for doctors who were too young and preachers who were also very young and who had hefted your derriere up a hillside.

The rich smell of good food prepared well met them when they went through the door. A long shelf of pantry goods for sale separated the area reserved for eating and the other half of the store, which was a wine shop. They had baby bottles of champagne for sale over there, and Mildred occasionally bought a small bottle that contained two glasses of champagne and chilled it in her fruit drawer in the refrigerator for when *Saratoga Trunk* came on late at night, and she couldn't sleep. She would join Ingrid Bergman when she drank champagne. Ingrid soaked peaches in her champagne, but Mildred never had peaches when that movie came on.

Ingrid was especially pretty in that movie, and when complimented by an admirer, she replied, "Aren't I lucky?"

Mildred's mother had been lucky like Ingrid, and when Mildred sipped champagne late at night with Ingrid drinking her peach-infused champagne and marveling at her good luck, Mildred thought of her mother and wondered what she was doing in heaven.

The dense smells of steaming food overpowered the memory of sipped champagne, and something happened to Mildred Budge that was uncharacteristic of the size-14 church lady: she lost her appetite. The sudden loss of appetite was so unexpected that Mildred looked quickly at Fran to see if the same thing had happened to her.

But Fran was busy scouting the entrees on the buffet, assessing the possibilities of fried chicken, fried catfish, a bar-be-cue plate (or a sandwich), and eager to give her friend, who always liked to eat lunch, a Sunday-quality good meal on a Monday after a near-death experience.

Her mouth dry, Mildred fell into step at the buffet behind Fran, who began to point out the entrees on the buffet as if Mildred couldn't see them for herself. But Mildred could see them. And she could see tables. And she could see the bottles of wine in the small room on the other side of the long well-stocked shelf.   And she remembered something that had gone deep inside of her when she sailed over the embankment.

A stillness rose up and overtook her. With the same clarity that she had observed in the people in the car as they sailed over the embankment, Mildred discerned in that moment a kind of restless despair in other people—a dislocated lostness that pulled at her causing her to want to shout, "Jesus saves!" to everyone in the room.

Then, as Mildred's mind stored the awareness of a present sadness nearby, a part of her that was deeply alive expanded, and the soul of her awareness began to whisper greetings to the shapes of people who were living in the limitless kingdom called Jesus Saves. It was a bigger dimension than the room they were in or the room of her mind's consciousness, and it had a shape. That shape was a hand as large as the universe which held them all—the quick and the dead-- and Mildred's spirit touched that hand while she listened to Fran announce:

"They have meatloaf today."

Mildred couldn't reply because the appetite for the things of the world had vanished, like the deer that had run across their path yesterday. In that moment, twenty-four hours after she had declared "Jesus saves," Mildred Budge only knew that she believed that, was experiencing it in a larger-than-life way, and her whole being pulsed expansively with a knowledge too great for the limited vocabulary that she called upon to point out the features of everyday living.

"You don't know what you want," Fran assessed when Mildred did not immediately choose. "Has the injection made you nauseous?" Fran asked, turning with concern.

Mildred smiled at her friend--her dear friend--who was pretending to want lunch in order to give her friend a meal that she usually wanted. 'How quickly we can shed our old selves and become new wineskins,' Mildred thought, 'and how hard it is to tell someone that. Husbands and wives must have a very hard time with that process, for to suddenly say, "I don't want any meatloaf or any of it really," was to say to a friend or a spouse, "You no longer know me. I am different now, and you do not know the new me. The old me always wanted meatloaf. The new me does not.'"

And so, with the disciplined graciousness that Fran had offered the meal, Mildred smiled, and said, "I will just have the bar-be-cue sandwich with one of those good pickles."

"A Wickles pickle is always welcome," Fran agreed readily. She met the gaze of the young girl who was waiting for their order on the other side of the steaming buffet, and said, "Two regular bar-be-cue sandwiches with extra pickles, please."

They went to the table they liked best by the window where they could watch people come and go on Cloverdale Road. Parking was tight and tricky, but people managed to back out safely into moving but respectful traffic.

And as they waited for their sandwiches, Mildred's consciousness continued to abide in that realm of Jesus Saves where she knew that down the street a girl who once had cut her hair was still cutting someone's hair in a salon that people who worked downtown used because it was on their way home.

She saw Anne Henry arrive and find a parking spot that had just become available, and Mildred's hand went up automatically to wave at Anne, but her good friend didn't see her. Anne was most likely going to Apropos, a small shop only a couple of doors down from Derk's that sold clothing and keepsakes and special jewelry, even some select pieces from Ex Voto Vintage for people who didn't want to drive the short distance over to Elizabeth's shop on Woodley Road.

Occasionally, Anne Henry showed up at church on Sunday morning wearing something special; and when someone asked her where she got it, she always smiled and said, "Apropos!"

'And that is how Anne Henry looked for every occasion,' Mildred thought. But her tasteful wardrobe wasn't the only reason Anne Henry always looked wonderful. Anne Henry was lit up from within--lit with the light of heaven that lived inside of her and made anything she wore look like a million dollars.

Mildred's attention returned to the present with Fran, but not all of it. Some of her awareness stayed in the dimension of Jesus Saves that was now taking a quiet tour of Cloverdale. She was remembering people with the kind of affection she had once known in the classroom when she walked down the aisles between the desks and patted the heads of children because a child's head seemed to need patting.

Memories of people she had loved often required that same affectionate awareness, a touch from her memory that brought them back to life. Mildred was acutely aware of people who had come and gone and were now abiding eternally inside the living love of Jesus. Her parents were there. Her grandparents. Other family members. Her Aunt Eileen. Uncle Joe. Uncle Sammy. Uncle Tommy. Aunt Faye. Aunt Betty. And friends. So many friends. Virginia Sellers. Esther Splawn. Hugh Luckie.

It seemed to Mildred that there were more people she loved living in heaven than were left on the earth, and a significant portion of her heart had already moved to heaven to be with them. In grief, her heart felt broken. In faith, she felt the communion with the saints and the pulsing, trustworthy love of one whose arms enclosed them all—those in heaven and the ones still sitting in Derk's or on their way to Apropos.

"It is a crying shame that we didn't buy more of those really good pickles when we could. Aren't you down to your last jar?" Fran asked, taking small bites of her sandwich.

Mildred took a tentative bite of her sandwich and quickly washed it down with a sip of iced tea.

"We have that one jar of pickles in the pantry and half a jar in the fridge," Mildred said, relieved that the food went down. The tea was good. She took another sip

"And then disaster," Fran said. "I didn't really know the Pickleman was sick. He just up and died."

"And took his pickle recipe with him to the grave," Mildred said.

"Maybe not," Fran replied, taking another bite.

Mildred copied her. Her chest relaxed. Her shoulders eased. The food was going down better than she would have predicted.

"His wife probably has that recipe. Or, she could have some left-behind jars of pickles that she would like to sell."

"Or, she might want to keep them for herself," Mildred said, as the people who lived in Jesus Saves retreated from her consciousness.

"Her husband did make them. They may be all that she has left of him that will taste like home."

"She could be sick of his pickles by now."

"Wishful thinking," Mildred said, as the experience of Jesus Saves took a different turn, surging up in her with a surprising motion like an iceberg that has been submerged and suddenly rises to the top of the water. She recalled that where they were sitting was, years ago, a music store. Wasn't it? Was it in this very building or in some other small neighborhood store? She used to go to Mary's House of Music, and buy sheet music the same way she ran the other errands of going to the dry cleaners, the grocery store, and the Farmers' Market where the Pickleman had sold his wares next to the table where Mrs. Parsons sold her wonderful jams and preserves made from the fruit that she mostly grew herself.

Sometimes Mildred wouldn't know the name of the song she wanted to learn to play, and the woman who worked there, whose name was not Mary, would listen to Mildred hum a piece of melody and then immediately be able to show her the sheet music she wanted to learn. *Here's Chopin. Here's Schubert. Here's Beethoven.* For while Mildred loved music, she had not had much formal training, and so her acquaintanceship with classics had become this kind of seeking out of a haunting melody that she tracked down to a piece of music that led her to a composer that took her to his body of works. She had learned Chopin's *Nocturne in A-flat* that way, and that one piece of music led to the other nocturnes. Sitting there holding the bar-be-cue sandwich to her mouth while Fran made small talk about pickles, Mildred thought of Mary's House of Music, and how she had known they were going out of business long before anyone posted a sign that announced: *Everything in the store half price.*

She had felt it as the shelves became emptier, and no new music arrived to fill them.

She had felt it when the keys of the store's piano went undusted. When the store began to show signs of aging and decay that no one tried to stop or repair. People were like that, too. You could tell when someone had given up long before hospice was called in.

"I didn't know the Pickleman was that sick," Fran said, waving at Anne Henry who was coming back toward her car. This time, their friend saw them and waved, her smile growing large and beaming. She pointed to her watch to signal that she was in a hurry, *forgive me for not coming in.* They both nodded vigorously and waved back.

"She always looks so good," Fran observed. It is what she always said about Anne Henry, and it was always true.

"She does," Mildred agreed, wondering if Anne had ever sipped champagne with

Ingrid Bergman while watching *Saratoga Trunk* and exulted in being lucky, too. "I did sort of know the Pickleman was ill," Mildred confirmed. "I just didn't speak of it."

Fran nodded. "You tend to know stuff like that sooner than I do. If you had told me I would have bought all of his pickles."

"I would have told you, but he died faster than the idea that he was dying came to my mind."

Fran nodded and chewed, and Mildred thought of how much better her life had become since she and Fran had adopted each other.

Fran helped Mildred see the world clearly, in ways. But Fran did not stop Mildred from seeing and recognizing the truth that there was dimension to living in the world of Jesus Saves when the way you see and experience eternity in the present moment was acutely personal and did not need validation from anyone else or to be shared in order for it to be real.

While Fran talked about a pickle recipe, Mildred was living in the world of Jesus Saves, and one dimension did not exclude the other.

"Someone could have gotten really hurt yesterday," Fran said suddenly.

Mildred nodded. She was halfway through her sandwich. And she did not want the rest. She did not even want the Wickles pickle on her plate and that was unprecedented. She wanted nothing. She was surrounded by a great cloud of witnesses who lived all of the time inside the realm of Jesus Saves, and she thought she could hear them off in the distance singing. A melody reached her from a distant place, and she tilted her head and tuned her attention to see if she could recognize it. She didn't, but she was drawn to it—wanted to hum it and store the sound inside where Chopin and Beethoven also lived.

"You do not have to eat it all," Fran said, reading her mind. "You have been through a lot, and it makes perfect sense that your appetite would be untrustworthy."

"Is that what it is?" Mildred said, laying down her napkin.

Fran nodded and laid down her own napkin. "Sometimes I am scared of facing food. You think I am just watching my weight, but there have been times when I have truly been envious of your appetite, Mildred. Mine is not trustworthy often."

Mildred stared into her friend's eyes. She had not known that about Fran. A near-death experience that had affected them both had brought the confession.

"What really happened in the car yesterday, Mildred?"

The whole answer to the question was not yet present in the experience of Jesus Saves, and Mildred Budge did not like to lie. So, she answered simply, "We could have died, but we didn't."

17

BECKONING JOY

Mildred walked as if in a dream, letting herself out of Fran's car with a wave. The experience of sailing over the embankment returned, and she heard herself chanting in that interior voice: *Jesus saves. Jesus saves.* And then the message shifted, as if her spirit needed to remember: *Jesus is the same yesterday, today and forever. His people must change, but he is the same.*

And with each chant of this witness to her spirit, Mildred became increasingly aware of life around her, of a pulsing harmony that sustained the universe and could not be adequately named by physics, and of a powerful joy calling to her to come home. This beckoning joy took hold of her with a fiercer possession than the simple appetite called hunger—and yesterday, survival—for she realized as the sailing over the embankment coursed in her like a wave that moves away from the shore and returns, that there was more to being alive than she regularly admitted even to herself. Before she placed one foot across her own threshold, she said out loud: "No eye hath seen nor ear heard what God has prepared for those that love him."

There was no response to that provocative idea—no way to predict what that could be. There was only the motion of turning, turning, turning toward the absolute truth of what holiness is and which signified what real repentance is. For turning toward the light of holiness is not an obsessive cataloguing of one's sins. That is the first baby step toward loving God—to get rid of guilt and make space inside yourself to receive more love. Rather, this turning was an awareness with some part of who you are that does not rely upon the senses for information to process that there is a hand stretched out across time and space beckoning members of the Invited to accept love and then more love in order to pass it on, and that hand belongs to the father who stands watch in the field, waiting for the safe return of his child that he would clothe and feed and celebrate over, and that celebration was what Mildred was feeling.

With the assurance that she had known in her spirit when she had declared to the members of the pulpit committee that Jesus saves, she said out loud to God and herself, while sorting the mail, "I feel a party coming."

Almost as soon as the words were out of her mouth, she saw the letter. It was addressed in a childish scrawl. The postmark was from the next county; and before she flipped it over and read the return address, Mildred knew it was from Janie in prison. Her Janie. Janie who was pregnant with the child of a man who was a liar—had lied not only to Mildred but to Janie, and now Janie, who had been caught up in his lies, was in jail for all sorts of offenses that the law had names for, but which Mildred Budge, church lady, simply identified as lies.

Mildred opened the envelope and read the young woman's letter:

Dear Miss Mildred:

I miss you, though it would not surprise me if you did not believe that. But I do miss you and I am still sorry for how we treated you but know you are a Christian lady who must forgive me and I hope you will. There is something I need to tell you but I cannot write it in a letter so I want you to come and see me if you will and I would be glad to see you and maybe you would bring me a Bible.

Come soon. It is important.

Love,

Your Janie

Her real name was Amanda, but she had used the name of Janie while Mildred had known her for those few days. Mildred had been planning to go and visit her in Tutwiler prison, but she had been busy with the pulpit committee.

She placed the letter on the table and told Jesus: "I think she's probably pretending and most likely is just asking for a Bible because she knows that I cannot ignore such a request. I think she is a liar, and that doesn't make any difference, does it? She is yours just like I am and but for the grace of God—and if that rock had landed on Liz's head and she had fallen in the ravine and died—I could be in jail, too, for murder or manslaughter. Liz could press charges for assault now if she wanted to. I, too, am a criminal," she said to Jesus, "And just as much as I did the first time I said it, I ask your pardon, your help, and give me the desire or at least the will to be obedient to visit those in prison because I surely do not want to go."

Mildred laid down the letter, and walking lightly at the pace of Jesus Saves, she went to her room and laid down for a nap, for she was very tired and not as steady as her daddy had told her she always would be.

18

LONESOME PRISON

Mildred Budge did not want to go and visit Janie in prison. She had no idea what the visiting hours were. She did not know how to call a prison and find out. She did not know what to wear to a prison, but she was pretty sure it wasn't red jersey stretch pants. She wore a good pair of black slacks and the sister version of her Sunday aqua sweater top; only this one was moss green.

She didn't like the drive toward Wetumpka, which was in the opposite direction of any other place she ever drove. But Mildred pointed her car in that direction anyway because Janie-Amanda had asked her to come, and when someone asks you to do something like give them the shirt off your back or walk two miles instead of one, you say 'yes.' Even if those verses hadn't been in the Bible, there was always Jesus whispering: *When you visit a prisoner, it's the same as visiting me.* Yes, there was no avoiding going to see Janie, so Mildred went.

At Tutwiler, she accepted a yellow parking form and placed it on her dashboard, parking her car in a space where the word 'Visitors' felt more promising than it ever had before. She sat inside her car for a few seconds to prepare her spirit to be loving rather than judgmental. She asked Jesus why she was so uncomfortable doing what the Bible urged believers to do: visit prisoners. And he said in that exquisitely subtle way that believers learn to hear: *Because you don't trust me completely. Not all the time.* And then she felt Jesus smile, as she had felt him smile through the years. She smiled back because it was true that she was a full-time Christian lady learning how to live in the dimension of Jesus Saves, and with as much heart, mind, and strength as she could discern and muster, she believed it, and there were times when "not all the time" told the truth, too.

Feeling the smile of Jesus inside her heart, Mildred walked purposefully across the hot parking lot, making sure that she wrote her name very large on the ledger inside so that there would be a record of her entering, for Miss Budge, who had been a public-school teacher and confined daily in small, airless school rooms with students for twenty-five years, had a revulsion towards being enclosed—a feeling she had not known existed inside herself until she walked away from teaching two years ago.

She smiled up broadly into the closed-circuit TV camera so that it would be a good video recording of her entering, and she mouthed her name for the camera, "I am Mildred Budge, and I am a free woman."

The guard who was standing post nearby had a face that showed nothing. Miss Budge recognized that expression. Church ladies wore it, too, from time to time but for different reasons.

Then, clutching her brown Grace Kelly handbag that had been examined for contraband materials, Mildred followed a yellow line painted on the floor that led to the waiting room with tables which were bare of what usually belonged on tables: napkin holders, sugar, silverware, or, at least, a tablecloth. There was no smell of something baking with apples and cinnamon in the next room. There was no welcoming aroma of coffee dripping or perking. There was no fragrance of hospitality of any kind. There was only a dank, fetid smell of too many bodies living too closely together in a building so closed up that the sunshine and fresh air couldn't get in.

Janie emerged from the far-left corner of the big meeting room. Although she was not wearing chains on her ankles, the young woman walked with the shuffle of someone who had learned to measure her steps because she now often walked along in lines with other slowly moving prisoners who were also being watched by guards.

Janie's appearance was a shock. Her once lustrous red wavy hair was dry and more brown than red now. Her skin, which had been luminous a few months ago with youth and rest, was pasty. She looked heavier and untoned. Her body had both a restlessness and a fatigue, as if she needed exercise that she wasn't getting and as if she hadn't slept well in many nights.

Miss Budge felt a quickening of deep concern.

Mimicking the expressions of the guards, Miss Budge offered Janie a disciplined smile of greeting. Light did not appear in the young woman's eyes that had once seemed ocean gray but now looked like the color of concrete blocks. Mildred knew a moment of great remorse: *It will be too late soon to stop the fatalism that will come to this girl if she doesn't have hope.*

"Miss Mildred," Janie said. She sounded nothing like the girl that Mildred still loved in spite of the better part of wisdom.

"You were sweet to come," Janie said, sitting down heavily and with the careful balance that mothers-to-be evidence long before their bellies reach the roundest they will become. Janie looked pregnant, though. She was due in a couple of months.

"How are you?' Mildred asked, lowering herself into the opposite chair. She would need a shower when she got home. It felt very sticky.

The girl's gaze roamed about the room. Her fingers were swollen from water retention.

Mildred looked down. The girl's ankles were puffy, too. Life in jail did not agree with pregnant women.

"How are you?" Mildred repeated.

"I am fine, Miss Mildred," Janie said with determination. She pressed a tissue to her mouth as if to stifle nausea.

"Still having morning sickness?" Mildred inquired.

Janie barely nodded, as if, yes, were no more significant than, no.

Mildred had seen this before—this resignation. She had seen it in young students she had tutored at home for a while, but they were, sometimes, terminally ill, and learning lessons had seemed pointless to both teacher and student. Her post-retirement effort to supplement her fixed income had quickly failed, and right afterwards, Fran had decided that they needed to open their booth at The Emporium.

"What does the doctor say?" Mildred asked, trying to sit back in her chair and adopt a posture of relaxed conversation. *Who was she fooling*? She wasn't sure how natural her smile appeared on her face. It didn't feel natural at all.

"The doctor says I am gaining too much weight. It is hard not to. The food here is mostly potatoes and meat. And processed cheese and peanut butter. And I eat it because I am hungry." Janie's gaze swept past Mildred as she surveyed the walls made of cinder blocks painted a grayish white. "I feel like a blimp."

Mildred asked the next question carefully. "Have you heard from anyone?"

She was tactfully referring to the man who had posed as Janie's husband. Janie had been arrested alone, newly pregnant, and because she and Mildred had bonded in the few days that she had been a guest in Mildred's home, the church lady had remained her only connection to the outside world.

"Have you heard from any of your family?" Miss Budge prompted hopefully.

The girl's eyes stayed dull. The hands holding wadded tissues moved to her belly and braced under it, as if she needed to hold her stomach up from resting too heavily upon her thighs. "My aunt in Georgia may come. She may take the baby."

"That's good, isn't it?"

Janie sighed noncommittally. Miss Budge could not read her thoughts. Something larger than the table between them separated them now.

Mildred waited to see if Janie wanted to say something more. She didn't. "Then you could go live with her when you are released in a few months. Maybe sooner, if the parole board will allow it. Is your lawyer helping you get ready for that?"

"He says I am to show signs of being sorry. To wear a good dress, not a sexy dress, on the day we go to the hearing. To get letters of support from a church." She looked over at Mildred meaningfully. "From the minister."

"I can get you a dress to wear to the parole hearing when that time comes, my dear. And I will. But we are between ministers right now," Miss Budge replied carefully. "You remember that, don't you?"

Janie stared back at the spot on the wall that had riveted her attention. The level of passivity was more than Mildred could bear. Her own current tension with Sam did not matter in that moment. "But maybe I could get Sam, one of our elders, to write a letter on your behalf to the board."

"I guess that would be okay," Janie said. And then she pulled her shoulders back. "How have you been?"

Mildred tried to think of something to say that would seem interesting. "I was in a car accident last Sunday," she remembered. The accident felt like it was a long time ago. Ancient history. But it had happened just two days before.

Janie studied her, checking for bruises. "You're okay though?" she asked.

Mildred offered a small laugh. "I am fine. It was more an adventure than anything else. I had to climb up a hill with a rope. Sam's car is totaled. Everything is back to normal now."

It was a lie. She had not meant to lie. The words flew out of her mouth automatically for courtesy's sake. *Small talk is dangerous, too. Nothing was back to normal.* Mildred was feeling things about Sam that she had never felt before. She had thrown a rock at the woman who had married Hugh Luckie. She knew moments of acute awareness—of abiding in a dimension of Jesus Saves that seemed rarefied and exquisite. The moments felt eternal and, simultaneously, fleeting. The paradox dumfounded her.

Janie's attention drifted and then returned. "Have you cooked that spoon bread yet?"

"No, I haven't made the spoon bread lately. I will make you some when you get out," Mildred promised as an atonement for telling the lie that all was the same as it had ever been.

The light came on in Janie's eyes. "You would really make me some spoon bread at your house? I could sit at your table again?" The girl leaned forward, and when she did, the light hit the girl differently. It exposed the beginning of crow's feet at the corners of her eyes.

They came to everyone, but Mildred hated it for her—for Janie, who was so young to have been lied to by a man who had left her pregnant. Abandoned her.

Mildred's heart ached for her. For her situation. For her youth. For the crow's feet. "Of course, my dear. I will make you some spoon bread, and you will sit at my table, and we will talk about anything and everything just as we did before."

But it wouldn't be as before. Trust had been broken.

The girl perked up briefly, patting her stomach as if to console the little baby in there whose father had deserted them both. She swallowed hard. "I have not seen my aunt in a very long time. I do not know what kind of mother she would be. She is younger than you are and has two children."

"I am sure she would love your baby," Mildred encouraged.

"My aunt would not be able to bring him to visit me. She couldn't, you know, living over in Georgia. And if I don't get paroled, my Little Mister will be almost a year old before I can have him back. If they will let me have him back. Will they let me have Little Mister back?" Janie looked at Mildred as if she could tell her exactly what would happen.

Mildred did not want to lie. But she didn't know what the truth was. "There is still time, my dear, to figure out what to do next. Take it one day at a time," Mildred said, regretting that she was speaking in clichés.

"One minute at a time, Miss Mildred," Janie clarified softly.

Mildred nodded consolingly, rising. If she were a different kind of church lady, she would have offered to pray with the girl. At the very least, Miss Budge knew that she should have quoted some Scripture that would not return void. But Miss Budge felt wordless, except for the clichés—empty of her own wisdom and sorrowful, because while she didn't like to say it out loud—Janie had touched her heart, and then broken it in a new way. It had been a surprising kind of heartbreak coming at the end of a period of refreshment that had consoled Mildred for the loss of her school children, offered her something else, and then broke her heart again. And Mildred Budge wasn't over it yet.

Janie stood up, too, when Mildred did, slowly. To compensate for her lack of spoken Scripture, Mildred attempted a reassuring embrace that the younger woman allowed. It was a clumsy hug, and Mildred wondered if there was any way to do anything right in a situation like this. The most she could manage was the forced bright promise that implied she would return and that sounded like a lie but it was not: "I will see you soon, Janie. And when it is time for you to wear a good dress, I will bring one."

It had not been a very good visit, but Janie asked, her voice achingly urgent, "You will come back?"

"I will not forget you, and I am sorry I keep calling you Janie. I know your name,"

Mildred promised, holding the girl's small swollen hand.

And the girl's eyes filled with tears. "I would rather be your Janie than anyone else," she said.

If Mildred had not known the girl to be a liar, she would have felt moved by the tears; but Mildred had been stung before, and she didn't trust them. She was sorry that she didn't trust Janie's tears—more sorry than she could say.

As the church lady left, she did not feel righteous or pleased with herself or aware that God was pleased with her for fulfilling the Scripture's admonition that she and the members of the Beloved remember those less fortunate whose sins had resulted in prison walls and chains.

When Mildred was back in her car, she thought about praying for the girl and all the other girls inside that complex of walls, but her desire to escape the situation was so great that she only tore away the parking pass from her dashboard and stopped long enough at the gate for the guard to examine her back seat and trunk. As soon as the electronic arm went up to allow her to leave, Miss Budge zoomed through, automatically choosing the right-hand turn at the corner, which was the wrong way to go. Relieved to be in motion, she drove off without a proper idea of her place or destination.

She wandered around for twenty minutes before she realized that she was thoroughly lost.

Only then did she ask God to help her find her bearings so she could go home. Carefully, she worked her way back to the prison; and as she passed it this time, she did pray at last but not with words. Her shoulders heaved, and the pain in her chest that had been heavy the day before came back and felt powerfully burdensome not just for the girl Janie, but for all the girls who had chosen a lie over the truth. And she moaned for the innocent baby and other babies who would be born in a prison not of their own making.

"God, please give Little Mister the right home and mother." And as the landmarks that felt familiar and comforting reappeared, she was dismayed to recall that she had forgotten to take Janie the requested Bible.

19

HELLFIRE PICKLES

Fran was in Mildred's kitchen stacking Mason jars when Mildred walked in. The countertop was loaded with two five-gallon jars of pickles, and there were boxes of pickling spices on the table. As if nothing very odd was going on, Fran loaded the granulated soap in the dishwasher's detergent dispenser, closed the appliance door securely, and pressed the "On" button. She picked up the cardboard box the Mason jars had come in, took it to the back door, and tossed it outside near the large green plastic trash can.

Mildred waited for Fran to explain.

Finally, Fran announced with a triumphant smile, "I called that woman and got the pickle recipe." Fran tidied a dish towel, hanging it over the edge of the sink to dry. Leaning with her back against the sink, Fran met Mildred's incredulous gaze. "Asking for a pickle recipe is not the same activity as circling her house like a vulture, trying to see if some poor widow woman has any extra jars of precious pickles made by her recently deceased husband who will never make another jar," Fran explained.

Mildred tried to process what she was hearing.

"You think I went too far, don't you?" Fran asked, crossing her arms.

Mildred looked once again at the two large jars of pickles. *Why were there so many pickles? Why weren't there cucumbers that would become pickles?*

"You got the pickle recipe," Mildred repeated dumbly, as she looked around at the clutter in her kitchen.

Fran's gaze followed Mildred's. "I will clean up this mess when we're done, really."

"I am not worried about the mess," Mildred said. "You actually called up a recent widow and asked her for her dead husband's pickle recipe while she was grieving."

Fran shrugged. "I didn't really think I was going to do that when I called her. I just called her, thinking I would let the conversation go where it would. Turned out she was lonely. We talked a good long while. His death was not a surprise. He had been sick for quite some time, but he refused to take to the bed. I told her I was a widow, too, and that I understood."

"How did you get to the point where you asked her for the secret recipe that was her family's means of earning money?"

"I told her I liked the pickles. I paused in case she wanted to offer me any remaining jars of pickles that could have been left for sale. When she didn't, I just asked casually for the recipe. She put me on hold. Went and got the recipe and read it to me on the spot. Is that so wrong?" Fran held out her hands innocently. "I mean—really. Our not ever eating again the best pickles ever invented by mankind does not help her in any way cope with her grief and loss."

"You have been volunteering for Hospice too long," Mildred said, sitting down heavily. The dishwasher was rumbling loudly. Mildred didn't recognize the sound. Fran read her mind and explained, "I have got the jars in there. I put it on the sanitize cycle."

"I did not know I had a sanitize cycle."

"It doesn't say that. The button reads, 'Dry heat.' In my mind, that's the sanitize cycle. When the jars are sanitized, I am going to fill them with my vinegar concoction and the spices, transfer the pickles from that jar to those jars, and fasten the lids.   We wait six weeks. Then, voila! Pickle heaven!"

Mildred focused on the big jars of pickles. "The Pickleman started with store-bought pickles, not cucumbers."

Fran nodded. "Yep. He didn't pickle them.   He just changed the taste of a pickle made by someone else. That is all."

"I paid five dollars a jar for his recycled store-bought pickles believing they were homemade?"

Fran nodded. "Now, don't you feel better about my asking her for the recipe?" Fran prompted. "I mean, really, it is not like it is some secret recipe that was passed down through their family. Actually, after she told it to me, I thought I remembered that I had read the same recipe in one of my cooking magazines. Only they called it something else. They called it something like "hell-fire pickles" which is, of course, why two upstanding church ladies like ourselves would never make them. But, after we make our first batch, we will call them quite simply "Sweet/ Sour Bread-and-Butter pickles". You mix up the spices, transfer the pickles from that big jar into the smaller jars, then wait six weeks. That is all there is to it."

"Six weeks," Mildred said. "I will have to make some room in the pantry."

"Don't worry about that," Fran said. "They need to sit in the dark. Let's put them in the guest room closet. They won't be in your way in there."

"You think of everything," Mildred said, but it didn't sound like a compliment.

"Well, don't eat any then, if you think I am so terrible," Fran said, growing offended.

"I don't think you're terrible," Mildred replied. "I have just come from visiting Janie in prison, and I have got a pulpit committee meeting tonight. Sam says that I owe Liz an apology--and I do. My actions have not been honorable. I would honestly rather be here transferring pickles from one jar to another with you than sitting at Liz's dining room table wondering if that bruise on her back is uncomfortable."

"You feel things too deeply, Millie. If you feel you must, just say you're sorry and get on with your life."

Mildred looked up at Fran. "Just say I am sorry and get on with my life," Mildred repeated. "It's that simple?"

"Of course, it's that simple. "Jesus makes life easy. He handled the suffering. We just have to admit we're wrong."

"I was wrong, and those are the best pickles I have ever tasted. And now we have got the recipe." Her face brightened, and Fran returned her grin.

"Yes, they are," Fran replied. "And we can make as many jars of pickles as we want. I love power."

"We're really going to have to wait six weeks before we can eat any?" Mildred asked.

Fran shrugged. "I can't do anything about that. Six weeks is how long it takes for them to marinate in the jars."

The dishwasher made a funny sound, and the two women turned toward it suspiciously. "I don't believe I have ever used that cycle before," Mildred said with a flash of concern. "Why didn't I see your car in my driveway?"

"I brought in the stuff and then parked my car down the street," Fran said as if that explanation made sense.

"And you are parked down the street because you don't want people who already know we are best friends to know you're at my house," Mildred concluded.

"Thinking I am here and knowing it are two different things," Fran said. "I am playing hard to get," Fran explained immediately. "Come to think of it. I am hard to get. Maybe I am impossible to get," she concluded, mildly surprised.

Mildred did not ask who Fran meant.

Fran turned, and the light caught her and her clear blue eyes were laughing. "Winston thinks he's in love with me big time, Millie. My old boy keeps asking me to marry him. And he said he wouldn't take no for an answer."

Mildred sat down hard on the kitchen chair she used when Fran was with her. She sat at the opposite end of the table when she was alone, but that was because she often liked to watch the evening news while she ate a light supper. When Fran was with her, she sat facing the sink and the stove because Fran was just as likely to be at the sink or the stove as she was.

"Winston said that he has simply made up his mind to marry me and that is that."

"He has made up his mind. I don't know how you can resist a sweet talker like that."

"It has been real hard," Fran said, shaking her head, and turning back to the pickles. "But I don't want to get married, Millie. I like my life just as it is. Still, it's something to think about. You can get set in your ways and miss an opportunity from God to change."

"Me, too," Mildred replied weakly.

"Why did you go to see Janie today of all days? I thought you didn't want to leave the house." Fran eyed the noisy dishwasher suspiciously and added, "I thought we had decided that I was going with you."

"Janie sent me a letter. I got it yesterday," Mildred said. "She has an aunt who might take her baby. She wanted to talk with me about that. And she will need a dress for her parole hearing. She also asked me for a Bible, but I forgot to take her one."

Fran sat down and listened.

"I love that child," Mildred said.

"You love everybody," Fran said.

"Some more than others and not Liz."

"I imagine you will get around to it. You usually do," Fran theorized softly.

Fran waited.

"I think Janie wants to come and live with me when she gets out of jail. She didn't say the words, but I think she wants that."

"With a baby?' Fran said. She struggled to keep the tone of her voice measured.

Mildred nodded succinctly. They each understood the problem. Christians are supposed to be hospitable.

"You don't want to live with her and a baby, do you?"

Mildred took a breath before answering. "I do not."

"We are in the same position. The details are different, but it's the same problem. I don't think I want to share my home life to that extent either," Fran said.

"Is that it? We don't want to share our lives?" Mildred replied.

"If we did, you and I would be sharing a house instead of paying double utilities. I am over here all the time. But I don't want to live here."

"I don't want you to live here," Mildred said. "But Winston wants to live with you."

Fran nodded and raised a hand of warning. "Just because I might be going crazy doesn't mean you need to go off the deep end and let that girl back in this house with a baby she's had by a man who is on the lam and could show up again anytime. You can be a Christian without being a fool."

The dishwasher began to scream softly, and the jars clanked inside. Mildred and

Fran looked at each other. Finally, Fran shrugged. "Que sera sera."

Whenever Fran started quoting Doris Day, Mildred changed the subject. "Sam says we women are jealous of Liz."

"He is probably right. Ordinarily, I don't care enough about other people to dislike them, but I really don't like Liz. There has to be a reason that I care enough not to like her."

"She did try to steal your Winston." Mildred declared.

"Did she? I really don't think that she is an intentional thief. She is more like a witless kleptomaniac who goes on her round of errands; and when she gets home, she finds stuff has come home with her."

"Like other women's men," Mildred said.

Fran nodded succinctly. "That she didn't mean to pick up, but she did."

The two women sat quietly for a moment listening to the dishwasher and surreptitiously glancing at the large pickle jars that they would need to open. Neither one of them had said the words yet, but there was a real possibility that they wouldn't be able to open the big jars of pickles.

The span of the jar's lid was almost bigger than the breadth of either woman's hand; and to break the airlock, they ideally needed to tip the jar over and rap it gently in circles on the floor. But it was heavy and holding it upside down would be awkward. If they dropped it and the jar broke, pickle juice would be all over the floor.

"So, do you think these pickles we make are going to be as good as the Pickleman's?" Mildred asked, as she got up and went to the silverware drawer. She found her biggest, sturdiest wooden spoon and walked over to the first giant jar of pickles. She began to rap on the edge of the lid, tapping methodically around its circumference.

Fran shook her head. "Nope. Food you make yourself is never as good as when someone else makes it. Am I going to have to call Winston to come over and open that jar?" Fran asked. That was the kind of favor that if one asked for in the midst of considering a marriage proposal would sound very much like a tentative, yes, I guess I will marry you if you promise to open all of my jars for the rest of my life in sickness and in health until death do us part.

Mildred rapped the jar hard two more times and then stretched her hand across the lid. It was an important move, like so many of the ordinary, daily tasks that single older women face each day. It was a battle every day to prove all day long that you could do everything that needed to be done, and to lose any battle—no matter how small-- signified the possibility that you could lose your independence and become someone others bossed around in an assisted living home—or worse.

Mildred thought suddenly of climbing up that hill Sunday afternoon with Jake on the other end of the rope pulling her up, and energy surged through her. Her hand stretched and gripped and twisted. The lid moved and then moved some more. Her hand twisted fast and hard as if she needed to do it in a hurry, and Fran grew quiet behind her, waiting for the moment of victory.

It came. Mildred lifted the lid and turned and showed it to Fran as if she hadn't been watching. By then, her best friend had imagined two kinds of futures: married or single. Mildred studied her eyes, but a veil came down over Fran's gaze as Mildred laid the lid on the counter. Had she saved her friend from the entrapment of matrimony or prevented her from making a call to Winston to come open that jar—a call that deep-down if Mildred were not watching and listening, she wanted to make?

Mildred did not know.

Maybe Fran didn't know herself, Mildred thought, as she headed toward her bedroom to change. "I have to go over to Liz's house for a meeting," Mildred reminded her. "Do whatever you want."

It was a strange parting sentence between two old friends who did not need to give each other permission to make herself at home in the house of her best friend.

THE ACHE OF GRIEF

Mildred stopped short of walking to the front door of Liz Luckie's house when she saw through the illuminated picture window in the living room two people standing too close together. She didn't have to look any harder to know it was Liz and Sam. Mildred felt the dull ache of grief over the foolishness of people and was just about to make herself walk up the front walkway when a voice came out of the darkness.

"Do you think she is going to kill Sam?" Belle asked and then appeared from the other side of a tree where she had been standing and watching the action inside the house.

Mildred considered her response carefully, then spoke, stepping closer to her good friend who was masked by the shadows of late twilight. "Sam knows Liz's reputation."

Belle was unapologetic about being in front of Liz's house checking up on her husband. Still, she offered an explanation. "Sam said he had a meeting, but he didn't tell me that it was at Liz's house. He kind of let me think it was going to be at the church. He mentioned you a lot."

"He is not very happy with me right now," Mildred said, and instantly regretted it because Belle might ask why, and Mildred didn't want to tell her why. She didn't have to.

"I heard you hit Liz with a rock because she wouldn't jump the ravine," Belle said quietly.

Mildred didn't know what to say in response, so she simply stepped closer to her friend. They watched what was happening on the other side of the living room window. Sam threw his head back and guffawed, and Liz patted him intermittently on the forearm, laughing brightly.

"Do you think she seduces men on purpose, or is the way she talks—that on-going flirtation with them-- the only way she knows how to communicate with men?" Belle asked, her voice tinged with sorrow and curiosity.

"How lonely would you have to be to do that?" Mildred replied.

"Bless her heart," Belle said firmly.

"Yes, bless her heart," Mildred agreed. "How long are you going to wait before you say something to Sam?"

"I don't know exactly what I am going to do. Not tonight when Sam comes home. Not tomorrow when my husband wakes up. Did

Sam come and see you early yesterday morning?" Belle asked suddenly, turning in the shadows.

"Yes," Mildred replied carefully. "Sam came to tell me about the meeting tonight."

Belle nodded seriously. She had expected Mildred to say 'no.' It would be a terrible thing to live with someone who told you where he was going and then not know for sure whether he was telling the truth or not. "He could have called you about that," Belle said. "He left so early," she added, but she dismissed the questions that arose from that curiosity. She wasn't worried about his meetings with Mildred. She was watching Sam flirting with Liz.

"My old honey has been restless for a long time. And now he doesn't have a car. He just walks out the door, and I don't hear a car leave. I don't know when he's going—or that he's gone—and then I discover he's not home. I wonder why he hasn't told me, and when I ask him, he gets mad and says he did, too, tell me—like he wants me to think I am going crazy, but I am not going crazy, Millie. Sam did not tell me he was going to your house. He just went outside to get the morning newspaper, and he didn't come back for a good long while." Belle looked at Mildred, frustration lining her face.

"Mildred, I came over here this morning, too. This is my second time over here today on foot. Can you believe it? I am checking up on Sam!"

"He was at my house for a few minutes yesterday," Mildred confirmed delicately. "We had coffee." Now she knew why Sam had left by her front door. He could have gone anywhere after he left Mildred's and Belle couldn't see which direction. Mildred turned and studied Sam through the window.

"Sam drinks too much coffee," Belle replied automatically, and Mildred wondered if she said that often to Sam. Mildred had seen wives whose husbands retired start watching their husbands' diets more closely and, in the watching, shift almost without knowing it from being a caregiver to a judge of their husbands' behaviors and natures and habits, until both the husband and the wife were at odds all the time, with neither of them understanding exactly why they were so tense with each other.

A retired husband could get too much attention from a wife, and the wife of a retired husband often wondered why he didn't want the attention he had once craved. Men didn't like being judged or watched, and women often couldn't see that they sounded more like they were judging their men rather than giving care.

"Sam is afraid these days of being older, and he is willing to be distracted from that reality," Belle assessed, and her voice felt as soft as the shadows that the early evening was creating around them.

"This ridiculous business won't last long," Mildred promised. "Sam is the kind of man who faces up to the truth eventually. I don't think he even knows he's doing anything wrong. It will come to him in time," Mildred said.

Belle nodded wordlessly, slipping into an interiority of married life that was distinctly her own: her private life. That still existed for some people in a society where many people blurted out anything at all about the deepest, most private aspects of their lives.

"Will you be okay?" Mildred asked, thinking it was time she went inside and stopped those two from getting into worse trouble. Besides, the sooner they got the meeting started, the sooner it could be finished and she could go home. She needed to tell God the truth about her day, and that always took a lot of time.

"Look at him," Belle said in response.

Mildred followed her friend's gaze, watching Liz and Sam through the window.

"She is acting like a hostess. He is acting like the head of the committee. And I am acting like a fool. I know how I am acting, Millie," Belle declared. "But look at him. Look at her. Swishing her hair and fluffing it with her fingertips, and my old honey keeps checking his belt buckle to see if it's tight enough and trying to hold in his stomach and occasionally he puffs up his chest, like a rooster. And each one of them is in there thinking—who knows what they're thinking? —but they believe they have nothing to hide—don't even know their own secrets. Yet, there they are, in full view of the world on the verge of having what people call an affair."

"I don't think it will come to that," Mildred murmured automatically, consolingly.

Belle stifled a bitter laugh as down the street a car turned the corner and headed slowly their way.

The headlights attracted Mildred. She turned toward them briefly and then back to Belle. "That's probably Jake."

"Do you think he knows?"

Mildred considered saying something neutral, then knew better. "He saw them." It was enough to tell.

That revelation startled Belle. "So, it has gone far enough so that another man can see it?"

She didn't have to add: men only see what's plain in front of them. They're not like women. If a man sees it....

Mildred nodded in the shadows.

"That's pretty far," Belle said, and a fresh mourning filled her voice.

A kind of mourning that might kill her, Mildred thought.

"I wondered. But I didn't know. Pitiful," Belle added. "We're all pitiful."

Jake steered into the driveway.

"He is going to see me standing here like this talking to you and looking through the window."

"Jake doesn't talk."

"Mildred, it hurts. I am standing here talking to you, but it hurts. It hurts to know you know. It hurts to know Jake knows."

Mildred reached over and patted Belle's back, then put an arm around her and hugged her lightly. "Trouble passes."

The car door of the silver Expedition Jake was driving slammed as he got out. Sam and Liz looked up at the sound but from their position they could not see Jake yet in the driveway or Mildred's car on the street.

Jake was about to call out, raised his hand in a big wave when he realized who Mildred was standing next to; and with a sudden flash of understanding, he simply nodded, and said, "Good evening."

He looked at the front door and then at them, and decided he belonged with Belle and Mildred. Belle backed up to hide in the shadows of the tree.

The front door opened and Liz appeared. "What are you two doing out there? People are going to start talking about you two if you don't come inside," Liz teased, and in spite of her own extended period of repentance, Mildred thought: *If I had a rock....*

Both Jake and Mildred forced a smile while Belle retreated behind the tree. Belle hissed, "Don't let on I'm here. Please."

Jake called back. "Budge and I will be there in a minute. She's broken her leg, and I'm setting it."

Liz understood his meaning: *'Go on.'* Offended, she closed the door loudly.

"I've broken my leg?" Mildred asked after Liz had retreated. "That was the best you could do?"

"Let them figure that out. Hello, beautiful Belle," Jake said. Then he did something churchmen didn't often do. Jake Diamond leaned over and kissed an elder's wife on the cheek. It was a consoling kiss—a kind of prayerful event that made Mildred Budge want to say "Amen."

"How are you feeling, love?" Jake asked.

"Rattled," Belle replied, reaching out her hand, and he took it. "Thank you—thank you for not letting them know I am here."

"Your old man is giving you a bad time," Jake said, and he smiled warmly as if to reassure her that what was bothering Sam wasn't worse than a case of flu and that he would recover.

Mildred was surprised that Jake spoke of Sam's indiscretion openly, but he was right, she saw. Belle needed the truth more than she needed her feelings protected, though she was not ready yet to face Sam and Liz. Men were different. Sometimes the way men saw the world was direct, tactless and refreshing.

"You walked?" Jake asked. He looked behind her and saw only Mildred's car.

"I've taken to walking in the early evening while Sam does his phone calls," Belle explained.

"He does phone calls," Mildred repeated the words.

"Then, he turns on the news channel and falls asleep in front of the TV, and...." Belle's voice trailed off as if there was no point in saying that each evening had become that routine—of living separate lives under the same roof with Sam's focus on anything but Belle.

"You want me to take you home, love?" Jake asked.

Mildred thought she would say no, but Belle surprised her.

"I am quite tired. Very tired," Belle admitted. "What would you tell them about being gone for ten minutes?"

"I wouldn't tell them anything. Why should we have to explain ourselves to them?" Jake replied. "You stand there a minute, and I'll bring my car alongside the street here, so you can get in. Mildred will go in and distract them."

"Just take my car," Mildred said, handing him her keys. "It's already on the street." She didn't add that none of the neighbors would think anything of her red and black mini-Cooper sidling up in front of the Deerborn house and letting Belle out. That big Expedition would attract interest and commentary. Jake understood and took Millie's keys. Belle had almost evaporated into the shadows when her voice reached Mildred again. "Sam is not as terrible as he looks right now.   He has got some kind of amnesia. It's like he has forgotten who he is."

"That is right," Jake assured her. "But your old man will remember in time. I am going to get you home, and then I will come back and take care of business here."

Neither woman knew exactly what Jake meant by that, but they were both glad to hear him say the words.   Women happily wait upon men who know how to take care of business—and do.

"Hey, Budge. When you go inside..." Jake began.

Mildred turned and waited.

"Limp."

21

MEETIN' TIME

Liz and Sam were very busy being busy.

Wearing his standard light-blue golf shirt though he didn't play golf, Sam was rotating his yellow folders around and making sudden important notes on little yellow Post-it pad sheets when an idea came to him. Then, he peeled the notes off, pointed, and Liz took them and stuck them on the correct folders.

She twinkled while she worked. The ruffled cuffs of her white blouse occasionally needed to be shaken back out of the way of her managing the notes. She kept offering small waves of her hand to move the cuffs back, and when she did the five diamond-bedecked silver bracelets she wore jangled. The serial widow was a very able assistant.

Mildred had three yellow Post-it notes on the front of her folder, and Jake had five.

Mildred had been watching the process since she had entered the room, when Sam had said, gruffly, "Take a load off." He was not intentionally rude. That was the way Sam spoke sometimes. There was no sign that he was still mad at her about throwing a rock at Liz.

For her part, Liz was sitting toward the front of her high-backed chair at the dining room table, and Mildred did wince when she realized that Liz most likely couldn't lean back with a bruise the size of a rock on her back.

Liz reached across the table and slid a paper napkin in Mildred's direction. It was not a cheap napkin either—the kind for which you spend three dollars to get five hundred, so you won't have to buy more napkins for at least six months. It was an oversized white napkin with a delicate, almost indiscernible flower pattern. The kind of napkins Liz Luckie bought cost three dollars plus for a package, and you only got eighteen napkins. Entertain a messy eater, and you would run out of napkins in one sitting. Good stewards of their money did not spend $3 on 18 napkins. Liz did.

No one condemned her for it, however, because Liz Luckie, a well-off widow, simply did not have to count pennies or clip coupons. "Those shortbread cookies have cranberries and walnuts in them," Liz promised.

When Mildred touched it, the napkin felt almost like cloth. It was that thick, that soft. Mildred considered the possibility that Liz might have paid more than three dollars for a package of napkins. Mildred rubbed it between her forefinger and thumb. 'Maybe she had spent even more. Five dollars? Six dollars? Who spends money like that?'

"They are one of the best cookies you will ever eat," Liz promised.

Mildred recognized the tone of voice and the gambit instantly. A small number of thin women in the church talked about desserts that same way. They were women who didn't really like to eat but knew the right words to say to trigger other people's appetites. They were pretending to be like people who have a hearty appetite for food, but they were thin eaters, which was all right. Only they encouraged other people to overeat.

Mildred took the napkin and politely picked up a cookie. "Did you bake them?" Mildred asked automatically. She wasn't intentionally throwing another kind of rock, but the question landed with a thud.

Liz cast an irritated glance at Mildred. "I use a woman who specializes in baking deluxe cookies. She has time to cook," Liz explained with a dismissive wave of her right bejeweled hand. "She pipes cheese straws, too, if you ever need them."

"If I ever need cheese straws, I go over to Richardson's Pharmacy and buy some. Mrs. Richardson always has what I need," Mildred replied, nibbling on the deluxe gourmet cookie. It was delicious. Very delicious. Mildred took another bite. It was almost the best cookie she had ever eaten. Then, she encountered a small chunk of white chocolate. Yes, it was the best cookie she had ever eaten.

"Have another one," Liz urged. "Don't leave them here for me to eat tomorrow. I don't need the calories."

Size small women never did.

Size large women looked ahead to the next day when a deluxe shortbread cookie made with cranberries and white chocolate would be very welcome indeed. Mildred wanted another cookie.

"I hate for them to go to waste," Mildred said, taking two more and placing them on the napkin near her folder. Maybe she could create a small collection of them; and when it was time to leave, she could simply fold up the napkin and discreetly take them home. Even as her brain created that plan, Mildred felt unfaithful to her friend Belle and uncomfortable that Fran might find out that she was eating these cookies, which did not stop her. They were very good cookies.

Sam interrupted. "We don't need to be talking about food. You women are always talking about food. Where is Jake? We've got to get down to business."

Mildred bowed her head instinctively, thinking that Sam would lead them in a prayer for guidance; but Sam picked up his mechanical pencil and pointed instead to the first item on his agenda. "I think we have seen enough to go forward in the hiring process."

Sam cleared his throat as if expecting one of the women to interrupt him, but neither did. It didn't occur to Liz, and Mildred, for a moment, simply did not believe what she was hearing. No discussion. No plan to go and hear Steev preach. Just decide—and without Jake present yet to vote or offer his input.

"We have heard two men preach, and we have met the other one who is obviously too young, so I am logically wondering if we even need to try and go hear him. Steev has met us. The boy saw our church; and if the kid has got half a brain in his head, he knows we are not a good match. So, I am thinking that we either need to go to the second tier of candidates if what we need is another candidate to consider...." Sam stopped and looked at Liz, who dutifully shook her head, no, and then at Mildred, whose face registered nothing because she was trying to figure out what was going on.

None of what Sam was saying was making any sense. 'What about the hiring procedure? What about praying through the issue? What about Jake's opinion?' Mildred cast a quick glance at the front door, willing Jake to appear and take care of business.

"Or we can hash it out among ourselves tonight and try to choose one of the first two guys to be our guy. Didn't we all like both of them, you know, basically?" Sam prompted.

A sharp rap on the front door stopped the women from answering. The members of the pulpit committee turned and looked at the front door when Jake let himself in.

Out of the shadows now, Mildred could see that he was wearing tan exercise clothes, the kind that joggers wore. He smiled warmly, gave a reassuring nod to Mildred that Belle had been delivered discreetly and safely home, and then asked, "What have I missed?"

Sam stifled irritation that had been with him toward Jake since the accident, when the younger man had taken charge so ably. "I was just explaining to the ladies that we have got two viable men as candidates, and it is time to choose one. Either one of them would most likely work out fine, but you all know where I stand."

Jake sat down, flashed a quick smile at Liz, who automatically fluttered in return, and asked innocently, "Which two men do you mean?" And then without waiting for Liz to offer, Jake snagged a cookie and said in an uncanny imitation of a cowboy to Liz, "Hello, Darlin'."

Liz's face registered confusion because up to that moment Jake had maintained a decided reserve toward her. He popped the whole cookie in his mouth and chewed, somehow managing to let his eyes keep smiling. Mildred was puzzled, and Liz was looking hurriedly at Sam, who was married, and then back at Jake who was not.

"I was saying that we have two men who would be a fine fit at Christ Church. Steev is too young, as we all know."

Jake spoke while still chewing. "I don't know that. Do you know that Liz?" Jake's merry forest-green eyes connected with hers and held on. Liz smiled at Jake, trying to read his mind but she could not.

"I was just trying to save us some time and some gasoline. I mean—really—do we need to go hear the boy preach this Sunday when it is obvious that he is too young for the job?" Sam asked, his voice testy.

"He does have a great deal of energy that younger men often have," Jake replied, looking about for something to drink. "I work on a college campus, and we appreciate the energy of the young there." Jake grinned. The implications hung in the air.

This time Liz read his mind and went to the kitchen and brought out a glass carafe of water with slices of lemon and ice cubes floating in it. They weren't ordinary square ice cubes. They were little frozen flower-shaped ice cubes that were melting slowly. Wordlessly, she poured Jake a glass, and he took it, his fingertips grazing her hand as he accepted the glass. Jake held up his drink in a toast to Liz and then drank it all in one big gulp. Liz stood nearby and refilled his glass while he smiled at her, his eyes sending some kind of message that was making Mildred nervous. Mildred pushed her saved cookie on its napkin away from her two inches.

When Jake did speak, his answer was firm. "No, I disagree with you, Sam. We need to go hear Steev preach. It is the right thing to do."

"That is an absolute waste of time and gasoline," Sam replied, sitting back in his chair. His hands rested on the arms of the chair, like a commander at his post. "I made a mistake when I let the kid's name get to the top tier. I was trying to be open-minded about the young when I should have tried to be sensible instead. I am sorry about that. It is my fault entirely, but we should just move forward now. At this point, I don't know about you all, but I am ready to wind things up."

That answer startled Mildred. "What do you mean? You should never have let his name go to the top tier?"

Sam waved his hands skyward. "The boy was a convenient candidate. He was close enough to drive to hear, and we needed a third candidate to round things out, but you have to know—and agree with me because I am right--the boy is too young to lead a congregation our size and age. He has just barely graduated from being a youth minister. Look at the stupid way he spells his name."

Mildred wondered about that, and instantly deduced Sam's master plan. Positioning a candidate who was too young in Sam's view into the top tier was one of the ways the efficient Sam Deerborn had planned to manipulate the outcome of the pastor selection.

She studied Sam with fresh regard, realizing in an instant that Sam had already decided that the first man they had heard preach was the one he wanted for Christ Church. He had always planned to discount Steev, and then they would have been left with two real candidates in his eyes; and at best, the vote would have split as it did 2-2, with Liz voting with Sam.

But Sam had not believed there would be a tie. *But why not?* Mildred wondered, and then she knew. Sam had counted on both women voting with him—Liz and his old friend Mildred Budge. Sam was not worried about what Jake thought.

In fact, she understood instantly. If Jake had cast a lone dissenting vote making him an outsider that would have suited Sam just fine. Mildred studied Sam and wondered if she had ever really known her old friend.

"We can't just dismiss Steev as a viable candidate because going to hear him preach is more work than you want to do," Jake argued, leaning forward with his elbows on the table.

No one had ever talked to Sam like that in front of Mildred Budge. Jake's gaze met Mildred's for an instant, and he offered her the quickest of winks.

Disoriented, Liz did the unthinkable. She reached out and took one of her own cookies. She bit into it the way she always bit into food in public so that her lipstick would be spared: teeth bared, her lips were pulled back, like a tigress attacking her food.

The expression on her face startled Mildred, and Jake's eyes widened involuntarily.

Sam's voice was steely. "I am not afraid of the work. I just think we should be as efficient as possible, and it is clear to me—and it should be clear to everyone that the boy is too young. All that praise singing in the van on our way home. That is way too much noise for me and for the people of Christ Church. And think back. He was wearing blue jeans at a time when he thought he might meet the members of the pulpit committee."

"He looked good in his jeans," Liz offered, taking another cookie and placing it on her napkin as if she were only going to admire it from afar. Then, temptation took hold, and she bit again as she said, "Jake has a point, Sam. We should go hear Steev preach. It is the least we can do. After he came all that way on Sunday and rescued us."

"He will have his reward in heaven for that," Sam said, undeterred. "I don't have a car now, and the church van is used to pick up old people on Sunday."

Liz considered that point. "We could go in my car, but I don't want to be the one who drives."

No one seemed to hear Liz.

Sam said, "Mildred, your car is too small for four people."

Mildred didn't argue. Her red mini-Cooper was petite, but four people could actually sit cozily in it.

"Jake drives a truck."

"I have an Expedition, too. It is parked in your drive right now. I just don't drive it much since the price of gas went up, but we can take it," Jake replied. "I drove it over here tonight because it needed a run. A road trip would be good for it. I will pick you all up this Sunday morning, and we will go hear Steev preach." Grinning, Jake added, "I won't charge the church for gas or mileage. I will just wait for my reward until I get to heaven." Jake's voice had a note of jocularity in it, but sternness too, as if he were daring Sam to find another reason not to go hear Steev preach.

"I don't think mocking the Lord is the way to arrange this trip," Sam replied coldly. He looked to Liz for agreement, but she was staring out the front window.

"Do you all see something out there?" Liz asked, rising. She walked across the living room and stared transfixed through the front window that faced the street.

Mildred stared, her attention snagged. She thought for an instant that she had seen a whirlpool of light, but it must have been only the reflected headlights from a car as it passed by.

"It must be my eyes. I see things out of the corner of my eyes a lot," Liz said in a troubled voice.

Jake leaned forward and sought Liz's attention. When she finally turned toward him, he said, "How about it, Liz? You want to go for a ride with me on Sunday?"

Jake's gaze was warm and friendly, his smile encouraging. Liz couldn't help herself. She smiled back at him, stifled a giggle, and said, "I don't see why not."

That surprised Sam. And angered him. He began to stack his folders noisily. "It is a waste of time, and we need to get down to the business of hiring a new man because I am about ready to turn over some of this day-to-day work to him."

It was something Sam said often. It was the kind of comment any veteran in the church might make from time to time when his season on a certain committee or with the choir had come to a close. Church work often had a season. Over the years, Mildred had learned to respect it—allowing the seasons to teach her in one more way that letting go of a job at church was as righteous a work as volunteering in the first place.

"After the last time, I said to myself, 'Never again.' Serving on the pulpit committee is a thankless task."

"We could dissolve this committee and appoint a new one," Jake suggested. "If you really think that is true."

Sam sputtered. "Of course not. We will get the job done no matter what, but I think this trip you want to take next Sunday is busy work. That is all it is. I don't have a lot of time for busy work anymore."

Mildred wondered if that were true.

Sam often said he was ready to turn over much of the administrative chores to a new preacher, but the last two preachers had each had a hard time weaning Sam away from being in the church office every morning. Sam regularly volunteered to be the person who communicated with the church as a whole on behalf of the preacher.

The other elders who were not retired from their day jobs had come to depend upon Sam to represent their central, collective view. After a while, it seemed like Sam was the Chief Executive Officer of the church's elders. When asked, Sam said he had the gift of "helps."

Mildred saw the truth about Sam suddenly, just like that. She saw that Sam had been controlling the church for years; and all that time, he was complaining about the work.

Something inside of her rebelled.

"I will be ready Sunday morning, Jake. Thanks for driving. Sam, if you don't want to go, just say so. Maybe you ought to stay home with Belle anyway," Mildred said.

Sam's head whipped around, and he glared at Mildred. "Belle is doing all right. The doctors can't find anything wrong with her, and I am beginning to believe that whatever is wrong with her is all in her head."

Liz studied the table top. Spying a few cookie crumbs, she reached out with one hand and began to dust them toward her other open hand.

"I hate leaving the church on its own again so soon," Sam explained, making one last pitch to not go on the trip.

"The church will survive our absence. We could all have gotten killed last Sunday, and the church would have gone on very well without us," Mildred replied.

"Spoken like someone who doesn't understand responsibility," Sam replied, and then realized that he had said what he was thinking out loud.

Mildred pushed back from the table. "I worked for twenty-five years teaching other people's children, and I do understand responsibility, Sam."

"You know me better than that, Mildred. I didn't mean that the way it sounded."

"I think you said exactly what you meant," Mildred replied, standing up. The legs of her chair scraped loudly on the floor, surprising her and everyone.

"Watch out now," Jake said, rising to his feet more calmly. "Let's not end the evening like this."

Sam remained seated. "Mildred Budge, you know very well that men and women have different responsibilities in the church and that yours are not as important as mine."

Mildred placed a hand on the table and considered carefully her reply. "I didn't know that a hand was more important than a foot. I thought we all had our good works to do and that none of us was in a position to assign importance. But let's see. We women teach the very young. We women tend the very old. We women handle weddings and visit shut-ins. Is any of that work less important than anything you men do?"

"Hold on," Sam said, raising both hands. "You don't have to tell me—me! —what you women do. I know what you women do. But, and with all respect due the lesser sex, Mildred, you don't handle the money, you don't teach adult classes with men and women, and there's a reason for that. Women don't understand men, which is what you're giving a good example of right now. Are you having one of your hot flashes?" Sam attempted one of his short laughs, but the hawking sound ricocheted in the room with a hollow effect that made Mildred want to sit back down and cry for him. And Belle.

She didn't though. "Am I?" and her voice rose.

"Men have a greater responsibility, and it says so in the Bible when it tells women to submit to the authority of men. I am wondering why you are having such a hard time doing that right now. You are old enough to have learned and accepted this lesson. Why don't you just sit down and be quiet until we get this whole business settled?"

"I thought it was settled," Jake said, interrupting.

Sam looked distant, almost as confused by what he had said as Mildred was that her long-time friend had said it.

"Did you tell me to be quiet?" Mildred asked, disbelieving.

Something outside caught Liz's attention, and she went over to the window again, staring, transfixed by what she saw outside as the night grew darker. "Who saw that? Did anyone else see it?"

No one answered her.

"We are riding in Jake's car Sunday to go hear Steev preach, and then we will vote after we have heard all of the candidates that you have allowed to be in the top tier. What I would like for you to explain is why none of us had a vote on which of the candidates became the three in the top tier," Mildred said.

Sam's eyes flashed while his voice carried an intensity that was new to Mildred. He controlled his speech, fighting against the tone rising. "Why should all of you have to waste your time previewing all the candidates? I winnowed them out because I know what we need. I was saving you the trouble."

"That is not the kind of good work for which there is a reward in heaven. I think you were doing more than that," Mildred said. "You know, I used to hear so many people rumble from time to time that you were trying to run the church. I always said, not really, that you were just a hard worker. I am beginning to think I have been wrong about a number of things, and one of them is you."

"If you are not happy with the way things are at Christ Church, you are free to go to any church you like," Sam replied. "It wouldn't surprise me what you might do next. Nothing about you has surprised me since you got lazy and quit your teaching job too soon. That is a clear indication to me that you are spoiled.

"And you are hard-headed, Mildred. You can't admit when you are wrong, which happens more often than you know, because people don't tell you. They just let you have your way. You are like too many women at church these days who have too much time on their hands.

"The Bible has a lot to say about that! This sad state of affairs has arisen because we have been without a strong man at the helm of our church too long, and you are making it worse by postponing hiring the right man.

A young boy like Steev will be run over by you women, and don't think I don't know that. You women will mother-hen him to death, and he will end up doing whatever you women tell him to do. The church will go down the tubes because the line of authority will be messed up by you women if we hire that boy."

"Why do you all keep calling Steev a boy? He is in his thirties, isn't he?" Liz asked from the window, but no one paid any attention to her question.

"Do you really mean everything you just said, Sam?" Mildred's voice was incredulous with surprise. The Sam she knew did not talk like that. Belle's husband never sounded like that.

Mildred spoke slowly, trying to figure out what was happening. "I am supposed to show my respect for your authority by just agreeing with everything you say?"

Sam stared at her hard, as if he were waiting for her to make a real point.

Mildred shook her head tiredly and picked up her purse. Sam was right about one thing. There was another church on a different corner, and she could just join it. One of the perks of living in the Bible-belt was there were plenty of churches on plenty of corners.

"Oh, Mildred Budge, stop being so perverse," Sam said, slamming his fist on the table. "You need to go get you some fresh hormones, because you're sounding like a crazy lady."

"I am crazy! I am perverse...." Mildred sputtered, "because I don't automatically agree with you about everything. And especially about this young preacher. You took a dislike to him because he rescued us after you ran us off a small cliff, which is what the truth is, and that is the real reason you don't want him. He has seen you as someone who drove us off that embankment, and it would be practically impossible for you to control someone that you won't have your bluff in on. You don't have your bluff in on Steev. That's enough of a reason right there to hire him."

Sam stifled one of his harsh chortles. His eyes gleamed angrily, and he sat back his chair and coolly replied, "You might want to stop talking because you are just setting yourself up for a major time of repentance later, Mildred. You know that parable about a speck and a plank."

"Which one of us has the plank in our eye, Sam?"

He adjusted his glasses, pressed them up further on his nose, and replied, "I can see just fine."

"And I see that this is getting way out of hand," Jake interrupted. "You two need to cool down and make up so we can finish the work of this committee," Jake suggested. He nodded seriously to Mildred. "Okay, one of you needs to say you are sorry."

"Sorry for telling the truth? Not yet," Mildred flashed.

Sam raised his hands as if to indicate `See what I mean? You can't reason with a woman.'

"Did any of you see that?" Liz said suddenly, loudly. She was still looking out the front window. "I mean—really—it was like a bunch of shooting stars all at once. But stars don't do that. Stars don't fall in a cluster."

"You need to go to the eye doctor," Sam advised distractedly. "I told you that before."

Liz ignored him. Whatever was outside had held her attention at the front window, and she stood still, peering into the dark neighborhood.

"I think we ought to end tonight's meeting with prayer," Jake suggested.

Liz did not return to her own table. Something outside had magnetized her.

"You could come back over here, Liz, and we could join hands."

Liz did not reply.

Neither Mildred nor Sam reached out to each other.

Jake prayed standing with his eyes open. "Lord, we need help and we need mercy and we need to be reminded that you are in charge. Amen," he said.

"Amen, and amen," Sam said, shuffling his folders. "I will see you Sunday, Lord willing."

"Lord willing," Liz repeated dutifully, as Mildred crossed the room first and left without saying good-bye and without any cookies.

Jake was close behind her, catching up with her as she reached the sidewalk. "What is up with you tonight, Budge? Why did you let Sam get under your skin like that?"

Mildred turned impatiently. "What are you doing—leaving them alone in there?"

"Isn't that what you're really mad about, Budge?" Jake asked. "You're mad at him for his disloyalty to Belle and are saying it this other way?"

"Am I?' Mildred asked, staring back at the window through which she could see Sam talking and talking and Liz listening, leaning forward as if Sam were the most interesting person in the world.

"Do you think that women are second-class citizens in the church?" Mildred demanded.

Jake took his time before answering. The evening was rich in tea olive and honeysuckle and starlight.

Jake answered finally. "I think anyone who is focused on making sure other people remember that they are supposed to be submissive for any reason other than respect and love doesn't get who Jesus is."

"Jesus," Mildred repeated emphatically, and when she did, she realized that even though she disagreed with Sam about many things, her old friend had been right after all: she was overdue for a long spell of telling God the truth about her heart and what she had been thinking.

"I am going home," Mildred announced.

"Do you want me to follow you?" Jake asked, handing her the keys to her car which he had hidden in his pocket after taking Belle home.

"I have been getting home by myself for most of my life," Mildred said tiredly. "What was going on with you—smiling at Liz and .... all of that?"

"I thought maybe I could become a distraction from Sam. It was just an idea," Jake added lamely.

"You were throwing yourself on a live grenade," Mildred said, feeling on her key chain for the ignition key.

"It's early. You want some coffee—or something?" Jake asked.

She shook off the idea. "I'm ready to lock myself in my house," she replied, and headed toward her car. Jake watched her, marveling that Mildred walked with such a purpose even just going home.

It was only when she was behind the wheel and halfway down the block that she understood what he had been telling her in that question. Jake had something else he wanted to say to her, and he had not wanted to go home before saying it. Only then did she wonder what it was.

22

AFTER CHURCH

Jake grinned when she opened the front door. "I was worried that you might have broken your leg," he jibed. "So, I have come over to check on you."

Mildred considered trying to laugh lightly in response, but she had never been able to do that upon command, so she did not try. She also didn't want to tell him the truth of why she had skipped Wednesday night church. The truth was that her life called for extended periods of silence in prayer and immersion in the Scriptures in order for her to feel whole and safe. There was no one else who could do that for you; and if she did not devote herself to that good work, the work of preserving her personhood with integrity did not get done. She had been in prayer for several hours which is why she had missed church, and she wasn't finished praying yet. Emerging from that deep place of solitude, she said only, her hands plucking self-consciously at the red jersey pants that she was very sorry to be wearing, "Something came up."

"Budge, you've had enough of Sam—and probably bossy men—for a while," Jake explained for her, as he stepped into the living room without waiting to be invited. He was wearing the same tan exercise outfit. He had paid more than three dollars for his pants. There was one of those little insignias on it that indicated he was serious about being athletic.

"You moving out or moving in?" Jake asked, looking around the sparsely furnished living room.

Mildred followed the movement of his gaze, pleased by how empty the front living room had become. She thought of it as lighter. Cleaner. Her living room was emptier of furniture than it was full. She liked the emptiness very much.

"Ever since we opened our booth at The Emporium, I find myself taking over pieces of furniture to add to the inventory. It has been wonderful to get rid of so much stuff," she added, with satisfaction.

"Are you going to replace any of it?" Jake asked as he assessed the minimal seating options. There was only the couch now and one chair that faced it.

Mildred studied the empty spaces where two chairs, an end table, and a small bookshelf had once been. "When I think about it, I wonder: do I need anything else to dust? The answer is, no."

"You'll come around," Jake said with good humor as he lowered himself to one end of the sofa. His was an indolent ease—the kind that American men are supposed to emanate and which few did.

Mildred admired the way Jake seemed to feel inside his body. Easy. Like he trusted himself. She had read a book once that theorized that the popular crooners from the fifties were singing songs written by Jewish immigrants who had envisioned the kind of American man they wanted to be.

The vision of some song-writing immigrants was of a man at ease with himself and his environment. She studied Jake, wondering if black men dreamed that, too. Was Jake the kind of man who even thought of himself in those terms? How long did one have to categorize someone else as a black man or a white woman? When would it be all right to just think, Jake? Mildred.

Mildred sat down on the other end of the sofa as Jake pointed a hand at the empty house across the street. "How long has that bungalow been for sale?"

"Two years," she said. "Ever since Mr. Garvin died. There was a family living there for a while. But they're gone now. I don't know what's going to happen over there," she said. She felt a pang of discord. It grieved her to see the house empty.

"The real estate market hasn't recovered yet. But that has been good for us at the university. When economic times are bad, the local university benefits because parents keep their kids home, but they still want them to attend college," Jake said as if Mildred didn't know that.

She did know that. She smiled, still dwelling in that remembered silence where purity and love could grow. Jake was trying to make conversation. Men didn't do that very often. She was grateful.

"Enrollment at the university is up." Jake gave her a thumbs up, and he grinned again.

He waited for her to ask something else, but she couldn't. The lingering silence of extended prayer held her close. Her eyes smiled for her but she didn't have any small talk to offer.

"The cat problem got solved," he reported, filling her silence. "You were right. The teachers were glad to get rid of the sand boxes. The cats don't bother the children now, and everybody thinks I am a genius."

She smiled and answered slowly, her voice sounding hoarse in her own ears. "I'm glad. It wasn't much of a problem."

"It was for me," Jake said, as his greenish-brown eyes grew more amused. "Are you going to offer me something to drink?" His eyes teased her.

"What would you like?" she asked automatically, thinking that she had lemonade, water, and she could make some coffee.

"I don't care. Surprise me."

She went to the kitchen, so very sorry to be wearing the red jersey pants. "God help me, Fran was right," she said as she went to the kitchen and opened the refrigerator. There were the little Cokes and a small bottle of champagne. She didn't want Coke.

Champagne sounded good. And it would surprise him.

She found two simple wine glasses that she and Fran had used upon rare occasions, and returned to the living room.

"Do you want to open this? she asked.

"What are we celebrating?" Jake asked, taking the bottle and quickly peeling the foil and popping the cork with his thumbs. She held out the glasses while he filled them. There was just enough for one glass a piece.

"Every day is a good day," she replied, as the bubbles began to settle down.

He took a sip and looked amused by the bubbles. "Do you drink a lot of champagne alone?" he asked.

"No," she said simply.

"Here's to you," he said, holding up the glass in the same way he had held up his water glass toward Liz.

"And to you," she replied politely.

"If you hadn't climbed up that embankment like you did, I don't know how we would ever have gotten Liz up that hill."

Mildred took another sip of the champagne. *Every day was good. Why did you have to come close to death to remember that? To toast the goodness of the day, to give thanks, to turn over the minutes of your life to Beauty and dwell there in peace and contentment, remembering how little you really needed to be happy.* She appraised her starkly furnished room and wondered what else she could take over to the booth at The Emporium.

"Do you want to tell me why you are here?" she asked, crossing her legs. Her body was beginning to feel the warmth of the alcohol. At the same time, she felt stiff from having been inside her house for so long. If it were not nighttime, she would go for a walk—a long, long walk all around Cloverdale under the starlight in the cool of the night, and she would speak to God without ceasing about anything and everything. She had an infinite number of things to tell God—but she had very few words for Jake.

For the first time, the sunny smile disappeared, and the frank warmth of Jake's eyes receded. "I don't know exactly," Jake replied honestly.

His body changed. A vulnerability surfaced that Mildred had seen a thousand times before in her lifetime, most often in children on their first day of school. She knew that vulnerability personally, too, and had learned to hide it, even from Fran most of the time.

But at this stopping point in an evening long prayer, her own defenses were down, and she sat and waited patiently for this man to explain himself. Her patience was all he needed from her to continue to tell the truth.

"I was thinking about last Sunday, Budge. We haven't talked about what happened Sunday because of Sam and Liz, and I guess we can call them that though it's awful. Just awful," Jake said, and he sat up straighter and leaned forward, concentrated.

"I don't want to talk about Sam and Liz," Mildred declared. Outside the stars began to sing to her. *In a little while, maybe I'll just walk out the door and keep walking*, she thought. *The whole world is out there, and I haven't seen much of it. Which way is the road to Emmaus?*

Jake nodded. "I didn't mean to, Millie. They were just in the car when we were-- when that happened. You and I were in the back of that Buick when it flew off that embankment, and we haven't talked about that. That's what I want to talk about."

Jake waited for Mildred to say something. She didn't. Her spirit had moved outdoors, and she was walking with Jesus, talking with him *"Kudos on the genetic code. Seriously! Kudos."*

"I think there's something to talk about," he prompted. "Something bigger than either one of us or all of us."

Starlight suffused her. She was living inside her prayer. And the laws of physics! Big objects suspended in space in perfect balance. Small elements ensconced like tiny universes living inside larger objects. We watch jugglers with fascination but look at what you do!

"Yes. Something did happen," she agreed, while inside she was considering if it was time to buy a telescope and use it prayerfully.

"Only I don't know what it was. Is. Do you?" He took a swallow of champagne and eyed the glass approvingly. "I forget about champagne."

She nodded and took a sip of hers before responding to his question.

"Do you mean when we were going over the hill—when we were in the air like that?" she asked. "Undeniably alive inside the breath of God like that?" she asked.

He nodded. "Yes. Alive and flying in that big vehicle safe in space. And your eyes came open, and I saw you, and I didn't recognize that expression on your face, like you were filled with wonder to suddenly discover that you could fly, and you said 'Jesus saves.' Something happened to me when you said that."

Something had happened to her, too. Mildred closed her eyes briefly to remember that moment—to relive it. Only one could never truly relive that kind of moment. She could feel the living words inside of her 'Jesus saves.' They seemed to always be there inside of her like some prayer that she could never stop saying.

When she spoke to Jake, her voice was softer. "He does save. He saved us. He saves us every minute of our lives, I think." Her voice grew smaller still in that pronouncement, and she heard the echo of it in her memory seconds after she had breathed it to Jake, and was amazed at how she, too, sounded as Jake did. Vulnerable. Filled with wonder. A child again. Only they were both of a seasoned age and alive inside the breath of God.

He nodded, his face growing bright as his eyes shone with remembering. "But it was something else. There was something else. I felt like everything was all right. I mean, truly all right. I didn't blame Sam or the deer and even old Liz. Poor old Liz stopped being a nuisance in the car while we were flying." He took a breath and let it out. "It was strange for just that small amount of time to cast off every burden. I have wondered since then if it is possible to live like that all the time—without a burden in the world. Without an opinion. Boy, wouldn't it be wonderful not to need to have an opinion?

At the university, you must have opinions to prove you belong there. It feels to me like it could be possible to go on living like that moment in the car with you—without having to judge every single thing all day long—to take life as it is, just be glad to be alive. To be thankful for everything. And that moment keeps happening inside of me. Wants to keep happening inside of me even when I can't pay attention to it. And, Mildred, what I want to know is if that is happening to you."

Mildred settled deeper into the sofa, and took another sip of champagne. "Yes, it keeps happening to me," she said.

"You are a lucky woman," he said. "And I am lucky to know you. Your house is really peaceful. Houses have personalities, and yours has a peaceful personality."

Mildred looked around the room as if she had not just looked around it. She was home. She heard the clock ticking, the hum of the refrigerator, the sound of the stars singing. She felt the presence of Jake in the room, only he was large and weightless, the way they had felt together in the Buick, and she knew inside of herself as if she had suddenly been told that at her age in life, she was now with child that there was a dimension to being alive that was not part of the daily routine, and you could have it every day, or, at least, more of it--more joy. *What a small word joy is to represent living in the heightened awareness of Jesus Saves.*

Jake leaned back against the sofa as if he might never leave. "Sam will be all right again. And Liz...." He stopped. "That woman needs a husband, but it won't be me," he declared. "Thank you for the champagne and for letting me barge in on you. It's so peaceful here," he repeated with wonder.

His mission accomplished; Jake stood up

"How was church?" she asked.

Jake said, "The same. Sam led the singing. Sam gave the homily. Sam opened the service with prayer, and Sam closed it. We need a preacher sooner rather than later."

"People could take turns preaching," Mildred suggested.

"Not everybody studies the Bible. I guess we need someone who has studied the Bible."

"I guess we do," Mildred relented. There were times, however, when Mildred Budge thought that all of the theology in the world didn't measure up to one sweet moment when you were all alone and felt Jesus smile. *Find a man who could smile like Jesus, and maybe that's all anyone really needed in a preacher.*

"I'm going to pick you up first on Sunday so the other two can sit in the back," Jake said.

Jake opened the door for himself and stood there on the threshold. The night was clear. The stars were singing. They never stopped singing, but people did not stop often to listen. Mildred Budge heard Ingrid Bergman say one more time, 'Aren't I lucky?' and Mrs. Budge's only daughter smiled broadly, more broadly than she ever had in the company of anyone but Jesus.

"You're a cool girl, Budge," Jake said.

She was afraid he was going to offer her one of those closed-fist, knuckle-rapping hand moves, but he didn't. Jake Diamond leaned forward and kissed Mildred Budge on the cheek. It was another prayerful event, like the kiss he had given Belle, suffused with good will that was released into the air and pulsed all the way to heaven. "Did you need stitches for that cut on your leg?"

Standing in the shadows, Mildred's hand instinctively reached for the small wound that had troubled Fran more than it had bothered her. Mildred had almost forgotten about it. She had learned through the years that the greatest victory over pain was to ignore it. "Just a tetanus shot. And, I have to go in on Friday for a follow-up visit."

Jake's expression changed as he stepped away from the foyer. "What kind of follow-up? If you didn't get stitches, there's nothing to take out."

"He was a young doctor. You know how young doctors are. He called me today and said he wanted me to come back tomorrow, but Fran and I have plans tomorrow, so I will go Friday. I imagine he just wants to read the results of the blood work out loud to me and charge me for it."

Jake didn't look convinced. "Are you sure that is all he wants to do? I mean, cause, Budge, doctors don't waste their time with unnecessary visits."

Mildred smiled benignly. It was funny having someone care about her or even sound worried. "I think when doctors call you back, they are just doing something to avoid getting sued."

Jake digested that information and then decided that everything was all right. "Don't let them do anything to you that goes against your own good judgment," he advised, with a wave over his shoulder as he headed to the car.

23

THE EMPORIUM

The aroma of scorched coffee greeted them at The Emporium. It was not a disagreeable welcome. Rather, aged coffee seemed to fit the kind of vintage merchandise and slowed-down atmosphere of a labyrinthine store comprised of independently operated booths that created a time capsule.

People who were living in the 21st century wandered down aisles where artifacts of history were arranged in artful tableaus and beckoned passersby to come to a different time and live there for a while or at least remember it. Long-brewed coffee seemed exactly right at The Emporium.

Mildred noted again the coffee station, which was positioned by the rocking chairs that encircled a table where platters of store-bought vanilla cream cookies gave men who didn't want to trail around with their wives something to eat. Men who did not like to shop sat and talked and stirred powdered cream and packets of sugar into the bitter brew and drank it.

Every now and then, a new vendor—a Betty Crocker type of woman who couldn't bear the sight of cream-filled vanilla cookies sitting naked on a plate without even a piece of cellophane to keep them from getting limp--brought in a cheery wicker basket with a blue-and-red plaid cloth and homemade muffins dusted in large granules of brown crystallized sugar. Even though a couple of veteran vendors always thanked the new seller for her generous contribution to the ambience of hospitality that The Emporium boasted about in their TV commercials, the periodic appearance of over-sized muffins was always a short-lived affair. Gourmet muffins simply did not fit the appetites or natures of the men who preferred cookies that crumbled and strong coffee that needed an extra packet of sugar. Streeter, the day manager and overseer of the coffee station, had put out a fresh package of cookies, and Mildred snagged one and began to nibble it on the way through the store to the far-left corner where their booth was located.

"How do you eat those things?" Fran asked.

"Just testing to see if it is good enough for our customers," Mildred replied, popping the last bite in her mouth.

Fran stopped a few feet short of their booth to take stock of its appearance. Mildred watched Fran assess: 'Would their current arrangement of merchandise draw passersby to stop and sit in a chair? Imagine how a chest would look in their spare bedroom? Did the arrangement of the selected pieces of furniture invite touching?'

Mildred's turquoise wingback chair was still waiting for someone to claim it. The pretty but backbreaking chair had been there since day one when Fran and Mildred had opened their booth.

"Hi, neighbors!" Liz said, poking her head out from behind a white French Rococo dresser. "I bet you are surprised to see me," Liz said, wiping her hands on a pink towel that was on top of the dresser. "I am kind of surprised to be here myself. But I am trying to branch out of my routine, and I thought if you girls could do it, why couldn't I?"

Liz was dressed in pink Capri's and a pink gingham shirt and was wearing an old-fashioned pair of white Keds. She had small feet.

"What do you mean—if we could do it?" Fran asked, and her voice was deadly while she processed what was happening right in front of her.

"I have been getting a bit of cabin fever since Hugh, you know, died. And the house feels very empty, and I have so much stuff, and I know you two girls cleaned out your attics by opening one of these booths here. Everybody talks about how successful you two are at church. Everybody is really, really impressed," Liz added, tilting forward as if that was confidential information, and she was giving them insight they might not otherwise have.

"Well, it is no secret that I have more than an attic full of stuff. I have a whole storage building that I have been renting since before I married Hugh where I have been storing my things that were, you know, left over from other days." Liz meant her previous marriages.

"And I thought, 'Why am I paying rent to hold onto the past which is over and done with anyway?' And I thought about you two girls, and I saw a commercial on TV that advertised The Emporium, and then at the end of it they said to inquire about renting a booth, so I inquired, and they had this spot come open, and I thought, 'We could be neighbors,' and here I am," Liz said, waving her freshly manicured hands.

"I thought I'd set up the French Rococo bed first, because while it is not everyone's taste, it might suit a young woman. That is how I see it anyway." Liz pivoted, surveying the set-up. Her floor space was the same size as Mildred's and Fran's, but it looked larger because everything in it was white.

"Yes, a young woman would like that white dresser," Mildred agreed, moving in between Liz and Fran, who looked like she was about to say something she would regret later.

"What is wrong with you?" Liz asked Fran. "You look like you have seen a ghost. Are you diabetic? Do you need some sugar?"

When it was obvious to her that Fran was biting her tongue, Mildred answered for Fran. "She is surprised right now. We had no idea anyone else was thinking about renting this booth. We were just talking about expanding our booth's floor space."

"If you snooze, you lose," Liz replied brightly, spinning on one girlish Ked-ensconced toe.

"You just go ahead and set up your booth," Fran said through a clenched jaw. "But my Winston will not be helping you move your furniture in and out."

"Winston?" Liz said his name as if she couldn't quite remember the name of Fran's long-time beau.

"I wouldn't have even dreamed of attempting this if I didn't know how I was going to get my furniture all the way over here from clear across town," Liz explained, picking up the pink towel again. "I might be able to help you two girls with that. I have found two of the most darling young men to move my furniture. We could go in together and save some money if you wanted." Liz said, and she shrugged, a small moue of movement that had probably been winsome in her twenties and maybe into her thirties.

The expression did not wear well over time. Mildred thought about that. 'Should a woman make sure that a lifetime of expressions fit her age, the way one monitored one's clothing and hairstyle so as not to dress too young?'

"We don't need to save any money," Fran replied sharply. "Winston is free."

"You never know when Winston might be discommoded," Mildred interrupted, for it had been her fear that if Winston and Fran broke up, they would indeed need to know another man with a truck, and they would have to pay him.

Smiling, Liz stepped closer and began to speak confidentially. "Anybody could have found them, but I, well.... you've heard of Two Men and a Truck?"

"Yes," Fran said, her gaze narrowing thoughtfully. Everyone knew the local movers who called themselves Two Men and a Truck.

Liz leaned against the turquoise wingback that had come from Mildred's living room; and when she did, the chair appeared older and more worn than it ever had before.

'It is never going to sell,' Mildred thought dully, and the idea grieved her, for she was afraid that one day the selling would stop. So far, Fran and she had done extraordinarily well; and because business had been good, Mildred couldn't help thinking surely it would have to come to an end sometime.

"Well, I have discovered Two Italian Men and a Truck," Liz declared, and her blue eyes shone. "They are very cute." She made the shrug with her shoulders again, and added breezily, "That is—if you think that tall, dark, and handsome is cute." Liz giggled, and then a movement over Mildred's shoulder caught her eye, and Liz raised one small forefinger and pointed.

Coming across the back of the store rolling a silver two-wheel truck were two of the handsomest young men Mildred and Fran had ever seen. They appeared to be brothers. They were both tall, had curly mops of black hair, chiseled Roman features, bright white teeth and sparkling black eyes.

"The grandsons of Gregory Peck. That is what I thought when I first saw them," Liz said. They have just started their own moving business, and I explained that I needed regular help, and they said they would make a special deal for me, and I thought to myself, 'I would pay you two boys just to stand around looking good in my booth.' They could bring in the ladies, I believe. Well, I wouldn't exactly do that," Liz added, waving her hands in a fluttering movement that Mildred had seen other women lapse into when they were excited.

"Have you ever seen two more beautiful, strong young men?" Liz asked. She turned and took a deep breath, as if inhaling their beauty.

Mildred was not accustomed to assessing the beauty of men, but she could not help but be impressed by their lean good looks and the quiet competent way they handled that big white sofa. Empire style. Brushed velvet. Cat's paw feet.

"Leave it to you to find the only two Italians in Montgomery, Alabama," Fran said, shaking her head in stupefaction.

"There are more than two Italians in Montgomery," Liz argued. "I found these two young men at the Catholic church near downtown."

"What were you doing at a Catholic church? You're not thinking of converting, are you?" Fran asked hopefully.

"I love the Catholic church. I mean, really, if you want to go to church, you really should go to a Catholic church," Liz said.

"What do you mean—if you really want to go to church? What do you think we are doing at Christ Church?" Fran asked.

Liz ignored the questions. "They have everything at a Catholic church. Beautiful buildings. Beautiful fixtures. Candlelight. Music. We could learn a lot from the Catholics, if we would just stop being prejudiced. I don't know about you girls, but sometimes I really need to be at a church with a capital C."

"So, what were you really doing at a Catholic church? Did you go in there to confess your sins to a priest?" Fran asked darkly.

Liz heard the slightly mocking tone, was used to it, and decided to tell the truth anyway. "They keep the doors open all the time. I love that. You can go inside any time you like and sit in the back and just be there. Someone usually comes in. I like for people to come in and pray. That way you're not alone. Sometimes they kneel. We don't usually kneel at our church," Liz added.

"That is because we are afraid we can't get back up," Fran said, though she had no mobility problems.

Mildred wanted to reach over and grab Fran's arm and tug with a motion that meant: 'Stop. Just stop. Don't bait her. Don't play her game.'

"I like to go in there and light candles sometimes." Liz added. "When you light a candle, it is like saying a prayer. Sometimes I cannot think of the words I want to say in a prayer; but when a candle is lit, it is like the fire speaks for you."

"You go there to pray," Mildred interpreted.

"I sit down in the back while the candle burns and try to think about things. I have a hard time doing that at home. Do you have a hard time doing that?" Liz asked.

She looked at Fran, who didn't answer her, and at Mildred who said, "No. I like it."

It was the truth. But Mildred's answer sounded as sharp as some of Fran's comments. It couldn't be helped. It was still the truth.

"Do you ever go in that little booth and talk to the priest?" Fran asked. She cast another knowing glance at Mildred.

"I would love to confess my sins to a priest. Can you imagine what that would feel like to tell a man the truth? But I think the priests assign prayers for penance, and I don't know the prayers they say with their rosaries. It seems disrespectful to accept a punishment that you cannot complete because you don't know the prayers they tell you to say. Have you ever talked to a priest?" Liz asked Mildred, turning away from Fran, who stepped back to let the two young men with the sofa maneuver past them.

Liz clapped her hands at the movers who looked at her for guidance about where to place the sofa. She moved back toward her booth, smiling at the boys and pointing to a spot, calling over her shoulder to Fran and Mildred, "This is going to be such fun."

Mildred and Fran watched the boys move the sofa back and forth as Liz decided how to define her space with the white sofa as an anchor.

"I'm in hell. I'm in hell. I'm in hell." Fran began to mutter. "I mean, really, Mildred, how could something like this happen?" Fran didn't say the words, but Mildred knew that she meant that if Mildred had not dawdled in coming over to sign the lease, they would not be in hell.

"It is not hell. And her booth doesn't have anything to do with our booth."

"Liz is the last person on the planet I would want next to me—not to mention we had decided to expand. She stole it right out from under us."

Mildred stared after Liz. "I don't think she intended to steal it out from under us. I think she just did."

"Same thing," Fran said bitterly.

"There is only one course of action. We are going to have to wait for another spot to come vacant, and we're going to have to get a second booth that isn't beside this one," Mildred proposed.

"There is another vacant spot already available. I have seen it." Fran reported. "But it is in the basement."

"The basement! That means stairs," Mildred said, staring toward the center of the large building where wide stairs led to the basement below and another level of booths.

"There is an elevator," Fran reminded her.

"But Winston would have to take the new stuff down there. Is he up for it?" Mildred asked.

"The elevator goes to the basement, too. There is only one decision to make. We can't let her beat us. We are going to take that spot, and we are going to fill it with the best merchandise we can find. It will be a lot of work—and not the way we wanted to do it-- but when we are standing on the cruise ship waving good-bye, it will all be worth it," Fran said with determination.

"It will all be worth it," Mildred repeated softly, as they watched Liz's booth take shape. "It looks kind of like some sex kitten's boudoir from an early James Bond movie."

"That is what I said. We're in hell."

24

JUST ROUTINE

After signing the paper for the second booth, Fran asked Mildred if she could meet her the next day at their second booth in the basement to talk about merchandise placement and where to find it, but Mildred said she couldn't. "I have to go to the doctor for a follow-up visit."

"For a tetanus shot? I have never heard of a follow-up visit for a tetanus shot. Is your leg okay?"

"My leg itches, but it's fine. They took blood, and he wants to talk with me about his findings," Mildred explained.

Fran stared silently at her best friend.

"I am sure it is just routine," Mildred shrugged. "Busy work doctors give themselves to do so that they won't be sued, and they get to charge me for another office visit."

"You haven't been to the doctor much, Mildred. They don't call you in to discuss blood work unless there is something to discuss. Otherwise, the nurse calls and leaves a message like 'Everything is fine. See you next year.' That message. What did the nurse say?"

"The nurse didn't call. The doctor did."

"That's not good, Mildred. Why didn't he just tell you the report on the phone?"

"I don't know. I figured he wanted to charge me more money."

"They don't do that, Mildred. They only call you in when there is news, and Mildred, what kind of news could it be?"

Mildred held Fran's gaze. "Not good news?"

"How long has it been since you had a complete physical?"

"Two years?" Mildred asked. "Last year got away from me."

"You had your eyes and teeth checked, but you let your middle parts go."

"I don't remember my middle parts very often."

"You are like a lot of teachers, Mildred. You think of your body as just something that carries your head around, but your middle parts have real importance."

"I don't think that. I don't think the rest of me exists to carry my head around."

"Do you want me to go with you to the doctor?" Fran pressed. She almost said 'we could go to The Emporium afterwards' but she stopped herself.

"I can take myself to the doctor," Mildred replied. "I'm sure there's nothing to it. I would have heard it in his voice. He sounded quite cheerful."

"That's how they sound," Fran replied mysteriously. "You call me when it's over and tell me what he said."

"There won't be anything to tell," Mildred replied staunchly, before she headed home.

Home was a ten-minute drive through parts of Montgomery that people still called the east side of town, but it wasn't as far east as Montgomery had grown.

Parked in her driveway, Mildred was resistant to going inside right away. Something was pulling at her—not nagging at her—drawing her. She looked over her shoulder as if someone were watching her from inside the vacant Garvin house. The grass was burned by the sun and needed mowing. Mildred had not seen anyone go inside in months. The power was turned off and maybe the water, too.

Without planning to, Mildred finally got out of her car and walked across the street and over to the house, her hand grazing the top of the black metal mailbox that was growing rusty. Careful where she placed her feet, for there were small holes under the overgrown grass, Mildred walked past the front of the house and around it to take a look at the backyard.

It was worse than she had imagined. The grass was much taller back there. There had been some infrequent mowing of the front lawn, but whoever was orchestrating the yard work had decided not to pay to have the back yard cut.

Mildred pushed open the wooden gate and stepped through and saw that the brick barbecue pit that Mr. Garvin had laid with his own hands was still there but was disguised now by an overgrown bush and tall weeds and grass. What had once been a well-tended flowerbed did not exist any longer. Everything was overgrown. Mildred peered closely. Submerged under dense weeds were some veteran plants and flowers that no one was tending any longer. What had happened to the day lilies, peonies, and what was the name of that plant? She couldn't think of it. "This is a mess," she told the Lord. "I'm halfway tempted to buy this place myself just so I can clean it up."

Mildred stayed inside that prayer for a moment, testing the suddenness of it, the truth. "I would like to clean up this place," she said. "If I weren't about to be told I have cancer I might even call up the realtor and make an offer."

Mildred Budge did not make deals with God. But the impulse that rose up in her in that moment took root, and she walked back home with the idea that all of her prayers to produce a buyer for this house could be fulfilled if she simply bought it herself. She could rent it out. The monthly rent would make the house payment. There was a lightness to her step as she began to imagine the feelings of accomplishment that reclaiming that backyard and the front yard could bring.

She tucked that idea deep inside herself and went into her own house and asked the Lord to either fan the flame of intention or let it die—whatever he wanted. Then she poured herself a bowl of corn flakes and sliced a banana on it for supper.

25

NO MORE SCALES

On Friday morning, Mildred walked with her Grace Kelly handbag past the various machines that flanked the hallway, not looking at the big weighing contraption that was ridiculously out of date and would be a better coat rack than a scale, she was sure.

In that moment, Mildred Budge decided that she would never step on a scale again. Never. She was old enough to say 'no' to being weighed, and she would, because if she had what they were going to offer her chemotherapy to fight, then she wasn't ever going to get on a scale again, so there.

"Miss Budge, thank you for coming," the young doctor said, and Mildred thought, 'He's even younger today than he was five days ago.'

He was visibly uncomfortable, moving restlessly around the room as if he had drunk too much caffeine. He fidgeted with the items on the desk and nervously adjusted the pencil holder, moved his name plate, and re-situated a plastic model of a skull that reminded Miss Budge of the x-rays that dentists take of the full face when they want to charge you double the amount you pay for the little wing x-rays that they take twice a year.

"How old are you, Miss Budge?"

"Old enough to know you have the answer in front of you on that form," she replied tartly.

He laughed as if she had made a joke; and unlike the effect of the forced laughter that Sam was coughing up these days, this self-

conscious chortle caused Mildred to relent--
to forget her own future and think of the boy
in front of her and how hard he was trying to
be a doctor.

"And so, it does," he said, his voice growing
louder than it needed to be. "Like I told you
on the phone, Miss Budge, the blood work
came back...."

She could not help herself. Mildred leaned
forward, her brow furrowing, for it is one
thing to know that you are saved and
guaranteed eternal life; it is another event
altogether to shake off this mortal coil before
you have finished completing all the chores
that you have on your to-do list. An image of
the Garvin's overgrown backyard rose up in
her memory, and she had such a fierce
appetite to weed the flowerbed, trim the
heavy branches back and have the yard
mowed. If her life were not about to be cut
short, she would do it all: her own personal
bucket list.

The young man circled his desk and then settled himself on the front of it, trying to cross his leg while standing. He looked like a pelican. A short pelican.

"Your blood work is great. Which made me look at your stats again. Your vital statistics, Miss Budge," he clarified.

Feeling as if he were invading her privacy, Mildred did not reprimand him because that would have simply drawn out the tension. A doctor—even a young one--talked. A patient—whatever the age--listened.

"Your blood is good. Your stats are good. And your blood pressure is something a 20-year-old athlete would enjoy."

She settled back in the chair. If there was bad news to come, he was certainly beginning in a strange way.

"You're pretty limber, too, aren't you?"

"I walk," she replied.

"How far?"

"As far as I need to go," Mildred said.

"Have you ever measured it—tested yourself to see what your endurance level is?"

She shook her head. "I walk. I enjoy the outdoors. The sunshine. The breeze."

"It would be interesting to know how far you could walk if you pushed yourself. I am a scientist, you know, and we like to measure things."

"I am not a thing," she replied, as the tension over a possible death sentence slowly evaporated, leaving behind a kind of dull surprise: 'Oh, it didn't happen to me after all. Not today, anyway.' She realized that her hands were gripping the arms of a faux leather chair. Brown vinyl. She made herself let go. The doctor didn't notice. He had something to say, and he was trying to say it.

"We have come a long way in geriatric care, Miss Budge. A long way."

"You are talking about taking care of old people."

"Not old people," he said, clearing his throat. "People whose ages fit inside a certain category."

"Old to you."

He shook off the characterization. "I am a doctor who is part of an ongoing study to collect data about people, like you...." He stopped.

"Like me?" Mildred confirmed, and she grinned because she knew there were many women like her. Church ladies. Southern church ladies. Mostly invisible Southern church ladies.

"Only there aren't very many people like you, Miss Budge, if one looks at the numbers. You, Miss Budge, are a lucky woman."

"I don't believe in luck," she replied.

"A figure of speech," he said, dismissing the need for a vocabulary or theology lesson that she was beginning to feel like she wanted to give him.

"You are very healthy."

"Praise the Lord," she said immediately.

The scientist ignored the comment that contained many secrets to long life, Mildred saw, and the teacher in her wanted to hold up one hand and explain that the reason people were born was to love God and that praise was the language of that love. From that language the very energy of life poured forth from the Father of Love and gave life to mortal people.

"Take these numbers and add them to the story of you climbing a hill with a rope after being in an accident, and you must be, well, really, some kind of super woman."

She grinned. "Praise the Lord," she repeated, hoping he would hear her, but he didn't, so she continued, "You just haven't been looking around you. There are many, many women like me."

He shook his head, no. "You might not think you are a rarity; but Miss Budge, in my world the population fits into sets of numbers with one percent of the population having the kind of health you enjoy."

"I am blessed," she affirmed, though she immediately had a running catalogue of the aspects of her anatomy that she did not enjoy: cushy thighs and arms, and if she looked at herself too closely in the mirror, she was dismayed by the changes in her countenance. Upon more than one occasion, she had been tweezing her eyebrows and asked with true wonder: "What has happened to my face?"

"And, what I would like to arrange with you is a study of sorts. Schedule some tests. Gather some more data. Find out more about what makes you tick. I mean, your heart ticks so doggone well."

Involuntarily, she pressed her right hand to her heart. It was ticking. It always had.

"And your lungs...I am almost certain that you have an immense set of lungs on you. When I asked you to take a deep breath the other day, I had to tell you to stop inhaling because you kept on going. When you did exhale, the lamp shade over there trembled." He pointed across the room.

'Had her breath traveled that far?'

"I can breathe deeply," she agreed, and she began to feel uncomfortable. What he was saying about her did not feel altogether like a compliment. Rather, she felt somewhat insulted to be told that her breath traveled as far as that lamp shade. That was more than her share of the room, really. Church ladies tried not to take up more than their share of space anywhere they went.

"Anyway, I want to study you."

"Like a book?" she asked, gathering her purse onto her lap.

He could feel the 'no' that was coming his way and automatically moved to the door to block her exit.

"It wouldn't take much time. Do some walking on the treadmill. Pee in a cup."

His words hung in the air as she stared at him in disbelief.

"What did I say?" he asked when she rose and moved around him toward the door.

She stared at her feet, embarrassed for his crudeness, and wondered one more time why young people who go to college do not graduate with a richer, more decorous vocabulary.

She stood in front of the door and waited for him to open it.

He didn't "You are so healthy. You can't leave here and take your secrets of a long life with you. I mean, Miss Budge, people like you have an obligation to share the secret of how you got to be the way you are."

His words stopped her. She waited, thinking.

"I won't ever say 'pee in a cup' for the rest of my life," he promised recklessly.

She froze. He had said the words again. She recoiled from them, but in its way, his pledge was a prayer of repentance, and he was young and she was not dying from cancer. There were just a few tests that might satisfy his curiosity, and she did know the secret to eternal life after all.

The Great Commission commanded people to go forth and proclaim that eternal life was in Jesus, in whom she had found her life and breath and being. Jesus was a threshold to eternal life that you crossed over by saying his name. Before you said it in faith, you lived in the world that the senses took note of; but afterwards, you inherited a vast array of sensors that saw so much more. The universe opened up on the name of

Jesus. Eternal life began, and one lived in the new dimension of Jesus Saves.

"I will think about it," she said, for she was both a Christian and a Southern lady, and Southern ladies simply do not say yes or no to much right away.

She met his gaze easily.

"You will think about it," he pressed. "I can call you in a couple of days?"

"You could," she agreed. "But you should know that I have pledged to myself that I shall never again step on a scale. What about that?"

The statement took the scientist aback. He stared down the hallway at the metal apparatus that was taller than he was.

He looked into Miss Budge's eyes and knew that opportunity was knocking. "I personally will never ask you to weigh again," he promised.

The church lady heard the words and knew that the scientist was now talking like a lawyer and had built in a loophole. A nurse could ask Mildred Budge to weigh.

Well, that was another day.

She wasn't dying today. The young still needed her. She had some wisdom to share.

"Okay, you may call me next week," she agreed, and because Jake Diamond had kissed her cheek, she stood there waiting, waiting, but a second miracle—a prayerful kiss upon the cheek--did not occur.

Mildred wondered how she would answer Fran's and Jake's questions about what the doctor had said to her, but even though she figured out a polite way to say he had just invited her to be part of an old-lady study, neither one called to ask her if she was dying.

The drama of her close call with death at the embankment and then the scary idea of a bad prognosis from the doctor was old news before it became any kind of news at all.

So, when Belle called Mildred and asked, "What's going on?" Mildred did not reply, 'I've been to the doctor who told me I am a super woman.' She didn't even mention the geriatric study. She just said, "Not much. You?"

"Could I come over?' Belle asked, and her voice faltered. The last time Belle had called with that tone of voice she had mentioned the problem with her pink underpants that Sam had not appreciated.

Mildred braced herself. Through the years she had often counseled her long-time married friends on how to navigate the tensions of marriage, which was tricky, since she had never been married.

"You know you don't have to ask," Mildred said. "I'm here. Come on."

Belle only needed to walk across the back field, and Mildred automatically moved to stand on her back porch to welcome her. How many times had she stood there and waited for her friend--not her best friend, like Fran was--but a good friend. And now, as her old friend made her way across the field that connected their two houses, Mildred Budge realized that Belle, who was known for her dancing and for her laughter, had lost the dance in her step. As Sam's terrible false laughter had taken hold on him, Belle had stopped dancing altogether.

Mildred pushed the door open and stepped back to make way for Belle to come through. Her friend was wearing an old-fashioned housecoat—the kind with pale blue flowers and snaps. She wore an old pair of brown penny loafers. She kicked these off at the back door so as not to track in dirt from the field onto Mildred's floor.

"I was going to make some tea."

"Could we have something stronger?" Belle asked, standing in her bare feet.

"Coca-Cola?" Mildred asked.

Belle nodded seriously. "Straight up out of the bottle. No ice."

Mildred went to her refrigerator and extracted two small Cokes from her crisper drawer where she kept them. She allowed herself one a week. Usually, when she decided it was time to drink a Coke, she placed it in the freezer and chilled it for fifteen minutes more, but there was no time to create a slush. She popped the caps and handed one to Belle, who lifted it up and said without equivocation, "Sam is actually cheating on me."

Mildred didn't know what to say, so she took a deep draught and asked God silently for help.

"And when I thought about it, Mildred," Belle said, leading the way to the living room. She hadn't been in the room in quite some time. "I love the way you've cleaned this place out. It used to be so cluttered."

Mildred ignored the criticism—one of the small reasons that Belle was not her best friend.

Belle sat down, locking her ankles together as she took the spot where Jake had been

Wednesday night. "When I thought about it, Mildred, I saw this craziness with Liz didn't just come out of the blue. In his way, my husband has been unfaithful to me our whole married life."

Mildred shook her head and almost asked, 'Don't you mean faithful?'

Before she could frame the question Belle added, "First, it was the military. It was always more important than I—than we were as a couple. When Sam finally, finally retired from the Air Force, I thought—maybe now. Maybe now my husband will stay home and put us first."

"But he got religion," Mildred interjected. She had witnessed the days after Sam retired. Until then he had been a faithful attendee of church. After he retired, Sam had gotten religion in a way that put him at the church all of the time.

It was amazing how many jobs one could find to do at the church, and all of them were sanctified as fruits that proved you were a justified member of the Beloved.

"He needs to be in charge of something," Belle explained. "You know what?"

"What?" Mildred asked, playing her part in Belle's discussion with herself about Sam.

"I have always hated it when things were going well—you know how things can rock along pretty evenly? —and you think, oh, well—the status quo—how I love it. But Sam doesn't. When things are going too well, Sam starts some kind of fire so he can put it out. Do you know what I thought when I heard that he had driven off the embankment?"

Mildred was afraid to ask this time, but she did. "What did you think, Belle?"

"I think a part of him did that on purpose. I am so sorry, Mildred. I didn't know he would do that. How can you warn somebody about something like that? But I am sorry for you and the others. For your having to go through that."

"There was a deer," Mildred confirmed.

Belle waved that aside. "If it hadn't been a deer, it would have been something else. If it hadn't been the embankment that day, it would have been some other kind of cliff to jump off or push someone off —trip them, really. Sam is very good at tripping people, and there are a lot of ways to do it. He is really good at it. Nobody knows that but me. But I know it. God help me. I know that about my husband, Millie.

"The truth is, Mildred. Sam isn't a bad driver, but he is a dangerous driver these days, especially when things are going well. I have been in the car when I felt his urge to crash into something, and I was the one in the passenger seat that would absorb the impact. I have thought about that, Mildred. I have really thought about that."

Mildred didn't know what to say. She didn't know what Belle needed her to say. It was not the first time, however, when one of her long-time married friends had suddenly begun to try and explain the tenor of a long, long marriage and the depth of loneliness that can exist inside a long, long partnership.

"You are probably wondering why I am putting up with this Liz business, when I could so easily call a halt to it."

"No, I'm not," Mildred tendered softly. "Liz is just a small fire, and you know he will put it out before it spreads."

"Thank you, Mildred. You don't think I am crazy then. Or self-deluded. You understand he sets fires and puts them out. You know a lot, Mildred. Don't think we don't all know how much you know. Why else do you think I would be talking to you?"

Because she had no one else to talk to—not really--except God in prayer, and sometimes a petitioner wanted a person who would say something audible back.

Belle looked suddenly tired. "I don't blame you for avoiding all this nonsense. Trying to be married to a man who starts fires, I mean, isn't it nonsense? Or it would be if the consequences weren't so potentially awful."

"Heartbreaking," Mildred argued.

"Yes," Belle agreed. "My heart is broken. But it will get well."

"Do the doctors think....?"

"Yes, yes, yes. The doctors and my terrible mysterious illness! Can't you see that it isn't me? It isn't me, Mildred. It is Sam. Whatever is wrong with him is making me— us—sick. I am worried to death about him."

That registered as true.

"I love Sam, and Sam loves me," Belle clarified.

"I don't doubt that," Mildred agreed hurriedly.

"But aside from our devotion to one another, a lot of what happens day-to-day is nonsense. You are not afraid of being alone, Millie. I envy you that."

Before Mildred could respond, Belle continued, "Whether we are afraid or not, we are all alone, really. Even us old married women."

"Is there anything to be done about Liz?" Mildred asked, as the clock chimed. Belle looked startled. And nervous. And anxious. And resigned.

"We need to find her another husband. That's the only answer."

"Fran says the same thing."

"That is because Fran has got good sense. It is one of the reasons you two get along so well. You need her, and she needs someone like you to boss around. You are probably saving her from making a mess like I am in by not marrying Winston.

Mildred did not understand.

Belle saw her confusion. "If Fran didn't have you to take care of, she would probably feel freer to marry Winston, but she won't let you down. Surely you know that she is that good a friend. But I was speaking of Liz. As much as I hate to say it, Liz needs a husband, and the man she marries will need a lot of prayer. Liz needs a lot of prayer."

That last sentence stopped Mildred cold. She had rarely ever mentioned Liz's name in prayer. Even after Hugh died. Even then.

Mildred Budge, full-time church lady, was convicted one more time of not loving her neighbor as herself. But before she could meditate upon that and plan a time of serious repentance by telling the truth of her lovelessness to God, Belle stood up. "I am taking this with me. You're the only person I know who still buys these little Cokes. What if I had wanted a beer?"

"I don't have beer," Mildred explained unnecessarily.

"Thanks for the Coke," Belle said, as she, relieved of her pressures slipped her feet back into her old loafers, and started the walk back through the field to her house.

"Any time," Mildred said, as she let the screen door settle. She fixed the little hook and eye lock and picked up her Coke. She looked at it, and she didn't want any more.

Instead, she walked over to the sink and poured the rest down the drain. As she did, she wondered if Fran was really not going to marry Winston because of her; and if so, what could or should she do about it?

27

GOOD COP BAD COP

"I borrowed Winston's truck," Fran said, meeting Mildred's gaze. Before Mildred could ask the question, Fran replied, "I wanted it to be just us. Winston understands." She took a breath, and added, "Maybe our business will want to buy a used truck. We could park it at your house," she said, flashing a grin.

It was the grin that hid the kind of questioning and discomfort that Fran didn't admit to regularly. It was her bravado grin. Mildred was too good a friend to argue with that grin.

"We can park it here or even over there," Mildred said, pointing toward the Garvin house.

Fran considered the idea. "I guess no one would know," she allowed, jangling the keys to Winston's truck.

"I would know," Mildred said. "But I think it would be a good idea to have some kind of vehicle parked there until I get it rented."

"What do you mean until you get it rented?" Fran asked.

Mildred's gaze shifted thoughtfully to the house. "I made an offer on that house, and they have accepted it. I will rent it out," she explained placidly. "Of course, the bank has to approve the loan, but the agent says they will. I have a golden credit rating."

"You don't buy houses without telling me," Fran said, stunned by Mildred's news.

"That car accident has jolted me into doing things I wouldn't ordinarily do."

"You don't have to jump off a cliff every day, Millie."

"The truth is I am tired of waiting for someone to mow the yard. Now, I will just have it done. That backyard is a mess. Where are we going first?" Mildred asked while climbing up into Winston's truck.

"Arrowhead is sponsoring their neighborhood garage sale, and once we turn into that subdivision, you pretty much follow the signs or balloons or the cars."

"It is too early in the morning for there to be many cars," Mildred remarked.

Fran ignited the engine. "You can never be early enough on garage sale day in Arrowhead. It is where the people who have really good stuff live."

"I was wondering where they lived," Mildred said, fastening her seatbelt. Or she tried to. It was much too small. It was where Fran usually sat. Mildred loosened it, and then loosened it some more.

"I withdrew two hundred dollars from our account in small bills. It's in there," Fran said, pointing toward the cigar box on the floor at Mildred's feet.

"Maybe you ought to buy one of those metal boxes that locks," Mildred suggested as she adjusted her window to let in some air.

The morning air was cool, offering the false hope that the day would stay cool. It wouldn't. By noon, you could fry an egg on the hoods of most cars and trucks.

Fran smiled and turned toward the Atlanta Hwy. "If we spend it all today, we won't need a metal box. Besides, who is going to think anything valuable is in a cardboard cigar box?"

Mildred held the box close to her face and sniffed. "I don't remember your husband smoking cigars."

"Gritz used to smoke one cigar in the evenings sometimes sitting out on the back porch. I didn't like cigar smoke."

"A pipe is better," Mildred said. She missed pipe smokers—wondered where they had all gone.

Fran nodded, and then they lapsed into a kind of ruminative silence for a couple of miles while the landscape passed by. There wasn't much traffic on a Saturday morning at 7:00 AM on the Atlanta Hwy. Most of the businesses that flanked both sides of the thoroughfare were not open yet.

Mildred did not understand how ten o'clock had become the accepted time for retail stores to open. Almost everyone she knew would prefer to wake up and go out and accomplish errands before the heat of the day set in, which happened around 11:00 AM. You had to really move to beat the heat in Alabama, which was unrelenting around noon in the summertime.

"How are you and I going to lift anything big that we buy and need to put onto this truck?" Mildred asked.

"If we need help, there will be some man who will help us," Fran replied confidently. "And if we take it right to The Emporium, those boys that work there will help us unload our stuff if we slip them a fiver."

Mildred opened the white envelope. There were many fivers and lots of one-dollar bills, too.

"Millie, it is standard operating procedure to take small bills. It is much easier to negotiate when you have smaller bills. No one offers to make change; and once someone sees a twenty, he wants the whole shebang. Now, are you going to tell me why you suddenly decided to buy the Garvin house?" Fran asked coolly; but like the grin of bravado, the tone was manufactured to hide a tender place inside where Fran wondered how her best friend could have not only made such an important decision as buying a second house but also to have thought about it and not told Fran what she was considering.

Mildred told her the truth. "I really didn't plan to do it, Fran. I have been sort of aware of the house, and then Jake came over Wednesday night, and we talked, and he asked about the house. And he said something I had been thinking.

"With so many people losing their houses these days, people will need to rent. And Hyundai always seems to be expanding. People are coming to town. People in town who lost their houses to foreclosure need to rent one.

"It doesn't feel much like a risk. It makes sense. I decided that I could buy that house and rent it out. The monthly rent will make the house payment. I am protecting my own property values. It is not good for the neighborhood to have one house going down like it is."

"Jake Diamond came over to your house after church Wednesday night? Does he come and see you often?" Fran asked, staring straight ahead.

"Never before," Mildred said firmly. "We drank some champagne to celebrate being alive," she added. She gave Fran a moment to digest that fact. She had not been keeping secrets from Fran; life was simply happening faster than they had been able to keep up with telling the details to each other. They were catching up in Winston's truck—his absence from the hunting-and-gathering adventure yet another piece of news that Fran had not explained with satisfaction to Mildred.

"Anyway, if the bank says okay and the paperwork gets done, I will have some serious house cleaning to do over there. That back yard is a mess."

"I will help you," Fran offered automatically. And in that instant, Mildred was forgiven for any suspected trespass, such as making a big decision without sharing the details of it with her best friend.

Spying a white balloon that indicated that the resident was participating in the neighborhood sale, Fran eased up on the gas and parked at that house. She turned to Mildred, fixing her attention on her.

"I know you must be all right or you wouldn't be buying that house. But are you going to tell me what the doctor said?"

"He is young."

"Everybody is younger than we are," Fran said.

"He said that I am some kind of superwoman and that he's conducting a study on how women get to be sixty years old and have the blood pressure of a young athlete. He wants me to be in his study."

"Your blood pressure is that good?"

"It appears that my lungs are really big and that if and when I am so inclined, I can leap over tall buildings in a single bound."

"If you can climb down out of the truck without breaking your neck, I'll agree with him," Fran said.

Fran hopped down out of the truck and slammed the door, not hard, just efficiently.

Mildred scrambled down while still holding the cigar box. Fran came around and opened the cigar box and took out the envelope. "Let's leave the box in the car and take the envelope. You are going to need your hands free," Fran explained, tucking the envelope of cash in Mildred's purse.

"Why are you giving me the money?" Mildred asked.

"We may need to play bad cop/good cop," Fran explained.

"Which one am I?"

"Oh, Mildred, you will always be the good cop."

"After we finish today, let's take the new load over to The Emporium. A lot of browsers come out on Sunday," Fran said.

Mildred winced. If there was a way to close their booth inside The Emporium on Sundays, she would do it. Making money on Sunday felt wrong. Spending money did not. That inconsistency in her theology did not bother her.

"There is nothing we can do about it, Mildred," Fran said, reading her friend's mind. "And if God wants us to be closed on Sundays, he will blind people from seeing our merchandise for sale. You could pray for that if it would make you feel better," Fran suggested, rolling her eyes.

Fran was a pragmatic person; and once she made a decision, she didn't spend time second-guessing her decision. "It wouldn't make me feel better if we did all this work, and God didn't bless our efforts. I just wish there was a way to be unspotted from the world." Frowning slightly, Fran added as an acknowledgement that she understood how Mildred felt, which was deeply, "I do wish there was a way to remain unspotted from the world. But the world spots us, Mildred. The Lord understands, and he can clean us up again."

"I know he understands," Mildred replied, and there was a trace of sorrow in her voice that she didn't want to hear in herself. After her retirement, a spirit of mourning had come upon her, and it had taken her two years to walk it out with the Lord. Now, when she felt grief's encroachment, she shook it off. She would not live in grief. She simply would not.

"Besides, isn't the pulpit committee itself working tomorrow by driving over to hear the boy preacher?"

"Yes," Mildred said, but she didn't take the bait. Church work on Sundays was exempt from being thought wrong, although it did seem to Mildred that even the most devout upholders of resting on the Lord's Day were the very ones who called non-essential meetings at 2:00 PM Sunday afternoon because it was the only time when everyone on the committee wasn't at their jobs. Sometimes it was hard to stay unspotted from the world even at church.

Mildred drew her shoulders back and confessed, "I am not looking forward to another long drive in a car with those particular people."

"That is mainly because, at your core, you are shy. You get out and you talk and walk, but you are shy. People don't expect someone our age to be shy, but you are anyway and working as a teacher for years didn't change that about you."

There was no reproof in that assessment, and it was true. Mildred turned to Fran with a kind of gratitude that her friend knew that and did not blame her for shyness or see it as a mark of deficiency. Fran simply saw it, acknowledged it, and went on. Mildred liked the forward motion of Fran and followed behind, realizing with a start that one of the reasons they got along so well was that Fran was a leader in social situations, and Mildred preferred to hang back, shyly. She did that while Fran approached a lady at the first table of merchandise.

"How much do you want for this?" Fran asked nonchalantly, pretending she didn't care what the answer was. Fran the Buyer was different from Fran the Seller.

"The prices are on the Masking tape," the woman replied, leaning forward to read the numbers that had been written with a black Sharpie on the square of tan Masking tape. "Two dollars for that and two dollars for that," she said, as if she now thought that the price of two dollars was too low for any item in front of her.

"I mean--how much would you take for all of this on this table?" Fran asked nonchalantly.

"How much would I take for all of this?" the woman repeated. She yawned extravagantly, and Mildred saw the residue of sleep in the corners of both eyes where she had not washed her face thoroughly—maybe not at all. It was awfully early to be doing business.

She caught the eye of a man who was walking in circles, unsure of what he was supposed to be doing at the sale in his own front yard and waved him over. Mildred imagined that her husband was supposed to be the bad cop, only no one had told him that. "How much do we want for all of this loot on the table?" his wife, the good cop, asked.

He looked at his wife as if she was a stranger, but they were old married people. Mildred wondered if he ever wore anything other than the outfit he had on: baggy beige camper shorts, a well-worn red Alabama football T-shirt and brown leather sandals without socks. He needed a pedicure badly.

He coughed to clear his throat and replied gruffly, "It's your stuff. You know what it is worth." While he said the words, he was trying to read the prices written on the items, but craning his head didn't work. He was up too early and having a hard time focusing. He scowled at his wife with a glare that said: 'Why'd you get us up so early for this?'

Fran had already added up the amounts. She was a whiz at reading and adding numbers upside down or sideways. Fran beamed the way she had years ago when she had been a New York model. She pointed like one of those beauties on *The Price Is Right* who helped the host direct the gaze of the contestant to multiple items that were part of the game: "Two dollars, two dollars, two dollars, two dollars, two dollars, plus two dollars could be..."

Fran let the conclusion dangle, adding, "Twel.... How about ten dollars?" She shrugged winsomely as if making a joke rather than shaving two dollars off the total of twelve.

Mildred was in awe.

"Ten dollars sounds like a deal to me." He turned to his wife and said, "The sooner you sell out, the sooner we can close up. There is a game on this afternoon," he said, and then rambled off to follow around other shoppers who were browsing other tables—tables of stuff that Fran had dismissed with a quick glance and instead focused all of her attention on this one array of merchandise.

"He had to get up too early," the lady explained as an apology for his rudeness. She reached under the table and withdrew a cardboard box. It was the movement of agreement, though she had not formally said, yes.

Fran interpreted the act quickly, hissing to Mildred. "We need two fivers."

The woman placed each item in the box but had nothing to wrap them in. Fran offered no complaint. At the last minute, she intercepted the problem of the cumbersome cake stand, and said, "I will just carry that cake stand. Thank you," Fran added as the woman pocketed the money.

Mildred took the box.

Fran led the way back to the truck, where she immediately started wrapping each item in the tissue paper she had brought.

"Are you sure this stuff is worth ten dollars?" Mildred asked when Fran moved the cake plate to a separate box where she had left some Styrofoam peanuts.

She settled it down and pressed the insulation around it. When she stepped back, one small white Styrofoam peanut clung to her palm. Fran tried to brush it off, but it only moved up her wrist, attached by static electricity. Fran slapped at it but it obstinately clung to her fingertips. Mildred reached over and calmly removed it, taking the Styrofoam peanut like a small bird and laying it down on the cake plate where it stayed.

"The cake plate is oversized. They are hard to find. We will get fifty dollars for it, and thirty bucks for the jewelry holder head. It is trimmed in 18-karat gold, and it is the kind of frou-frou knickknack people who wear a lot of jewelry like. That's seventy dollars profit right there. And we have just begun. Onward, Christian soldier," Fran said, climbing back into the truck and behind the wheel. "And, we can lift all this merchandise ourselves."

They spent an hour of their time and another eighty dollars at five more houses and filled four more boxes of knickknacks.

"I'd say this is enough of a haul for one day if you do," Fran said. "Let's head to the barn."

The barn was The Emporium. Mildred nodded her agreement.

28

BETTER DAYS

"We can just park out front and carry this stuff in ourselves," Fran decided for them, as she parked near the front door of The Emporium.

Each woman picked up a box and walked purposefully toward the front door, where the fellow who greeted people saw them and hurried over to hold the door open for them. Fran winked at Mildred. Streeter was a likable man, a natural at making people feel welcome. He swept off his baseball cap and bowed as Fran went through first, followed by Mildred. "Ladies, my day just got better."

Streeter talked like that.

Mildred smiled when Streeter took the box from her hands—wondered why he didn't help Fran, who was the kind of petite pretty woman that men liked to help. Ignoring her protests, Streeter waved to the young man at the front reception counter that he was accompanying the ladies to their booth. The young man didn't seem to care. To him, Streeter was an old geezer who didn't know he was an old geezer, so let him go make a fool of himself over these two old ladies who were cleaning out their hope chests, finally.

The young man adjusted the ear piece of his iPod that was nestled in the front pocket of his shirt and flipped another page in a magazine about Tony Hawk and skateboarding.

"I can carry my box," Mildred protested, when Streeter moved ahead of Fran and led the way.

Before Fran could say, "We are going to our second booth in the basement," Streeter led them to their first booth Liz in the back on the first floor, where a strange light was emanating that had not been there previously.

Mildred felt that something was wrong before she caught up with Streeter, and Fran was close on his heels when he reached their booth and turned and asked, "Now, where do you want me to put this?"

Mildred looked up. And then over. As she did, Fran's gaze tracked with hers. Overhead of Liz's booth were five different types of crystal chandeliers, all of which were plugged into the ceiling electrical unit and shining like floodlights on Liz's merchandise below. Everything below was either white or glass. There were two mirrors that were positioned opposite each other, and they reflected the light from above and seemed to magnify the floor space of Liz's booth and eclipse the merchandise in the next booth: theirs. The light, the white, the mirrors so attracted the attention of anyone nearby that Mildred's and Fran's floor space was practically invisible. Certainly, by contrast their merchandise was now in the shadows— on the outskirts, the same way girls at a dance who were not asked to dance became wallflowers.

Fran registered the implications first.

Streeter looked down at his feet as if he didn't want to be a witness to what they were feeling and thinking. Then, having placed Mildred's box on the floor beside the forlorn turquoise wingback, Streeter tapped the brim of his hat with a Boy Scout salute and said, "That new lady has been really busy. She has got a couple of young men who've been working up a sweat." His eyes swept over Mildred, then Fran. Streeter mustered a consoling smile. "You ladies call me if you need anything." It was what he always said.

Then, turning, Streeter became a businessman who had once upon a time been a soldier. His military bearing took hold, and Streeter went back to his post, where he would greet both vendors and customers with the same welcoming air of hospitality no matter how the world treated him.

Fran swallowed and sat down hard in the turquoise wingback. Mildred leaned against the chair. Maybe she would have to take it home in defeat, place it back where it had once been—fill that empty space that Jake said made her house appear that she was moving out. No, she simply would not. No. If it came to that, she would ask Winston to take it to Goodwill. Some poor person would be glad to have a turquoise chair to sit on.

"I saw a movie once about Thomas Edison," Mildred recalled softly. Her voice had that air of grief in it again, and she coughed gently to dispel it. When she spoke again, her voice was stronger. "In the movie, Thomas Edison used mirrors in a room with lots of lanterns to create more light because a doctor needed to operate. The doctor needed more light," she said, repeating herself.

"Liz must have seen that movie, because she is really operating in here," Fran said, eyeing their cardboard box. All of their treasures from the morning's great shopping adventure now seemed lackluster and undesirable. The rush of achievement and anticipation that had been with them throughout the morning drained away.

Fran's eyes met Mildred's. "It is time for us to recognize that we may have underestimated Liz Luckie. The serial widow yelps at every occasion, flaps her hands when she is excited, cannot work a cell phone, and knows exactly what she is doing."

Mildred nodded soberly.

Then, Fran said the most amazing words that one church lady could say to another church lady: "It has come to this," she said pointing toward the well-lit booth that had eclipsed theirs. "It has come to war."

29

STEEV

The minutes inched by, held down by dawdling seconds. Rather than the animated conversation that should have followed a sermon as exhilarating as the one Steev had given, polite chatter punctuated the longer periods of silence as the members of the pulpit committee shook out their white cloth napkins and nodded with strange smiles of recognition to their sisters in the faith who were serving the lunch.

The ladies of Steev's church provided a proper lunch for the four visitors, knowing full well that the guests were very likely going to try and poach the best preacher anyone in the dining hall had ever heard.

Even as Steev had been speaking, Mildred kept telling herself: 'Now remember that. Remember that part. It's important. And that part, too. And the way he said that.' They were not new ideas. Not new words. Indeed, a part of Mildred Budge that kept an on-going record of her life, complete with footnotes and commentary, and retold it to herself privately in the lifelong human pursuit of finding and holding onto the kernels of meaning and disposing of the chaff, nudged her with the strange words: 'That's from the Bible, you know that verse— those verses. But think about it this way now.'

Afterwards during the lunch that was served by ladies who looked like Mildred and her friends, she recalled that the sermon had been drenched in Bible verses, built in Bible verses, gilded with glory, so fragrant with truth that bits of her began to dissolve instantly. Crusty parts fell off. Stagnant waters inside of her drained away until all that was left felt like fresh spring waters.

And then they had lunched on fried chicken and deviled eggs and corn muffins and green beans wrapped in bacon and sliced tomatoes and iced tea and chocolate pound cake that at first seemed disappointing because it lacked a glaze; but after the first moist bite, one realized that the cake was so moist—was the secret chocolate syrup used as the liquid and not milk? --that it didn't need anything else.

Temporarily talked out, Steev ate with gusto and gratitude, seemingly oblivious to their reactions to his sermon. When Liz said as they sat down, "That was simply wonderful. You are wonderful," Steev had held up a hand for her to stop and replied, "The Holy Spirit goes where he goes. I just happen to be in the same place."

Sam cast Steev a disdainful look. He didn't like mystical talk like that. A preacher needed to speak plainly.

The women who had brought the covered dishes for their lunch kept patting Steev on the shoulder as they passed by with the iced tea pitcher to offer refills or the plate with more corn muffins, and then they had stood in the kitchen beaming at him, all three of the ladies smiling, like proud mothers.

Steev answered their few polite questions, but there weren't many questions from Liz, Jake, or Mildred. Even Sam couldn't do a good job of interviewing. They knew the facts of his biography, and they all seemed to understand that the call on Steev's life was something beyond framing or pigeon-holing. No perfectly executed Q & A session could explain it. The sermon had put the members of the committee in a different position—a silent one.

Then, Steev ushered the committee back through the sanctuary and out to the parking lot and into their vehicle where Liz hurriedly jumped into the front seat next to the driver, Jake. Mildred and Sam took the back seat while Steev stood nearby, shading his merry eyes with his hand and waving like a kid as Jake steered the lumbering vehicle back to the street that led to the interstate and home to Montgomery.

It was only after they were on the interstate that Liz finally broke their silence with, "I vote for Steev."

Sam shook his head and dismissed her opinion with the brusque comment, "It is not time for a vote, Elizabeth."

"I don't see why not," Liz replied, unperturbed. "He was magical." She turned in her seat and stared at Sam. "Didn't you think he was magical? I don't see how you couldn't think him magical. He was magical. I knew it from the first time he materialized out of nowhere, like some angel had dropped him off from a passing cloud. That's what he is, some kind of angel—angel of life."

"The boy is no angel. Read your Bible. People aren't angels. They don't become angels when they die, and magical is not a word we want to use about a preacher. Being magical is from the devil," Sam said, reproving her with a glare.

Jake steered, his eyes hidden behind sunglasses, but Mildred felt him check the rear-view mirror for a glimpse of her and a clue about what she might be thinking.

He could not read her mind, because she did not know what she thought. Not yet. That simmering sensation was inside of her again, and she was having a hard time not saying aloud, '*Jesus saves. He saves us all every minute of our lives all our lives long.*' But she didn't. Women were trained to keep silent, and part of their wrestling with salvation was the on-going tension of when to testify and when to keep silent. Somehow in her life, Mildred Budge had decided that silence was more often the better choice. It suited most occasions, and it didn't make men nervous. Or angry. Some men could get nervous and angry. Women, too.

Sam looked like he was anxious—and mad. Some of his anger was aimed at Mildred; and in that moment, Mildred knew she had participated in not keeping the peace. Her hands, which had settled in her lap, fell to either side, and the interior voice that communed with her began a prayer of repentance that would continue throughout the day and into the next. Maybe longer. *'I have hated. I am a murderer. I want more than my daily bread. I covet. I am ungrateful. I am petulant, arrogant, greedy, and fearful.'* The prayer began and hummed and hummed, punctuated by the intermittent undeniable phrase: *Jesus saves, Jesus saves, Jesus saves.*

"I say we just let the dust settle and reconvene when we have all had a chance to let that tasty lunch wear off. Decide in haste; repent at leisure. I say we let the dust settle. That's what I say," Sam said.

Since Sam was not inviting comments, Mildred decided to let her silence be her answer, and she closed her eyes as if napping. The sun felt warm on her face, and through her almost-closed eyes, she kept tabs on the others in the car. What she felt was a lessening of resentment toward Liz. She would not be at war with Liz, and she would explain that to Fran. She felt more at ease in the presence of Jake—that everything was all right-- and she experienced a profound pity for Sam that was so great that she knew no words to express it. *Was all of that love? All of it?*

She recalled how Sam's hands had looked on the steering wheel the previous week, white knuckled, holding so desperately onto the steering wheel even after the crash.

Mildred studied Jake's hands. His were praying hands—hands that trusted that everything was all right. His movements declared that. There were all kinds of ways to worship, and Jake told the truth of God with his hands. They rested easy on the steering wheel; and as she watched him drive, Mildred had the strangest and most welcome sensation that they were all moving forward toward home with a kind of mystical and holy assurance that the author and finisher of their faith would ensure that each one of them would ultimately arrive safely at their destinations.

30

TIME TO VOTE

Sam stacked and restacked his folders.

Liz watched, paradoxically easy with Sam's unease. Occasionally, she tried to trade some kind of knowing glance with Jake, who sat across from her. But Jake, who had apparently laid aside his plan to be a distraction for Liz from Sam, was wearing his public face.

Belle turned on the faucet in the kitchen. She was stacking the dishwasher.

Mildred wondered if Belle was always as noisy as that. Was she aware of the members of the pulpit committee seated at her dining room table doing the Lord's work? Or, had she tuned them all out, abiding in that place where worried wives wait on their husbands to return even when they are still sitting at the dining room table on the other side of the closed swinging door?

Mildred wondered about herself at home, wondered if she was noisy or quiet when she was working alone in a room in her own house, and it seemed to her that the answer mattered. She saw herself as a quiet person with contained motions and movements that respected space and air and, especially, other people's space and air, but for the past several days, Mildred had been caught up in a whirlpool of emotions and sound.

Oblivious to Liz's watchful ease, to his wife's noise, and to Mildred's interior questioning, Sam called the meeting to order. "So, just to recap. It's two against two. Is that right?" Sam said loudly.

Jake spoke up. "We don't have to say it quite like that. You and Liz now prefer candidate number two, and Mildred and I are voting for candidate number three."

Jake and Mildred could not look at Liz, who had switched her vote from Steev back to Sam's selection.

Sam was impatient, feeling that Jake's comments were in some way a sign of disrespect. "We all know how everyone voted. What we need is someone who is able to compromise. I can compromise," Sam said carefully. "But I would be more inclined to change my vote from candidate two to candidate number one. He is the safer choice. How about you two? Is either of you willing to compromise?"

Although Mildred still had a great well of compassion for Sam and his need to control, she found that she simply could not bear to be manipulated by one of Sam's classic moves.

First, he had foreseen the tied vote, had lined up Liz to vote with him for their second choice; and now if he could make Jake and Mildred feel guilty enough to say they would compromise, they would change their vote, candidate number two would be left behind, and candidate number one would receive a unanimous vote of approval, and that was a lie. The number one candidate had been Sam's preferred choice all along.

Mildred remembered the original vote. And Mildred didn't want to imagine herself sitting in the pew week after week listening to candidate number one with his safe sermons and three carefully crafted points when she could be listening to a young man who was just learning who he was as an evangelist come into his own. What kind of an adventure would that become? To have a preacher grow up in front of her?

"No," Mildred said.

"You're being awfully hard to please, Mildred," Liz said from across the table, and then she got busy scratching at a shred of loose nail polish on her pinkie finger. "I don't know why you are making such a big deal out of it. All three of them were fine. Let's just pick one and get on with our lives. I have a new business to run." Liz glanced up and smiled. A kind of ruthless shrewdness shone through the smile, and it startled Mildred.

Sam looked down at his stack of folders. He took a deep breath. "Okay. Since Mildred is not willing to budge, what about this?" Sam began, and he picked up the folders again and laid them to the side. "Our real problem is that we are two against two, and that won't do. What if?" He hesitated. "What if we bring in a fifth person, describe the candidates, and let the fifth person break the tie? Is there any rule about not adding a fifth person at this stage of the game?"

"This is not a game," Mildred commented in spite of her very best intention to remain silent. "We are supposed to be discerning the will of the Holy Spirit in this matter, and it is not a game."

"We needed a fifth person all along," Liz said, talking over Mildred. "You told me that another person wouldn't fit in your car, but we could have taken the church van. Maybe we should do that next time. Have a fifth person and take the van."

Sam cast Liz a firm gaze that translated: *if you will just keep quiet there won't be a next time.* With all the resolution of a retired colonel, Sam marched up the hill carrying the flag he wanted to plant. "We could bring in a fifth person now, take a fresh vote and see what happens."

"Who?" Jake asked.

But Mildred already knew who, and so did Sam.

"Is there any reason we can't call in Belle right now and lay it out for her?" Sam asked, raising his hands innocently. "I have maintained complete confidentiality. Belle doesn't know anything about anybody. She is a member of the church—and because, recently there have been some accusations that I have been unfair to the women of the church, it might show my personal good faith if we let another woman—a friend of yours, Mildred...."

"Your wife," Mildred said without inflection.

"You mean, tell her about all three candidates and see which way she leans before she knows we have got it narrowed down to two," Jake clarified.

"Unless you all don't believe that I haven't tried to persuade Belle to vote with me. I haven't. I can promise you that."

Mildred did not say anything. Liz watched Mildred. Jake kicked Mildred under the table. She kicked him back.

Without further discussion, Sam called out, "Belle, come in here a minute."

"Are you ready for the coffee and cake?" Belle called back. They heard some more rattling.

"No," Sam yelled back. "We are not ready for refreshments. We need your brains," he said, with a wink that made Mildred wince.

Belle pushed open the door and stood there on the threshold to the kitchen, nodding to Mildred and willing herself not to see the other woman who was sitting at her dining room table.

"Hey, Honeybun. We have got a problem that only you can solve," Sam declared, raring back in his chair. He had finally let go of the folders and was now gripping both arms of his captain's chair. He rocked back gently on the rear legs as he made his case.

Belle waited, accustomed to Sam's flattering preambles when he was trying to finesse something.

"We need an objective opinion about our candidates.

"Are you going to be the one to describe the candidates?" Mildred asked coldly.

Sam teetered precariously on his chair's back legs. "Well, I thought I would," Sam said. "There's no reason to make Belle have to read through the resumes and listen to the tapes."

"That would be the best way to do it," Jake interrupted.

"I would like some coffee if it is decaf," Liz spoke up, and she brushed the bits of nail polish from the table onto the floor with one sweep of her hand. Belle would have to vacuum now.

"You all can't make up your minds. Is that it?" Belle said. "And you're asking my opinion about what?"

"Well, Honeybun, you don't have to know everything. We just wanted another person's opinion about which one of these men would fit in best in our congregation, which is mostly older..."

Mildred was about to stop Sam from characterizing the discussion and slanting Belle's decision in his favor when Belle waved a hand. "Did the first two preach grace?" she asked. "And that last one asked all of you if you knew Jesus?"

They nodded. Preachers who were trying out for a job often chose a safe sermon to give on grace.

"It is not as simple as that," Sam said.

"You are wrong, Sam. It is that simple. Grace matters, but Jesus matters more. I like how that young man asked all of you if you knew Jesus. You told me all about it when you got home, Sam. You didn't like that, but I like that. That is what a preacher should be asking. Everything else is secondary. If you're asking my opinion, I pick the last guy—the one who goes after the lost, finds them, and then points them to Jesus. That's what a preacher should be able to do. The coffee will be ready in a minute. And it's not decaf, and I'm not making any decaf because I don't like it," Belle told Liz, and then she disappeared back into the kitchen.

"Well, obviously that didn't go well," Sam said, as the front legs of his chair hit the floor. He leaned forward and whispered confidentially, "Belle is not herself these days. The doctors can't seem to figure out what's wrong with her." He cast a familiar worried glance at the now closed kitchen door.

"Belle heard enough," Jake said. "She just didn't vote for your man."

Sam stopped himself from showing his anger. He was clenching his jaw and visibly preparing what he would say next when Liz said, "She voted for Steev. You lost, Sam. I lost, too," Liz said with the same cool ruthlessness that Mildred had glimpsed and which she now understood was not reserved for other people. Liz was ruthless with herself, too, and in that moment, Mildred respected that. Liz stood up, resting her fingertips on the freshly waxed table. "Think of it this way. Nobody died exactly." Liz pushed her chair up against the table.

"It is not over," Sam told Liz. "Calling in Belle was a bad idea. We are just going to have to talk some more if we can't get some action out of this hung jury, or I hate to say it, we may have to start the whole search over."

Sam's head began to move up and down as he said the words. "It is a hard job. But I can post another advertisement. I can handle the resumes. I can even put together another committee if anyone wants to resign from this one."

"It is over, Sam," Liz said with a surprising firmness. "The job is done."

"No. Those two cannot hold me to what I said about Belle being the tiebreaker. She wasn't willing to listen or read or hear us out. If she had heard us out...."

Liz waved her hand. "No, Sam. Your wife heard just right."

"It is still two against two," Sam argued.

Liz shook her head. "No, I am changing my vote. I vote for Steev. Now, it is four against one. How is that for a compromise? It is over, and we can all go home and get some rest."

With startling suddenness, Liz picked up her purse, and with a curt nod to Mildred, an imitation of a twinkle at Jake, and a cold glance at Sam, Liz let herself out the front door.

Sam's face expressed disbelief. He began to fuss with the folders again.

Belle brought the coffee and cake. Her voice was bright, and she pretended she didn't see that Sam was angry and frustrated and that Liz had left.

They each took a slice of carrot cake and accepted mugs of coffee. Jake slurped his, but Mildred only took polite, hospitable sips.

It was simply too late at night to be drinking coffee.

"Anything else?" Belle asked brightly, and when Sam did not reply, she disappeared.

"I am sorry it turned out this way for you, Sam. But fair is fair. You laid down the rules," Mildred said.

Sam stared at the tabletop, lifting his eyes finally to face Mildred. He could barely look at Jake. An old friend could see him up close and broken, but it was hard for Sam to have a younger man see him fail at a task that he was skilled in: administration.

"The question now is who should call Steev and make him the offer," Jake said.

Sam shifted his gaze and stared down at the steaming cup of coffee in his hand. He fought the urge to throw the cup at the wall. The urge almost won.

Jake scratched his head, tried to make eye contact with Mildred, couldn't read her mind, and repeated his question. "Who should call Steev?"

Mildred whispered, "Later."

Sam said, "No. Jake is right. We've dallied long enough, and this is what has happened. Considering the circumstances, I don't think I should make the call. If the boy doesn't accept the offer, you will all blame me, and maybe you would be right," he added.

With one move, Sam shoved the folders toward Jake. "I don't trust what I would say to him. And you two don't trust how I will say it. And to be perfectly honest, I don't want to say it—not to him. He will destroy our church. I can see it coming." Sam settled back in his chair, pushing back until he was poised on the back two legs again. He could crash at any moment, and he seemed to know that and exult in the possibility. "He's not my choice. He never will be."

Jake accepted the folders and the delegated authority.

"All right, then. I will call Steev tomorrow and tell him we want him," Jake said, unperturbed by Sam's declaration.

"That's right. You just go ahead and do that," Sam said with bitterness.

Mildred wanted to play the role of peacemaker: *'Let's stop—we could start all over.'* But a deeper part of her didn't want to do that. A deeper part of her was grieving that Sam was hurt and that Liz was going home alone and that Belle's voice was too bright and that Jake was trying to step in without Sam having to feel as if he wasn't in charge anymore.

Jake needed to finish the job, and he needed to offer the job to Steev because Steev and his question, "Do you know Jesus?" was exactly what the congregation needed. He wouldn't be a peaceful pastor. Steev Emory would be a life-challenging, faith-challenging preacher, and that sounded very good to Mildred, who was usually slow to budge, and she was not the only one.

Belle reappeared in the doorway, and something mysterious had happened inside of her. She cast an approving glance at Liz's empty chair and asked, "Are you all finally finished with this business?"

31

A FORGIVING LIGHT

Liz was waiting in her parked car in front of Mildred's house. As soon as Mildred realized that Liz was parked in her driveway waiting for her to come home from the Deerborns, the car door opened and the overhead light in the car illuminated Liz.

Light can be forgiving, unforgiving, and something else: revelatory. One more time Mildred saw Liz in a different light, and that evening she saw the other woman's aloneness. Liz was not alone the way Mildred was. Mildred had an easy companionship with solitude. Liz not only disliked solitude, she suffered with hers. Mildred saw the strain in the stony expression on the other woman's face, in the way she moved, clutching her purse in front of her, in the gentle tilt of the other woman's body to the left as if she expected to be able to lean on someone. Only no man was beside her gripping her elbow, steering her, whispering sweet nothings in her ear on the pathway to her home or to anyone else's home.

Mildred opened the front door before Liz could reach it and didn't ask her what she wanted. Instead, she stepped back and waited for Liz to come in, silently. She did, stopping as most people did in Mildred's airy foyer to get her bearings and then, still wordless, looked to Mildred for direction.

Mildred pointed to the living room and the sofa.

Liz did not obey the rules of decorum for dropping in or even fulfill the patter of Southern woman chitchat by making up an excuse. She spoke like a man in that moment, going straight to the point. "I want to talk about what happened," she said, sitting down heavily.

Mildred sat on the sofa beside her. She didn't bother to offer refreshments. Instead, she braced herself for the reproach that, according to the stony expression on Liz's face, was about to come. And it was deserved. Liz was going to demand an apology for that thrown rock, and Mildred, having considered her own conduct, was ready and very willing in that moment to give one.

"This whole thing has been a fiasco from the very beginning." Liz announced. "The others thought I didn't belong on the pulpit committee. I know that," Liz declared, and she held Mildred's gaze.

Gone was the flirtatious former cheerleader. Gone was the bereaved widow. There, finally, was Liz who had been appointed to the pulpit committee to help choose the next minister for the congregation. "I know some of what people think about me. Feel about me."

Her shoulders went back, and Liz said, sitting taller, "I know that I am not well liked by the women in the church, and the men who do like me don't really know me. They just like how I look," she said.

"Some people think being pretty is a blessing, but I can tell you, it can also be a curse." Her mind drifted, and she looked around the room, noticing for the first time the sparseness of the layout. "It looks different in here," Liz remarked, but her tone was not disapproving.

"I have cleaned out my house," Mildred replied quietly as her thoughts began to organize the long, overdue apology. *'I am very sorry for throwing that rock. I didn't intend to throw the rock. But my hand did it without my permission because....no, no. I shouldn't bring up the reason because in its way that is another kind of rock. No. I am sorry for throwing the rock.'* But even as Mildred planned in her mind what she would say, an interior pressing pushed her to consider that the apology she had in mind was insufficient to achieve peace, maybe even justice, inside the love of Jesus Saves.

"You, only you, Mildred seem to understand what I was trying to do on the pulpit committee. And I know it went horribly wrong. I know that. Do you think I don't know that?"

Mildred sat quietly, practicing, perfecting her soon-to-be uttered apology: *I am very sorry for throwing that rock at you. I was wrong. Please forgive me.*

"Know what? What do I know?" Mildred asked.

"You know that Sam forgot himself. I forgot myself. We forgot what we were supposed to be doing. I think something is wrong with Sam. Have you seen that? I think Belle knows. Do you?"

The presumptuous question by this other woman about Sam's status offended Mildred Budge. Whether something was wrong with Sam was none of Liz's business.

"Well, what do you think is going on with Sam?" Liz demanded.

Before Mildred could think of a tactful response, Liz shook her head again and said, "I am not asking idly. I am asking because they are back, and I believe that you have seen them, too."

Mildred sat very still. She was not following Liz's meaning.

"And I wanted to thank you for trying to run them off with that rock."

"What?" Mildred asked dumbly.

"When we were out by the gulley. You saw the angels too—the angels of death. They swarm me like hornets from time to time. You threw a rock at them to try and run them off, and it worked for a while. I can't tell you how grateful I am that someone else finally saw them, too."

"Angels of death," Mildred repeated dully. The apology she had been framing began to evaporate.

"But they are back. And when they're back, usually somebody dies. Do you think it is going to be Sam?"

"You see angels of death and then someone dies," Mildred summarized.

"I can't tell you how glad I am that you understand. It has been terribly lonely being the only one who knows about them. And before, they wouldn't show up until after I married, and then they would start swirling about just out of eye range. I could sense death coming, and I have tried everything I know to run them off—to run away, too—but they come and go as they wish. After you threw that rock, they stayed gone for a while, and it was such a relief."

Liz looked at Mildred with such hope, such gratitude, such stark, undeniable aloneness.

'I didn't see the angels you are talking about. I threw the rock at you, because I was mad at you about Sam and Hugh.' Those were the words Mildred needed to say for her own peace of mind, but would those words do good or harm to Liz?

Mildred sent a prayer to Jesus, *what's your pleasure?*

"Sam doesn't seem like himself. I mean, really. And now what happened over there just now. It's clear as a bell. He is losing it." Liz paused. "I have seen this before."

"Sam is losing it," Mildred repeated. And as she did, she understood. Sam was losing his grip. His legendary grip.

"But it just goes to show that when people say that God is in charge and can make good come out of anything, that he actually can, because after all is said and done, we are getting the best preacher for the job."

"Steev Emory," Mildred confirmed.

Liz clapped her hands suddenly and soundlessly in the way some former cheerleaders do who learn early in their lives that men love to be cheered. In her mind, Mildred imitated the motion: her inner Miss Budge clapping, clapping.

But as she practiced the idea in her mind, Mildred was stopped from doing it in real life because Liz Luckie reached over and took Mildred Budge's hand and said, "Why can't we be friends? I know that you and Fran are friends, but does that mean you can't be friends with other people?" Liz asked.

Mildred did not look down at Liz's hand on hers. Her mouth went dry. The apology that Liz Luckie deserved was stuck somewhere deep inside of her with the question of what was just and what was gracious, and Mildred didn't know the answer. She only knew for certain that Liz Luckie, just as Sam had said, was a woman in the church like every woman in the church was and that she had a place.

Mildred finally uttered her apology this way: "I will be your friend. Will you forgive me for taking so long? And I am sorry about throwing that rock."

"I don't blame you," Liz said. "I have wanted to throw things at them too," she confessed. Liz waved her hands in that fluttery way. Her face pinked with emotion, and she stood hastily. "I have never been very good at all that kind of church talk." And then she leaned forward and offered an air kiss—the kind of air kiss that Mildred Budge had never perfected. Soundless. Easy. Immaculate.

Mildred automatically imitated the motion, her lips puckered, and even though she meant to return the air-kiss of friendship, she made that strange and awkward intake of air, like catching her breath, that was less than genteel. Liz waved away the sound, walking toward the front door, twisting the knob, ready to go home alone through the dark in a car where no man sat beside her who could change a tire if she had a flat or help her up the next embankment should she find herself in one again.

"Ta-ta," Liz said breezily, as she let herself out.

When the door was closed, Mildred tried the light clapping sound again—didn't feel natural at all—then, she looked up toward the heavens and offered Jesus an air kiss, and something like pity was rained down upon her.

Mildred switched out the lights through the house, resisting the urge to call Fran and explain to her that they could not be at war with Liz because Liz was now a friend, so she prayed instead, "Lord, be merciful to us, we're sinners."

32

I NEED YOU

"Miss Mildred, I need you."

"What is it, Janie?" Mildred asked, holding the phone closer.

"Miss Mildred, they are going to immediately extradite me back to California," Janie declared over the phone.

"I don't understand."

Janie's voice became high pitched. "It means that they are going to send me back to California where I will have my baby, and they will put my son in foster care there. In California! That's clear across the country."

"What about your aunt?" Mildred asked, pressing the phone closer to her ear.

"I haven't heard from her," Janie said.

"I thought you were hopeful that she was going to come and take the baby to her house."

"I mailed her the form to sign, but she never sent it back. When I call her—I have to call her collect—she doesn't accept the charges." The admission cost the girl more than she had wanted to show. Stripped of her dignity and abandoned by her lover, Janie had tried to maintain the illusion that somewhere an aunt lived that was dependable. The aunt would not accept her niece's phone calls.

'Heartless. Cold and heartless,' Mildred thought before she checked that impulse too. *Who knew what the aunt was dealing with? How dare she—renowned sinner Mildred Budge—dare to cast a stone at another woman? Any kind of stone? Any woman?*

Mildred inhaled, her gaze attracted momentarily by something outside her window.

Janie misunderstood the silence and grew nervous. She started speaking rapidly. Urgently. "I can't let a stranger have my Little Mister. I can't go to California. I can't...." Janie wailed.

The sound of the young woman's voice was like that of so many young mothers who had brought their children to Miss Budge when she was a schoolteacher. A young mother always and very sincerely explained why her child was special and needed more attention than the others.

Hidden deep inside that description was the confession of a good mother who was cautious about trusting the welfare of her child to anyone else. Mildred thought of a pin she used to wear of a baby in a basket, symbolizing Moses who had been placed in the river and sent off to his destiny. During her years of teaching, she had worn that pin every day. Each child was that baby, basically alone, floating helplessly, depending on the current of God's sovereign love to deliver him or her to a safe shore. Luck never had anything to do with it.

"What do you need from me, Janie?"

The girl came to attention. This was no time to be polite or to offer Miss Budge an alternative. "I need you to come sign the form that says you will take my baby even if you decide later that you can't. If you sign the form today, that will stop the extradition. They will let me stay here until after the baby is born. Otherwise, my baby will go to strangers out in California," Janie whimpered.

"I will come, and we will talk. Don't worry. We'll figure something out." Mildred said. "I will bring Fran. She is good at solving problems. Do you need anything else?

"I want to come home, Miss Mildred. When I get out of here, I want to come home."

It was what everyone wanted: to be home. Mildred didn't have the heart to tell the girl who was in jail that while people have home places in mind that represent the security of dependability called sameness, the nature of home itself kept changing even if you lived in a city your whole life and even if you had a family homestead that is passed down through the generations in a neighborhood as lovely as Cloverdale. The boundaries of home inside the vibrant love of Christ keep changing.

"We will see what the Lord will provide for you, Janie," Mildred said, apologetic for relying on the language of faith as a way of not committing further. "You will see me this afternoon."

The phone clicked in Mildred's ear, and she pressed the button that cleared the line and dialed Fran. When her best friend answered, Mildred said, "Grab your purse. We must go to Tutwiler."

Fran didn't ask, why do I have to go? She didn't say, I am busy today. She didn't demand an explanation. She heard the tone of her best friend's voice and answered immediately, "I will be ready. Just sound the horn. I'll come right out."

"You have to sign the form. You simply have no choice," Fran declared, after Mildred explained the situation in the car.

"That is not entirely true. I guess I could let her go to California. I could let the baby go to strangers. I could just...do nothing."

"That is not you. That is not us. We're not do-nothings. If we were, the Lord would spit us out of his mouth."

Through the years, Mildred and Fran had become like each other—as each one of them was changed to become more like the One who had called her to Himself and had said, "I am your home."   For all of the theology that people memorize and assigned to a proof text, the living reality of Christ was as simple as that: Christ was home, and His expansive love was bigger than one's sense of mortal walls and flesh.

Mildred steered around a logging truck— the kind she usually retreated from.   It wasn't really an emergency. They had plenty of time to get to the prison while visiting hours were still in operation, but once she had a job to do, Mildred didn't hang back.

"It is peculiar how you can just be living your life and then something like this happens. Look at you. You love living alone just about as much as anyone I know.   I mean, you really like your solitude, and the

Lord is going to give you a baby. You don't even have a dog."

"I love dogs, and I have considered getting a dog but then I think about us traveling one day, and I wonder who will look after the dog? So, I don't get a dog," Mildred replied.

"Winston would look after a dog," Fran offered. And something in her manner changed slightly, but then that had happened quite often since Fran had become the other half of Fran and Winston. Mildred registered the delicate shift in Fran, but she did not try to decipher it.

"Winston can't look after a baby. We may have to postpone our travel plans if I take this baby."

"But you probably won't have the child for very long. I mean—really, how many more months will Janie have to serve before someone lets her out? The prisons are overcrowded. She wasn't even the real bad guy. She was a young girl who got mixed up with a bad guy, only they haven't caught him yet."

"I am not sure her lawyer has done her much good."

"I have been wondering about that myself. I have been wondering if we need to look into finding her a different lawyer. Someone who won't take 'no' for an answer. Certainly, we need to make sure she stays in the state near her baby. They wouldn't let you keep the baby and then send her to California anyway, would they?"

"I don't understand it all. We are going to have to get all of that figured out."

"Today we're just going to look at that form and see what it says." Mildred had a sudden start of anxiety. "What if I am too old? What if they think I am too old to sign the form? The poor girl hasn't thought about that."

"You are not too old. They let grandmothers take babies all the time," Fran said unconvincingly. "And remember, it is in their best interest to find a guardian for the baby. They don't want to keep up with a baby. The childcare system is overloaded."

Fran sounded like she knew what she was talking about, but she was making up her opinion from what she had heard on various TV news shows.

Mildred knew the same words and where they had come from, but it was comforting to have Fran reassure her.

"I am not too old to take the baby for a few months. I will do it, and then she will get out and take away the baby that I will have learned to love. It will break my heart, but I can get over that."

Fran reached over and patted Mildred's forearm. "You can, Mildred. Many of our friends have had their hearts broken by their children, and they are able to recover."

"That is right," Mildred agreed. "A lot of our friends have had their hearts broken by children who desert them, and they get over it."

33

HOME

Mildred repented immediately of thinking that Janie wanted what everyone wanted: to be home. Only that. Because jail was a terrible place to be and wanting to come home wasn't just about coming home. It was about escaping dark and cold and meanness in other people that was the same on the faces of prisoners as it was on the faces of the guards.

They were all in jail together, the innocent and the guilty, and the hapless and the too young and the ones who had been too smart for their own good or too dumb—or simply, like Janie, followers.

Mildred believed that Janie had been a follower.

Janie was waiting in the open meeting room where inmates could visit with their families. When the guard tapped the blank line on the sign-in sheet that identified the type of relationship, Mildred just shook her head. She would not lie. "We aren't blood kin."

The guard shrugged and pointed toward the door. Fran signed, too, at first hanging back and following behind Mildred. Then realizing that her friend needed her, Fran stepped closer and kept stride as Mildred led the way to the meeting room.

"It is horrible here," Fran hissed as they stepped through. Hard looking, tired-looking women of all ages were only mildly interested in Mildred and Fran.

Janie's head went up. She was sitting on a plastic-covered army-green couch in the corner. Mildred saw her think about standing and then change her mind. If she stood up, someone else could get her seat. If she stayed put, they would have a place to sit together.

"I hope you brought your little disinfectant cloths. It is nasty here," Fran said as they walked solemnly across the big room to the green sofa. "What's happened to her hair? I thought it was red."

"That was a rinse," Mildred said, tight-lipped. She had already told Fran that, but after you saw the change in Janie, you had to say something out loud to let go of the surprise. Janie had aged in the jail. The young girl had aged quickly. Hopelessness and abandonment do that to you.

Janie stood up then, uncertain about whether she would be embraced.

Mildred put her arms around Janie, and the girl collapsed against her. She began to sob then, and Fran nodded vigorously, not part of the embrace but encouraging the two to make up.

Mildred opened her purse, and the guard came to attention and stepped forward. Mildred felt the attention in the room shift. She opened her purse, which the other guard had cursorily examined when she signed in, and withdrew the packet of Kleenex that she always carried with her. They each took one, including Fran, who was never able to be near other people who were crying without shedding a few tears herself.

"It is wonderful to see you, Miss Fran. It is awfully good of you to come to this place." Janie looked around the room through their eyes and shook her head. "You don't belong here. I kind of do. But you two don't. I am very sorry for calling you. If it weren't for my baby—and if my aunt." The girl faltered then. "Everyone is gone. There is only you, Miss Mildred."

"And I am here. Now tell me again what they said."

"It wasn't they. It was my lawyer who called. They—I guess the people in charge--notified him that I am being extradited for what happened in California—something about a bank statement--and they wanted to know what plans I had made about my baby. And my lawyer told them about my aunt, and they called her and she said that she wasn't going to take it. It. That was her word. She called Little Mister 'It'."

That was a shade different than what Janie had told Mildred on the phone.

That difference caused Mildred to sit back. A little voice whispered: *Listen carefully.*

Mildred listened carefully.

Janie wiped her eyes, and Fran reached into her purse and withdrew some Spearmint chewing gum and offered her a piece. She put it in her pocket, "for later" and when she said that, Fran gave her the whole pack. Janie offered her a smile of thanks and sat back on the deep sofa, crossing her arms across her belly.

"My aunt wouldn't take my phone calls, but she took that one from my lawyer, and she said to him what she wouldn't say to me, which was she didn't want to be responsible for my baby. Because he's not due till October, they can move me, and they want to because it's overcrowded here and start the paperwork there and find a foster family to take my baby--people whose names I wouldn't even know."

Janie looked at Mildred with alarm. "I don't know anybody in California." She stifled a sob of despair. "And I told my lawyer that, and he said that if someone here would sign the guardianship forms, they would keep me here until after the baby was born. If you had my baby, you could bring him here for me to see. My baby." She repeated the words and then looked at Mildred with such beseechment that Mildred could only reach over and pat Janie's hand and then hold it.

Mildred listened to the interior voice that helped to convict and urge, and she felt and heard stillness and a kind of benediction: *Even if what she is saying isn't the whole truth, wouldn't any mother say anything she had to say in order to provide a safe home for a newborn baby?*

"Your baby is going to be a boy?" Fran confirmed.

Janie nodded. "They did a sonogram. He has got what he is supposed to have. They say he might be really big."

'Too big for her to lift? To handle?' Mildred wondered. The anxiety began again with questions about the physical doing of it—not just babysitting—but the hours of holding and lifting and getting up at night to feed Little Mister and rocking him.

Even though Mildred had given up teaching after twenty-five years because she didn't want the heartbreak anymore of troubled children passing through her classroom and then going off into their hard lives, Mildred Budge felt a quickening, a sense of awe, a strange and wonderful sense that after all these years, God was about to give her a baby for a little while; but, isn't that how long any mother had a baby?

She tried to look ahead at the future and plan how to manage it, but she could not predict what the future would be. Mildred wasn't sure if she could take care of him. She only knew that Janie needed her. A baby needed her, and her best friend agreed with her, because Fran leaned forward, and said, "Mildred, you have got to sign that form."

The deed was accomplished with alacrity. The office personnel were pleasant and efficient in ways that bureaucracies often are not. Fran and Mildred took note of that in the administrative office, where they were treated with uncommon courtesy.

Here's the form.

Here's where you sign.

Here's your copy.

We will fax this one to her attorney. He will take it from there.

The clerk smiled and asked, "Is she your niece—granddaughter?"

"Just a girl—a friend," Mildred explained, folding up her copy and putting it safely inside her purse.

The clerk eyed her with interest and said, "She is lucky. A lot of them get abandoned by their families, and very few of them keep their friends."

Fran and Mildred left the prison somberly, passing along cold hallways that smelled vaguely like a nursing home but not quite— airless, close, with the floors and walls emanating the aromas of harsh detergents.

They were glad to be outside again.

Glad of the fresh air.

When they reached the curb that led to the parking lot, Fran stopped suddenly and grabbed Mildred's elbow as if pulling her back from traffic, only there wasn't any traffic. They were standing on the sidewalk; their feet poised near the curb that led to the street. It was the kind of step that each helped the other to make with their routine warnings: 'Watch your step! It's a steep curb. Don't fall.' They each knew the words, the warnings, the need to be cautious.

The curb was not a steep embankment, but it felt like a very big step into a very different future.

"I have something I want to tell you, Millie," Fran announced, and her shoulders went back, as she inhaled the freedom that people who are not prisoners forget is theirs. Christians, too.

Mildred stopped, waited, listened with the same sensitivity that Fran exercised when she had called her earlier that day.

"Winston has asked me to marry him." Fran announced solemnly, as if she had never said the words before.

Fran needed to say it her way in her time, and she had made a decision about Winston. Maybe she had made it in that very moment.

Fran looked up at the sky. It was clear and blue. The clouds were billowy, unthreatening. As she took the step off of the curb, Fran announced, and there was pure joy in the news, "I am going to say yes to Winston. If you can change, Millie, so can I."

34

FRIENDS AND MORE FRIENDS

The women were laughing, laughing. Drivers who ordinarily zipped past the church, who had learned how to tune out the church bells chiming when it was time for worship, slowed down because of the laughter that reached the streets as the women—friends of Mildred Budge--stood in the parking lot gathering their baby gifts and balancing their trays of party food.

It was a Tuesday. No one expected laughter from a church on Tuesday.

And it wasn't a usual ladies' circle meeting.

It was a baby shower for Mildred Budge who had never been the guest of honor at any kind of shower at all.

The packages were big and wrapped in different shades of blue paper and the women—coupon-clippers mostly-- had spent extravagantly, paying extra money on large, ridiculous blue bows.

The new preacher liked the laughter. But then Steev Emory wore laughter in his eyes the way some preachers wore clerical collars around their necks. When people teased Steev about how he spelled his first name, he laughed some more. "My name has two e's in it. Why should you care where I place the second one?"

They teased him about his old blue van. Many of his new congregants tried to get him to buy something a little more dignified. Steev listened, tucked his hands in his jeans pockets, and asked them what they were doing at their houses. Before the conversation was over, he usually said, "If you ever need help hauling something, give me a call. That van has helped move many a person."

Inevitably, the person who had at first a negative opinion about the van—usually the same person troubled by the spelling of his name--eyed the van with greater, more approving interest.

Steev was controversial. Any new preacher would be. He was a man in motion. Steev worked. He blew off the sidewalk, something that hadn't been done with thoroughness since Hugh Luckie died.

He didn't ask what needed to be done. He didn't wait. He didn't send out a form with little boxes on it for you to check the work you were willing to do. He worked. When others saw him working, they thought: 'He shouldn't be doing that. He's the preacher.' And then without worrying about making a commitment themselves, they leapt off the embankment of self-protection and got busy.

When the women came into the church laughing, Steev heard the enlivening sounds of sisters coming together, and held the door open to the fellowship hall. The tables were arranged, and extra care had been used. Fresh flowers were in vases on the tables that had the good cloths. Chairs were set in a circle in the middle of the room because they would be eating with plates balanced on ample, practiced laps.

All the ladies had brought their signature dishes. Patty's pimiento cheese sandwiches. Virginia's olive and cream cheese sandwiches. Julie's deviled ham sandwiches. Jennie's cheese straws. Lori's baked brie with cherries. Betty's stuffed dates. Lola's fresh vegetable platter. Sue's fresh fruit platter. And the petit fours from Sallie Brooks with a dot of blue icing on the top to signify that the baby was going to be a boy.

Petit fours were Sallie's specialty at baby showers. For family and fellowship suppers, she made a roast that had no equal—so tender you could eat it with a fork. For special occasions, Sallie baked a caramel cake that no one could duplicate. Her icing was dense and chewy, a caramel fudge that took years of practice to perfect. Sallie Brooks was the most versatile cook in the church and one of the most faithful friends any person could have.

"You women are living the good life," Steev commented when he saw the food.

"Stay and eat!" Several women invited. And he didn't pull back. Didn't find a way to excuse himself.

"I didn't know you allowed men to come to one of these parties," Steev replied, still holding the door for the stream of women who continued to arrive. "What goes on?"

"We open presents. We sit and talk. We eat. We talk about men and marriage, and we close in prayer," Fran explained. "We pray for the baby. For the baby's life. For the parents. Then, for all the babies in our church and in our lives. Sometimes we pray for the people on our lists in our Bibles at home. We pray for the preacher."

"Sounds good to me," Steev said as the telephone in his office rang. The sound could be heard throughout the building.

Fran thought he would use that phone call as an excuse to change his mind and escape all the women. Steev read her mind and grinned. "They can leave a message," he said.

"The guest of honor sits in that rocking chair. It's the mother-to-be chair. We've used that rocker for almost a hundred years. The wife of the man who donated the property for this church donated that rocking chair. It was her contribution to the growth of the church."

Steev assessed the rocker. The light wood gleamed. The women kept it well polished.

The door opened again, and Mildred Budge entered.

Steev walked over and embraced her. "The guest of honor," he acknowledged.

"Something like that," Mildred concurred.

Steev took Mildred's hand, and tucked it through the crook of his arm. He escorted her to the rocker as the other women filed through, laughing.

When Liz Luckie arrived, she looked around the room, waiting for someone to see her and speak to her: to choose her. Mildred smiled and waved. "Come over here, Liz. Right here," she invited. "Sit beside Dixie and me."

Dixie, the newest member to the congregation before Steev, looked up at the mention of her name. She always had the look of someone just waking up, and in that moment, she seemed to be fighting the impulse to yawn. Dixie was new to the congregation but attended all the meetings.

She came to everything with her bag of sewing, but she didn't say much. She always sat near Mildred for security, and everyone knew that Mildred was her protector. Liz took the seat next to Dixie and Mildred.

Mildred reached out and patted Liz's hand. "Thank you for coming, Liz. We would have missed you if you hadn't come."

The other women heard the words and automatically murmured agreement. Those automatic murmurs of agreement began a delicate shift in the way Liz Luckie would fit into the body of the church. Outside on the horizon, the clouds of change that had been keeping her company began to keep their distance.

"It is a nice day for a baby shower," Liz said.

The women smiled and murmured yes, yes; it is a nice day.

Mildred wondered if Belle was coming. She was not getting out of the house much—

not since Sam had started a round of tests to find out what his problems were. There was some discussion of mini-strokes and, maybe, Alzheimer's. As her friend's health was declining, Mildred's health was being documented as superior. She had said yes to the young doctor and his study of people like her.

Because no one was going to the refreshment table just yet, Sallie Brooks decided to get things started. With a slight limp from a car accident years ago, Sallie walked slowly around the room with her platter of petit fours and offered Mildred one first. Sallie had a lovely smile that reminded Mildred of her son—a boy Mildred had taught years ago. He was all grown up now— tall and handsome and as smart a boy as any mother could want.

Mildred smiled; her head tilted up as she nodded to Sallie just as Fran found her place. The other chairs filled up, and Mildred looked around the room at the faces of her dearest and oldest friends—women who were mothers and had become grandmothers.

There were some great-grandmothers in the room, too, and every one of them had a story to tell. In that moment, Mildred Budge wanted to know their stories, wanted to ask: "What has it been like for you? Loving God? Growing older? Reading the Bible? Trying to think only to realize that thinking isn't the key to living? It's just one more way of being?'

Some people referred to those recounts as testimonies and praise reports, but they were really, more authentically, the stories of their lives told at their fullest inside the larger context of Jesus Saves.

Oblivious to her curiosity, they were fully in the moment of the celebration of a baby coming, and they were all talking at once and laughing, laughing.

"Girls, do you want to get started?" Anne Henry asked. Mildred had not seen her arrive, but there she was. *The last time I saw you we were both in heaven, only I was sitting in Derk's and you were going to Apropos.* Anne Henry was dressed in her signature combination of red, white and blue, for she was very patriotic. She walked straight over to Mildred holding out her present wrapped in the familiar oatmeal-colored gift box from the local boutique. The label said Apropos.

"This isn't for the baby directly, but it will help the baby if you remember why I am giving it to you," Anne Henry said. "It's for you because you are going to be taking care of the baby, and you really need this."

Mildred looked up at her friend. The room became quiet. It was a small box and opened easily. Inside was a necklace of burnished gold chain links and the pendant was an old-fashioned key. "The girl who makes those necklaces is the daughter of the former art teacher at the university. Her business is called Ex Voto Vintage. She has a shop over in Old Cloverdale, but they sell her jewelry at Apropos, too."

"I know who you mean," Liz said, leaning forward. "Elizabeth's work is exquisite. Each piece is one-of-a-kind and made from precious artifacts that she collects from everywhere."

"Like that key," Anne Henry said. "The key is tried and true. It's from Scotland. It looks like you, Mildred."

Mildred slipped on the necklace. She liked the weight of the gold chain and how the key pressed close to her heart.

Anne Henry wore a similar necklace but hers had a different key.

"Remember, Mildred, when the baby comes to you, don't lose yourself in caring for him. We will be here to help you be yourself and stay yourself. Don't let taking care of a child swallow up your life. That is key, Mildred. Live your life. Don't forget who you are. You are one of a kind. Like that necklace."

"That is key," other mothers and grandmothers and great-grand mothers in the room murmured. "Motherhood can steal your real identity. Don't let it. It's not good for the children when you do."

Steev heard the women discuss motherhood, and his smiling eyes began to pray. The warmth of love emanated from him, and Mildred saw him slip simultaneously into that domain of communion where one can go to be with the Eternal One. Steev lived there. He went in and out of that green pasture where everything was just as Jake had told Mildred: all right all the time. Every woman in the room knew that place and came and went in the same way at their own pace in a timing that was beyond their control and, simultaneously and paradoxically, their choice.

Mildred nodded her gratitude to Anne Henry, patted the key at her chest, and promised simply: "I will remember what you have said. Thank you."

Fran handed Mildred the next gift to open. The lady who had chosen it called out, "You are going to need that, Mildred. That will help when Little Mister gets fussy."

Mildred had never announced the name that Janie used for her son, but word got round of what he would be called until a proper name was chosen.

Little Mister will need that. This. More of those.

There was a diaper bag.

Lots of diapers.

Different sizes of bottles.

Crib sheets for the crib that Mildred and Fran had bought at an estate sale and already sanitized, painted and sanitized again.

Blankets.

A baby room monitor.

Outfits. Blue ones and yellow ones and green ones in sizes that started small and went up to two years.

The women had gone all out, as if they were giving presents to a daughter who needed everything instead of one of their own: a woman old enough to be a grandmother.

The notes on the gifts promised faithful friendship. "Call me. I will be there." They had written their phone numbers on the cards as if Mildred didn't know most of them by heart or couldn't look them up in the church directory.

The last and largest gift was from Liz. It was too big for one person to have bought. Big gifts were traditionally bought by several women who shared the expense. But this big box had Liz's signature card on it etched in silver.

Mildred tried to open it. She couldn't.

Steev whipped out his pocket knife, and cut through the heavy-duty sealing tape and the thick cardboard. He extracted a stroller and a car seat: two expensive items that Liz had bought. It was too much. Way too much.

"Thank you, Liz." Mildred shook her head. "The days will be cool when he arrives, and I imagine he will enjoy a stroll."

"I will come over and help you," Liz began, but her voice faded away as she expected to be ignored or rejected. The other women busied themselves loudly.

Mildred Budge spoke plainly, loud enough for all to hear. "You have a standing invitation to come to my home anytime, Liz. I am going to need you."

It wasn't an apology only. It was the love of Jesus moving through her reaching out to welcome all his people, redeeming the time.

Liz sat back in her chair as the gift portion of the baby shower came to a close and the ladies began to eye the food table, wondering which one of them would rise and start the line.

Steev wouldn't do it—not at a ladies' function.

A veteran who understood what needed to happen and when, Sallie Brooks rose again and signaled to the others to go to the refreshment table. *'She was a magnificent woman, standing there inside the smile of Jesus—inside heaven-- the way she was,'* Mildred thought.

Fran leaned over to Mildred, and asked her best friend, "Who are we, Millie? I feel like I am getting younger. How can that be? You look younger than you ever have, and you just bought that house. Our business is growing, and there's more adventure to come! There is all this, too! So much love everywhere you look!" Fran said, waving at the baby gifts which attested to the future unknown, out of their control, and shared always with friends.

Mildred glanced at the new engagement ring on her best friend's finger and her brown eyes glowed. "We are the same women, but we keep changing. You are Fran Applewhite, and you are going to get married. I am Mildred Budge, and I am going to have a baby. I guess it just goes to show that anything is possible."

The Mission of Mildred Budge   Book 2
Miss Budge Goes to Fountain City   Book 3

New Series: A Mildred Budge Friendship Story

Belle: A Mildred Budge Friendship Story
A Gentle and Lowly Christmas

Stand-alone Novels

Christmas in Fountain City
Lovejoy, a novel about desire
Tricks of the Mind

Essays and Memoirs

A Cookbook for Katie
What Makes a Man a Hero? Stories about Men for Father's Day

Caregiving Books:

The Long Good Night a memoir

What Al Left Behind   Stories about Caregiving: Book 1

Blessed: Stories about Caregiving Book 2

Memory Care Books
for Activity Directors and Caregivers

Popular Culture Creators of the 20th Century Jan-Feb-Mar Book 1

Popular Culture Creators of the 20th Century April-May-June Book 2

Popular Culture Creators of the 20th Century July August Sept Book 3

Popular Culture Creators of the 20th Century October November Dec Book 4

11 DIY Holiday Small Talks Book 5

DAPHNE SIMPKINS

To keep up with new releases, follow
Daphne Simpkins on Amazon, Facebook,
BookBub, and Goodreads.

www.ingramcontent.com/pod-product-compliance
Lightning Source LLC
Chambersburg PA
CBHW051928020726
47501CB00001B/28